TAMING OF THE
SIREN

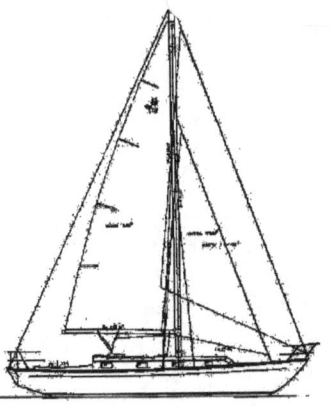

ALBERT REICHARD

www.albertreichard.com

✪ Gulf of Alaska ✪

"Twenty years from now, you will be more disappointed by the things you didn't do than those you did. So throw off the bowlines. Sail away from safe harbor. Catch the wind in your sails. Explore. Dream. Discover." — **Mark Twain**

This book is dedicated to anyone who has ever struggled to find themselves.

⚓ FORWARD ⚓

In life, the biggest struggle we all face is the struggle to find ourselves, for some we find ourselves in our careers, some in our families.

For others, it is different; we spend most of our lives feeling like a piece is missing, until that is we meet a special someone who is the Yin to our Yang.

Many people find those of us who engage in power exchange relationships to be strange and bizarre; However, the reality is that we are very much just like you, other than how we choose to live our lives behind closed doors; which is in an environment with a consensual power exchange dynamic!

For those of you who have never met a submissive with masochistic tendencies, there is something that I hope you would understand; that is deep down they are people who usually care very much, and because they care so much they often tend to suffer from stress and anxiety.

This is because they try very hard to make the people around them happy, it is in their personality to want to please the people around them, especially those they care about.

What this means is that when they make mistakes, they tend to be very hard on themselves and will punish themselves mentally and often physically.

At the same time, they can frequently be perceived to have bad attitudes and be incapable of accepting criticism; this is because whatever you are criticizing or punishing them for, they have already done far worse to themselves.

Then what happens is, they store all of this emotional pain up inside and begin to feel an emotional hurt that just stays there looming and lingering in the recesses of their mind.

The funny thing about the brain is that it cannot distinguish between emotional and physical pain.

This becomes a problem when the person begins to feel so much pain inside that the brain begins to feel an overwhelming need for the body to experience physical pain so as that it can rationalize why it feels so much emotional pain.

With the application of physical pain, it is like a pressure release valve, and how it works is through the act of being punished or even humiliated the brain can let go of the bad feelings it has stowed up inside, and the submissive can begin to feel better.

Therefore many turn to self-harm manifesting itself in the form of cutting or self-mutilation or performing degrading/humiliating acts.

However often times this creates a vicious cycle of self-harm and guilt perpetuated by the act of harming themselves. Which adds to the emotional pain they feel, and thus further perpetuates their desire for self-harm creating a downward spiral that can have severe negative effects on themselves and their loved ones.

By entering into a D/s or Dom/sub dynamic relationship, the masochistic submissive can find a situation where they can receive "punishment" when they are feeling bad about something instead of punishing themselves.

And can do so in a safe environment where their needs are being looked after, and they are truly being cared for.

Additionally, when finding someone to "serve" in a power exchange dynamic relationship, it means they can focus on making that person happy, and assuming that person is a good leader; they can find a great degree of happiness and fulfillment in their life and will do almost anything to please their Dominant.

If you are not into kink yourself but you are reading this book it is important to understand this so as that you can understand Caitlyn the main character of this book.

When the book begins, Caitlyn is carrying a great deal of internal pain with her, and it comes out as a bad attitude perpetuated by her temper.

As well upon reading this, you may find that this applies to someone in your own life, and you may find some answers to what makes them the way they are.

If you have someone who is like this in your life who is struggling, I hope that if you could take one thing away from this it is that they are not broken, there is nothing wrong with them, they just are not in a situation where they are getting what they need to be happy, and that likely they are being overwhelmed by the pain they feel inside.

If you would like more information on kink based relationships, please see the resources page on my website www.albertreichard.com

- *Albert*

⚓ ONE ⚓

Caitlyn walked down the gangway pulling her rolling suitcase, the wheels made an echoing wirr, and her high heel shoes made an echoing thud every time she stepped onto the aluminum deck.

As she stepped from the gangway out onto the floating dock, she became encapsulated in the beauty of a foggy morning on Seattle's Lake Union.

Off in the distance, the outline of the Space Needle and skyscrapers downtown were barely hewn outlines through the morning fog. The air was still and peaceful the water calm; aside from a few seagulls squawking the city had not yet awoken on this beautiful Sunday morning.

As she stepped along the wheels on her suitcase thumped and bumped over the creases in the concrete floating docks. Passing each boat, she noticed how all looked mostly the same, white fiberglass hulls with various bits of wood and stainless about them covered in either blue, green or maroon canvas except one.

At the end of a pier sat a Royal Blue sailing yacht, it had no canvas covering the cockpit to speak of, it seemed better cared for than the rest.

Instead of gray wood bits of polished stainless steel and anodized aluminum, adorned it's exterior, making it a smart well cared for boat.

As she approached the stern, she could see the name "My Way" hand painted across the transom. Seeing as that this was the boat she was looking for she called out

> "Hello anyone home?"

In her thick Irish accent as she knocked on the side of the boat.

Moments later a man's head popped out of the companionway hatch looked her up and down then he said: "Howdy, how can I help you?"

"Are you the captain?"

She asked.

The man chuckled as he let a soft, warm smile emit from behind his beard

"If you want to call me that, you must be Caitlyn?"

"I am indeed; I am assuming professor Ames contacted you then and told you what I was seeking?"

"He did, I'm Mike Black."

The man stepped from the companionway and up into the cockpit, it was only then Caitlyn realized how big he was, she was short being only five feet tall, but even standing above him on the dock wearing six-inch heels she still had to look slightly up at the man.

He reached out with his paw of a hand extending it to her

"Here why don't you come aboard. However, you will want to lose the shoes, though."

Caitlyn smiled kicked her heels off, handed her suitcase over picked up her heels, took his hand and then stepped down.

"Here come down inside I was just finishing breakfast."

Mike led her down into the cabin of the boat which turned out to be much larger than Caitlyn had imagined it would be. The interior built of finely finished wood accented with stainless fixtures had a very warm inviting cozy feel.

As she looked about, Mike gestured to her to have a seat at the dinette across from him.

"So Doug tells me you want to go to Alaska by boat?"

Mike asked while pushing his fork through his omelet.

"Yes, I am writing a research paper on whales, and I need some firsthand observations for my work.

I had paid another boat to take me, but the man disappeared with my money. Professor Ames told me you might be able to help me."

Mike didn't say anything as he thought for a moment, Caitlyn nervously began to fidget.

She had come all this way from Hawaii only to get seriously disappointed when the previous captain she had hired took most of her hard-earned money.

Now she was practically begging this man to take her north so she could fulfill her dream of seeing and photographing whales in the wild.

Being humbled like this wasn't easy for Caitlyn having the famous Irish Temper to go with her long curly red locks.

Finally, when the silence had become very uncomfortable Mike asked:

"This is important to you?"

Caitlyn swallowed hard and replied:

"Yes, it's been my dream ever since I went to Sea World when I was a little girl."

Mike then asked the question she dreaded

"have you got any money?"

Caitlyn paused and looked down embarrassed then replied:

"Well you see, I had saved up three thousand, but I paid another boat twenty-four hundred of it, and he ran off with my money, so all I have now is five hundred fifty left."

Embarrassed having to reveal she had been ripped off, Caitlyn had a hard time looking back up at Mike and when she did she noticed he had stopped eating and had begun to stroke his beard as he looked at her deep in thought.

Caitlyn felt as though she were about to be rejected again and had begun to resign herself to this fact when Mike broke the silence.

"Five hundred and fifty dollars aye?"

"Yes, It's all I have."

Caitlyn sulked through her thick Irish Brogue.

Thinking a moment more Mike spoke up:

"Well you had best keep your money, you're going to need to buy some foul weather gear as I have none on here that fits you."

Making eye contact again Caitlyn looked up a bit puzzled, then Mike explained:

"I am going to Alaska anyway; it wouldn't hurt my feelings to have some company for the trip, although understand I will expect you to help out around here as well."

Caitlyn beamed realizing her dream was going to come true.

"Oh, thank you so much!"

She exclaimed hopping out of her seat practically climbing over the table to give Mike a hug knocking his plate over in the process.

"Woah easy there tiger!"

Mike said as he caught the plate as it slid across the table. Caitlyn just sat back and smiled and giggled.

Mike peered across the table and looking at her long flowing curly red hair surrounding a freckled face that had broken out into an ear to ear grin.

He thought for a moment and then spoke up.

"We will need to get you some foul weather gear, and any other supplies you need. Everything here in Seattle is incredibly cheap compared to what it will be once we get to Alaska, so you will need to stock up.

Don't worry about food as I have plenty on board, and what we don't have we will catch on the way up."

Then he thought for a moment more.

"I will sleep on the pilot berth aft; you can have the Vee birth cabin to yourself so you can have a little privacy."

Caitlyn smiled even more and replied:

"Oh, thank you so much!"

Mike stood up and grabbed some of his things from the Vee Birth and then showed her in setting her suitcase on the bed.

"Why don't you put some proper shoes on and we will run into town."

Mike said stepping from the room.

"I will let me get changed!"

Caitlyn replied, shutting the door then throwing her blouse and skirt off a moment later emerging in Jeans sneakers and a hoodie.

When they got back from town, Mike helped Caitlyn bring all of the bags of supplies they had bought for her down from the borrowed marina truck.

They then loaded and stored everything onboard, and after a talk about safety they untied the lines, pushed off the dock and motored their way to the locks.

Entering the locks was an adventure all of its own, they waited near the entrance as another yacht emerged, then the shore crew signaled them in. They tied off to the side, the gates closed behind them, then suddenly the water began to pour out, as they dropped down to the level of Puget Sound.

Emerging from the locks Caitlyn found herself totally immersed in the sense of adventure that gripped her; everything was so pretty and serene.

As they reached the drawbridge and the heavy riveted iron structure swung up and out of the way, she had a hard time convincing herself this was not a dream as they passed under the old but beautifully kept structure.

Past the mouth of the harbor into the open sound the fog lifted and the wind began to pick up, Mike pulled the cover from the main and hoisted it, the sail began to flutter and flap wildly making a tremendous amount of noise.

Jumping back into the cockpit, Mike released the line that unfurled the jib, then he pulled the jib sheet around a winch, pulled it in, then he pulled it in the rest of the way by shoving a handle into the top of the winch and cranking rigorously on it.

Then he repeated the process for the mainsail and as he did the sails billowed to life, and the boat heeled over.

Mike pressed a big red button on the console killing the engine, and in doing so the boat was suddenly enveloped in the quiet sounds of a sailboat, the water rushing by, the wind in the sails.

The peace and tranquility of it all made for an amazing morning slipping along in relative silence carried by the wind.

Caitlyn found herself standing at the front of the cockpit arms rested on the top of the cabin looking all around delighted by the sights sounds and smells as they worked their way north through the sound.

Mike noticed too as he stood at the wheel keeping an eye out for traffic in the normally busy sound that today was a bit slower than usual for whatever reason despite being a perfect morning for being out on the water.

Finally, an idea came to him he yelled out to Caitlyn

> "Hey, you ever driven a boat before?"

she turned around and shook her head no.

> "Well come here, take the wheel!"

With this Caitlyn's eyes lit up with delight, she darted around behind the wheel and grabbed it with both hands, Mike pointed to the compass and said:

> "Here you see this heading 340?"

> "Yes."

She replied.

> "Just keep her pointed that way, you'll be fine, I will give you new headings to steer to as we need them"

He said before stepping away from the helm settling down into a seat resting his foot on the opposite side of the cockpit where he could relax while observing.

Caitlyn stood at the wheel smiling like a school girl overwhelmed with joy; this was the first time she had ever been on a boat like this let alone driven one.

As they worked their way north, Mike kept reading out new headings to Caitlyn.

Approaching the Western side of Whidbey Island they passed by the Port Townsend ferry a few hundred feet off of the port side.

Caitlyn could clearly see all of the people on deck on the heavy ferry as it lumbered past, some smiled and waved, she smiled and waved back several times.

She quickly found there was a rush that came from being more than just a passenger!

Rounding the north end of the island the calm water began to turn rough the wind whipped the surface into three-foot seas.

As the yacht plunged over the swells sending spray flying from the bow, Caitlyn began to dance with the rhythm of the boat anticipating its next move giggling and laughing all the time.

Mike from his seat in the cockpit looked to her with a sense of subdued amazement. Most people by now would be puking their guts out, but this little red-haired siren was taking to the sea like a mermaid!

As they approached Anacortes the sun hung low in the sky, Mike lowered the sails and started the engine before taking the wheel back from Caitlyn who by now was exhausted from her adventure.

Taking back the wheel Mike said to Caitlyn:

> "Hey I will get us moored, how about slipping below and starting up some dinner for us."
>
> "I can do that!"

Caitlyn replied as she bounced off down the companionway.

Inside Caitlyn searched through the fridge finding the fixings for a roast.

She pulled a pot out from behind the stove, cut up the vegetables and threw them in the pot with the meat along with water and some seasoning from the cabinet, she lit the stove and set the pot to cooking.

Once that was done she leaned back against the counter top and drifted off into a daydream, the day had been so amazing, starting with the sheer disappointment and rejection; with the first ship that had taken her money, then she had been brought back to a happy place through Mike's kindness and generosity.

She started to wonder about the man, how old was he? Did he have a family? What did he do for money? Where was he from?

Her train of thought was seriously derailed when the hatch slid open, and he came stomping down the companionway steps.

Stowing his jacket in the locker next to the ladder Mike plopped down at the navigation station and peeled his boots off placing them next to the bottom step of the ladder.

"I'm going to plot our course for tomorrow."

He said, then followed up with:

"What's for dinner?"

"I'm making a roast."

Caitlyn replied as she settled into the dinette opposite of him.

"Very good!"

Mike replied as he dug into his charts and started looking about them tracing a line with a ruler before plugging waypoints into the GPS creating a route taking them further north.

Caitlyn once again got lost in thought spiraling off in a day dream when all of the sudden she was startled as Mike said

"Are you going to answer that?"

Peering over the top of the nav table at her, confused for a second she realized her phone was ringing and she hadn't even noticed, she quickly clutched it and pressed it to her ear as she darted off to the Vee birth.

As she slid away the only part of the conversation Mike heard was "Hey babe, " and then the door closed.

Some moments later Caitlyn emerged, checked on how dinner was cooking then resumed her seat at the dinette.

"Was that your boyfriend?"

Queried Mike.

"Not exactly..."

Caitlyn replied as a sense of uneasiness overtook her, she started to wonder how she was going to explain herself, but before she could he asked:

"Was it your girlfriend?"

In a matter of fact way.

Damn!

Is all Caitlyn could think as she muttered somewhat embarrassed:

"Yes."

Mike simply responded with:

"I see."

Not sure if he approved or disapproved Caitlyn continued:

"It's, it's just really new and, well I just… I don't know; I was getting tired of boys and their games."

Mike held up his hand indicating for her to stop.

"You don't have to explain yourself to me."

He said with a half-smile and with that the silence that formed was interrupted by the pot boiling.

Caitlyn was ever so thankful for the disruption to pull her away from Mike's inquiry.

She pulled the pot from the stove, cut up the meat and served it up. As she set the plates down on the table, Mike Joined her after pouring himself a drink and one for her as well.

As he took the first bites he proclaimed:

"This is good! You keep cooking like this I may have to keep you on as crew!"

He chuckled, and Caitlyn smiled warmly, and the questions she had been thinking of earlier began to boil back to the front of her mind, finally she asked:

"How old are you?"

Mike responded with a twisted grin:

"How old do you think I am?"

Caitlyn puzzled for a minute twisting one of her curls around her finger.

"I don't know, perhaps forty-five?"

Mike laughed a big guttural laugh and bellowed:

"Forty-Five eh? Not quite."

"Well then how old?"

Caitlyn repeated a bit annoyed at being forced to guess and a bit embarrassed for being wrong.

Mike stroked his beard realizing it made him look older than he actually was, then he spoke:

"I am Thirty-Five."

Embarrassed Caitlyn returned to her meal, but before she could dive back into her train of thought Mike spoke up and asked:

"What part of Ireland are you from?"

Caitlyn paused setting her utensils down and replied:

"I was born in Dublin, but I was raised between Cork and San Diego California."

"Really?"

Mike responded with surprise in his voice.

"Yes, my mother is Irish, she took a job working in Dublin while she was in college, she had a one nighter with my father, an American Sailor from San Diego, nine months later I showed up.

My father didn't like it at first, said he felt trapped, they made a go at it, but in the end, it didn't work out.

When I was about six, I started spending time with him every summer if he wasn't deployed.

Then it was back of to Cork for the school year."

"I see."

Mike responded before launching his next question:

"How old are you?"

Caitlyn responded:

"Twenty-one I'll be Twenty Two in May."

Mike laughed and shook his head as he spoke:

"A red head and a Taurus, what have I gotten myself into!!!"

Caitlyn fully aware of her temper just had to laugh along with him, little did Mike know what a defining feature of this trip that famous Irish temper would become!

They talked late into the night, by the time it was over Caitlyn sleepily stumbled into the Vee Birth and crawled into her bed.

She lay there, smiled and reflected on the day and it was only then she realized she had gone on and on talking about herself all night.

She still knew nothing really about Mike other than his age and that he too like her father was in the Navy.

This puzzled her, and a shroud of mystery began to build around the man.

She lay there in bed thinking about this as the waves slowly lapped against the side of the hull.

Everything grew quiet, and the slow rocking motion of the boat gently sent her off into a deep sleep with a feeling of warmth, contentment, and excitement for the voyage to come.

TWO

Wumpf... wumpf... wumpf... a rhythmic noise brought Caitlyn out of a dreamy sleep.

She awoke still not totally realizing she was still on the boat.

Sitting up she became more aware thinking about the previous day then there was that noise again wumpf... wumpf... wumpf in slow, steady succession.

Caitlyn arose, pulled on her jeans and hoodie, stuffed her feet into her shoes and stepped out of the vee birth, she called to Mike but didn't see him anywhere. But then the noise was louder, over her head now wumpf... wumpf... wumpf... still in that same slow rhythm.

Up the steps she peered over the top of the hatch to be greeted by the crisp morning air, as she looked forward, she found the source of the noise. Mike was spread across the deck holding the hand rail doing slow, steady pushups one after the other.

He had not yet noticed her; he just kept pushing.

One after the next.

Caitlyn could not help but stare, in the night he had cut his beard back and trimmed up his face and now shirtless on the deck doing pushups she got her first real good look at the man.

As she watched him press the deck, she was mesmerized by the muscles rippling in his arms his chest and his back.

His muscles bulged and twisted as he pushed up and down, then suddenly it hit her she was finding herself very attracted to him.

Before she could continue with this thought however she was startled back to reality as Mike blurted out without looking at her:

"Good Morning Caitlyn"

Blushing she said the first thing that came to her mind:

"Good morning, would you like breakfast?"

Mike stopped still holding his body inches from the deck looked to her and nodded and said:

"That would be great!"

Oh fuck me! He is just showing off now Caitlyn thought to herself as she ducked back down the hatch her face almost as flush as her hair.

She wasn't used to getting caught looking. Actually, she hadn't had much as far as men go to look at lately anyways.

Something about Mike was different, most men either instantly wanted to fuck her, or they were sheepish and intimidated by her looks.

Mike, on the other hand, was different, in fact, she finally put her finger on what it was, he was indifferent towards her, and she now realized it drove her crazy!

With that realization spinning through her head Caitlyn set to work making breakfast, as Mike tromped down the companionway a towel draped around his shoulders tee shirt clenched in his fist he grabbed some clothes out of a cabinet and stepped into the shower.

When he emerged, he sat at the dinette Caitlyn set an omelet down in front of him smiling waiting for his approval. Mike slid the plate up smiled at her and thanked her and waited for her to join him before digging in.

This struck Caitlyn as odd, so many times while still living at home she had sat down to a breakfast table on days she cooked where everyone had eaten, and she had nothing but a bunch of empty plates to keep her company. She was finding there was more to this man that just being an old salty sailor.

"Did you sleep well?"

Mike asked.

"Oh yes I did, I slept like the dead."

She said with a smile.

"Sleeping on a boat will do that to you, I always sleep the best on the water."

As Mike finished his sentence, she sensed there was something more to that remark that he was not telling, what she didn't know.

Before she had much time to think about it, Mike once again interrupted her thoughts.

"I want to make it up to Vancouver today I have a previous engagement there I have to attend."

"Oh?"

Replied Caitlyn pressing for details.

"Yeah, speaking of which have you got a dress?"

Thinking for a moment, she replied:

"I don't think I brought one; I wasn't expecting to need one."

"Well I would invite you, but I'm afraid you have nothing to wear."

Mike responded with a slight hint of sadness in his voice.

"That's ok; I have a lot to do on my Thesis anyways, I wouldn't want to be a bother to you."

Mike chuckled and said:

> "Yeah, and I don't think anything I have would fit you!"

To which Caitlyn had to laugh considering Mike was three times her size.

A bit later they fired up the engine and motored from the harbor once again catching the wind with the sails, heading northward.

Patches of rain filled the sky mixed with patches of sun as they made their way up past the San Juan Islands.

Caitlyn couldn't help but marvel at the beauty of the low hanging clouds over the islands sending light dancing off the water.

She took what would be the first of several pictures on her Journey of these islands; she wanted to remember this forever.

That evening they tied up at the pier in Vancouver, after checking in with the harbor master and customs Mike stepped into the head to take a shower, Caitlyn settled into the big U-shaped dinette under a blanket with some hot chocolate and her laptop to edit the pictures she had taken earlier in the day.

When Mike emerged from the head, she was stunned by what she saw, where the old seaman had stood was now a handsome young man wearing a black suit with a fine pressed white shirt and a black tie. His beard trimmed neatly into a goatee and his hair combed back Caitlyn was amazed at how handsome he was.

Mike spoke up:

> "How do I look?"

> "Fantastic!"

Was all Caitlyn could say.

"Do you need anything before I go?"

"No I'm ok, you have a good time."

She replied. About then Mike's phone rang, and he answered telling the person on the other end he would be right out.

Caitlyn being a bit nosy followed Mike up the companionway onto the deck, she watched as he walked up the gangway to a limousine that stood there waiting for him.

As he approached the car the driver opened the door, and a woman stood up wearing a fine evening gown, she was a bit younger than he was, blonde and very pretty.

The woman gave him a big hug, and Mike's jovial laughs that echoed across the water made the fire in Caitlyn's guts start to burn.

She was jealous! And it made her crazy!

Then when another woman emerged from the car and hugged him in the same way she lost it and darted below not waiting to see them get in the car and drive away.

Returning to the dinette, she sat thinking to herself:

"So, this is why he was so indifferent to her; he had a woman already!"

Then other thoughts drifted into her brain; he seemed a bit conservative was he put off of her by the fact that she was dating a girl? Did he not like her freckles, her red hair, what why was she not good enough for him.

These thoughts were interrupted by another she realized she was hot for Mike, she was crushing on him so hard, and she barely knew him.

She felt so stupid for being so easily won over. So what if he did have his stupid boat, and so what if he had been nice enough to bring her along after her ordeal with the other captain stealing her money.

She pondered for a minute leaving the boat, that would show him, she could just take off and never see him again. Maybe then he would realize what he had lost. Maybe he would come find her then?

But no, she realized he wasn't the type to chase her.

With that realization, she got up and stuffed another small log into the little stainless fireplace flickering away in the corner of the cabin and burrowed back into her blanket to sulk.

Jealousy was not something Caitlyn did well.

⚓ THREE ⚓

Hours later Caitlyn shot out of her sleep awoken by voices on deck.

She could hear Mike's booming laugh and that of the two women in tow as they boarded the boat.

The companionway hatch slid open, and Mike stuck his head in with a grin and asked:

> "Hey, Caitlyn are you decent?"

> "Yes come on in."

She replied not knowing what to expect, then she thought:

> "Was he really going to rub this woman in her face?"

She sat silently as Mike climbed down, followed by the two women both fine dresses barefoot carrying their high heels in one hand as the came down the ladder.

The blonde from earlier much taller than her probably about five foot nine extended a warm smile as the other woman a brunette about two inches shorter came up and locked arms with the blonde smiling as well.

> "Caitlyn this is my sister Monica and her wife, Abby."

> "Pleased to meet you!"

> Monica said extending her hand. Caitlyn returned the greeting and shook her hand and then muttered in her thick Irish accent

> "I'm sorry, I was asleep when you got back. Would you give me a moment?"

> "Certainly."

Monica replied.

Caitlyn got up and stepped into the head, realizing that she did have to pee she sat down to do her business, feeling stupid and embarrassed!

She had gotten all worked up for nothing; it was his sister and her wife. Her wife. His sister was a lesbian, which is why it was no big deal to Mike, she had totally read him wrong.

She figured him for a conservative fuddy-duddy and yet what she found instead was that he was charming and accepting of people.

Finally, she composed herself and emerged from the restroom to find everyone sitting around the table, a bottle of wine had been pulled out, she sat down and joined the group.

> "Care for some wine?"

Mike asked.

> "Please."

Caitlyn nodded.

Then Monica spoke up:

> "So Caitlyn I wish you could have come this evening, you missed quite the party."

> "Oh?"

She responded:

> "Yes, didn't Mike tell you?"

> "No?"

Caitlyn replied looking a bit confused.

> "Monica is an artist; tonight was a big gallery opening for her."

Mike replied.

"Oh wow, do you have a website?"

Caitlyn asked.

Monica dug in her purse and produced a business card and handed it to her.

Caitlyn pulled out her phone and punched in the site; she was greeted by fabulous paintings, portraits of horses and other wild animals that were almost photo realistic.

"WOW, THESE ARE AMAZING!"

Caitlyn gasped!

Monica smiled politely thanked her and took a sip of her wine.

The four talked late into the night with Monica and Abby finally stumbling up the stairs back into their waiting limousine at about 3 am.

When Mike reemerged into the cabin, he put the boards back in and slid the companionway shut locking it from the inside. As he sat on the pilot berth taking his shoes off Caitlyn stood up and approached him.

"Mike?"

"Yeah?"

He said looking up a bit tired and bleary eyed.

"I just wanted to say thank you for taking me, I have had a really nice time so far, and it was very nice of you to introduce me to your sister."

Mike smiled a big smile at her and his eyes went soft and warm.

"Good night Caitlyn."

He said as he rolled over into the bunk pulling the blankets over himself to fall asleep.

⚓ FOUR ⚓

The next morning Caitlyn woke rolling to the side of the cabin and almost out of bed in the space that separated the two sides of the V Birth.

She sat up in bed and realized the yacht was listing hard to one side it took her a moment to realize that they were moving at a fairly good rate of speed.

She pulled her clothes on and stepped out of the Vee birth she could see Mike sitting at the helm through the open hatch.

"Good morning did you sleep well?"

He half yelled down to her.

Confused she stepped up through the hatch looking around, sure enough, they were sailing, the sun was up, and Vancouver had all but disappeared behind them.

About then the smooth water turned into chop as the boat plunged into it Caitlyn turned green, all the wine and food from the night before decided to make an appearance and she was not ready for it, so all she could do was hang her head over the side of the boat.

"I was wondering how long that would take."

Mike remarked reaching out to pull her hair back, feeling foolish Caitlyn held up her hand to signal she was ok, then she stumbled back down the ladder into the head, washed her mouth out and brushed her teeth.

When she emerged, Mike was in the galley making breakfast.

"I'm guessing you're not hungry."

He said with a smile.

Caitlyn just shook her head no. Food was the last thing she wanted right now!

Caitlyn stumbled forward and this time crawled into the bed on the starboard side of the Vee birth since it was downhill, there she laid trying to go back to sleep, her stomach still upset.

As she lay there wrapped up in the blankets staring off into space, the cabinet of drawers on the other side slowly took over her curiosity.

Finally, unable to take it she reached out and pushed the button that latched the drawer closed, it slid open, but there was little inside of interest, just socks, and underwear.

The next one down contained pants and shorts.

Then she pushed the button for the last one, and as it slid open, she was shocked to see two pairs of handcuffs and some other odds and ends tossed into the drawer.

The sight of the handcuffs startled her and she closed the drawer quickly reminding herself she was a guest here.

Hours later she awoke again when the boat listed hard to port and once again she rolled towards the center of the boat.

Feeling much better she emerged from the Vee birth wrapped herself in her coat and climbed the ladder to the cockpit.

There Mike sat next to the wheel book in hand seeming content.

"Feeling better?"

He asked peering up over his book at her.

"Yes, what time is it?"

Caitlyn replied as she looked around to get her bearings.

"It's sixteen thirty, you've been asleep all day."

Lethargic Caitlyn rubbed her face and stretched her eyes. She sat down on the opposite side of the cockpit.

"I didn't even hear the engine start this morning?"

She said a bit puzzled.

Mike grinned and replied:

> "That is because I didn't start it, the wind was blowing perfectly across the dock, all I had to do was shove off and unfurl the sails, and we were on our way. You didn't even wake up until the wind picked up."

> "I didn't even know you could do that."

Caitlyn replied in amazement.

> "Not many today know you can, but being able to operate completely under sail is a good skill to have, one I try to keep sharp."

Mike said as he scratched at the five 'o clock shadow that had started to grow back in.

About then a few hundred feet from the boat there was a spurting noise accompanied by a plume of water shot skyward.

Mike pointed and said "Whales" this was all it took to send Caitlyn scrambling for her camera, she dove down into the Vee Birth, ripped her camera bag open, grabbed her camera and went charging back up on deck.

The whales surfaced again, and she began clicking pictures, laughing smiling and giggling.

Finally, the pod ran out of sight; it was only then that Caitlyn realized as she went to check the pictures that she had left the memory card in her computer and had captured nothing!

Her heart sank, and she slumped over.

She felt like throwing her camera overboard, and had she not spent months saving the thousands of dollars to buy it and the big fancy lens hanging on the front she probably would have.

Dejected Caitlyn stepped back down the companionway steps camera slung loosely in her hand. She pulled her memory card from her laptop and placed it back in the camera so next time she could be ready, then stowed the camera back in her bag after making sure it was turned off, and that the battery was charged.

Then she slumped into the Dinette with her laptop.

She felt so silly; she had worked so hard to get here, now she wasn't even sure she wanted to be here anymore.

She could have just downloaded images off of the internet for her project; she could have just used other people's research. Why did she have to come up here herself? Why was she doing this?

The feeling of failure consumed Caitlyn, the emotional roller coaster of the last couple of months became too much for her, and she began to cry.

⚓ FIVE ⚓

The next morning found them anchored off of a deserted island.

It started the way almost every other had, with Mike doing his exercises on deck, Caitlyn made breakfast and then Mike got the boat underway.

They pushed north and even though the wind was with them so was the rain, it was a gray day, the sailing was technical the water that fell from the sky stung Caitlyn's face like icy needles, she now understood why so many men who were mariners had a beard.

Caitlyn finally couldn't take the cold any more, she retired below deck, stoked up the fireplace and let the heat from the stove soak into her aching hands before curling up with a blanket on the Dinette.

As she sat at the Dinette with her laptop it crept up on her slowly but surely, Caitlyn was horny. She started thinking about the handcuffs in the drawer in the cabin. She wondered what it would be like to wear them.

At times when she was younger, she had experimented with tying herself up although it was something she had not thought about in a long while.

She had never worn a real pair of handcuffs before, sure she had the play ones when she was a kid, but never real locking ones.

Her mind raced, and she began to ponder what it would be like to feel helpless, to lose control.

Slowly the feeling began to overwhelm her, she checked to see that Mike was busy on deck and then she made her way to the cabin, she closed the door behind her, then sitting down on the bed she pulled the handcuffs from the drawer.

Holding them in her hands the steel was cool to the touch, she worked the bracelets through the ratchet over and over again, and the clicking feeling started to drive her wild, and the compulsion overtook her.

This was all she could take! Caitlyn dug in the drawer and found a set of keys for them, and then she checked to see that the cabin door was locked.

First, she locked one side around her left-hand Click! Click! Click! Click! Click! Click! Click! The cuff locked shut and the desire inside of her burned.

Then she had an idea, with the cuff dangling from her wrist she dove into her bag, inside she dug out her toy, turned it on and shoved it herself.

With that, she lay face down on the bed stuck her hands behind her back and locked the other cuff around her right wrist Click! Click! Click! Click! Click! Click! Click! Click! And she was locked in.

Caitlyn's head began to swim, as the vibration took hold she struggled against the cuffs, the sensation and feeling made her head swim with warm and fuzzy feelings.

It didn't take long before she came hard having to bury her face into the pillow to keep quiet.

Gasping she continued to rock then moments later she came again, then again.

After the 4th time she came, Caitlyn could take no more; she expelled the toy, then she managed to shut it off then pushed it to the side.

She collapsed into the pillow her head swimming out of breath her entire body tingling, the sensation of still being in the cuffs giving her a pleasant light headed feeling.

Finally, she composed herself, pulled her hands under her butt and over her feet bringing the cuffs in front of her.

She grabbed the keys and to her horror, they didn't fit!

"Shit! Shit! Shit!"

She gasped.

Quickly she dove into the drawer frantically searching through it, but there were no other keys...

PANIC!

Panic was the only thing she could feel. Then the worst thing happened, she heard Mike's voice down in the cabin shouting for her.

Like an acrobat, she stuffed her legs into her pants, stood up and popped her head out the door hiding her cuffed hands behind it, but her blushing face gave everything about her predicament away.

Mike looked at her puzzled for a second

"Is everything alright?"

He finally asked after standing there for a moment examining her with his gaze.

"Well, um, yeah, I mean no, well I have a problem."

Caitlyn grimaced as she exposed her cuffed hands from behind the door waiting for Mike to lay into her.

He simply pulled his key ring from his pocket, uncuffed the cuffs, placed them back in the drawer and headed back for the cockpit.

As he exited all he said was:

"If you cared to make some lunch it would be greatly appreciated; seas are getting a little difficult."

As the companionway hatch slid shut Caitlyn darted into the head and splashed water on her face, looking in the mirror the wave of embarrassment that overtook her was worse than anything she had ever felt before!

She wanted just to run away but she couldn't they were on a boat in the middle of nowhere heading up the inside passage, and it would be days before they were in Ketchikan!

She was stuck here whether she liked it or not.

Finally composing herself, Caitlyn made her way to the galley to make up some sandwiches and potato salad.

She dawned her jacket and took both plates up to the Cockpit where Mike was seated peacefully by the wheel just watching for other traffic enjoying the day.

The rain had let up Caitlyn sat down across from him still reeling in embarrassment.

Finally, she found some words:

>"I am so sorry..."

Mike cut her off holding his hand up then said:

>"We all have our things, we all have compulsions, you don't have to explain yourself to me although in the future I would appreciate if you wouldn't go through my stuff."

Caitlyn swallowed hard then looked down and away as she mumbled:

>"I'm sorry it won't happen again."

Just then the familiar spurting noise of a whale breaching sent Caitlyn bounding back down to the Vee birth to get her camera, this time she began clicking away and was sure she had the memory card in the camera!

She snapped photo after photo smiling all the while and then one of the killer whales breached hard not 200 feet from the boat slamming back into the water sending spray flying and Caitlyn got several frames of the whole thing!

"DID YOU SEE THAT!"

She exclaimed! Her voice riddled with laughter.

"That was amazing."

She continued before Mike could get a word in edgewise obviously incredibly excited beyond belief at the marvel she was experiencing.

The whales continued to breach for several minutes more near the boat before going off their separate way.

As they did Caitlyn turned to Mike who was now standing next to her watching them wrapped her arms around him all of the sudden almost knocking him back giving him a giant hug then she scampered off back down into the cabin to look at the images she had taken on her computer.

Mike smiled and laughed to himself as he resumed his position in the cockpit thinking how silly the little red headed firecracker who had taken up residence in his Vee Birth was.

⚓ SIX ⚓

Caitlyn awoke to footsteps on deck over her cabin, odd she thought that Mike would be walking on the front of the boat so early, he usually didn't come up out of the cockpit before she had woken unless it was to lift the anchor, but they were sitting still, and everything was calm.

Then splashing next to the boat and more footsteps on deck, then a thump and all was quiet again.

She dressed and stepped up the companionway, as her head poked over the top she could see him standing on the bowsprit compound bow in hand, aiming into the water.

Just then he let loose of the arrow, and it plunged below the surface of the water followed by much splashing as he reeled the fish in with a string attached to the arrow.

He dispatched the fish and threw it in a bucket with the previous one he had shot, then turned and brought everything back to the cockpit.

"Good morning, you hungry?"

Mike said with a smile.

"Yes, STARVING! What did you get?"

Caitlyn replied trying to peer into the bucket despite being way too short from her vantage point.

"King Salmon"

Mike replied with a big smile then he continued:

"I've been waiting all year for these bad boys to start running. Let me show you how to clean them."

Mike pulled a cutting board from one of the side compartments in the cockpit; it fit into a holder on the rail, there he took one of the fish, cut along the top just to the side of the spine, and the bottom just outside of the rib cage, then up behind the gills.

Then he cut down across the tail; then he ran the knife underneath to separate the fillet from the ribs, he placed the fillet to the side then flipped the fish over to do the other side, explaining the whole time to Caitlyn what he was doing.

Moments later the fresh fish was sizzling in a frying pan on the stove with some lime and herbs.

The delightful smell of the fresh fish cooking permeated the cabin.

As he cooked the meal up Caitlyn couldn't help but think about how different Mike was from so many of the men she had known, he was quiet, reserved, seemed as though he had nothing to prove to anyone, that he didn't need anyone.

She liked that.

Most men in her life were immature and obsessed with sports or video games, yet she didn't even see a TV on Mike's boat anywhere.

She had been on board for almost two weeks now, and she realized she still knew very little about him she didn't even know where he was from or if he had any siblings aside from his sister.

Mike had a funny way of turning the conversation away from himself, silly she thought because she had told him so much about herself, she had told him all about the situation with her mother and father, her time at University, her research paper.

She didn't even know if Mike's parents were still alive, if he had been to college or if he had any siblings or children, what about children?

She was abruptly interrupted from her thoughts when Mike set the plate of food down in front of her then sat himself down across the dinette.

> "We should make Ketchikan today if you need anything there are a few stores there."

Mike said pausing for a moment before speaking again:

> "Also if you want to take pictures it is a very pretty town, you may want to have your camera ready. It may make some good background material for your paper.
>
> Then tomorrow we will continue north, should be lots of whales in the passages out there with the salmon running."

Caitlyn smiled and thanked him. She thought about asking him more questions but the time just didn't seem right, so they finished breakfast mostly in silence.

As they finished their meal Mike asked her:

> "So you think you can get us under way today?"
>
> "ME?"

Caitlyn gasped in surprise.

> "Yeah, you've been paying attention and doing a bit of driving, how about seeing if you can get us under way, it's a perfect morning for it, light wind and calm water, you won't find a nicer day to try."

Moments later they were on deck, Caitlyn worked her way up to the main sheet, untied the lines that secured it to the boom, then stepped up to the bow, she grabbed the control for the anchor and pulled it in, then stepped back and started hoisting the main sail.

With the sail at the top of the mast, she hopped down into the cockpit and released the line for the jib furler, then she started pulling the Jib sheet around the winch with the rapid whirring noise of the ratchet mechanism in the winch humming as it spun.

The wind bellowed the sheets, and the boat began to move, a couple of turns on the main sheet winch and they were on their way, Caitlyn grabbed the wheel and steered them out towards the open water from the anchorage finally looking to Mike for a nod of approval.

"You did good kid."

Mike exclaimed with his big grin piercing out from his "sea beard" that was growing back in thick and full.

Caitlyn ate up the praise and smiled from ear to ear giggling a bit as the boat began to heel over and ride on the breeze.

Within a few hours off in the distance, a jet punched through the low hanging cloud layer then disappeared over the horizon.

The noise startled Caitlyn as the screeching of jet engines was so alien to this pristine environment.

"We're getting close now."

Mike said acknowledging the Jet was landing at Ketchikan.

Soon over the horizon, an island appeared off the starboard bow that was very different from the others due to the many buildings lining its coastline.

As they grew closer, Caitlyn could see an array of beautiful old rustic looking buildings that dotted the coastline of the island that jutted skyward out of the water.

She wondered to herself what it must have been like back in the 1800's when the gold rush brought people to this once barren land.

In all actuality the sights here had not changed all that much since then, well then the thought was interrupted by the sight of cruise ships, ok so they hadn't changed that much since then.

As they sailed past the ships, they waved to passengers aboard who were snapping pictures and hooping and hollering at them.

It made Caitlyn giggle that she was on a bit of a private cruise, not the floating tourist hell filled full of noise and people they were passing!

Finally, they dropped sail and motored up to a dock in Ketchikan Harbor.

As they tied up, Caitlyn couldn't help but marvel at the beauty of the city built on pilings and docks clinging to the edge of a mountain that rose from the water.

The place was quite beautiful as though it were something out of a dream.

Mike went up to the Marina searching for a few parts for the boat, leaving Caitlyn free to roam about the town.

She headed from the Marina walking along admiring the old buildings when she came to a road called Creek Street; there she found several old houses built on pilings.

A placard bolted to the railing stated that these homes were built in 1903, then she had to laugh when she realized all of the charming old buildings were brothels up until the oldest trade became illegal in 1954.

She snapped several images of the old houses of ill repute before walking further uptown.

However when she got there she was a bit disappointed, with the cruise ships in town everyone was out combing the town, people packed into the shops, loud, noisy children ran everywhere.

Just people everywhere made it uncomfortable and spoiled the ambiance and beauty of the quaint coastal town.

She decided to see if she could find gifts for her parents, she entered a shop and began to browse the trinkets they had for sale.

Alaska-themed merchandise hung everywhere, and bits and bobbles of the same nature filled the shelves with about every variety imaginable from shot glasses to fake license plates.

Then she heard it; she heard that voice from the past, nothing could be confused with that thick bitchy Irish accent.

Caitlyn wheeled about, and she saw her before she could duck out of sight the woman sighted her and made laser-focused eye contact then realizing who she was called out to her:

> "Caitlyn, oh Caitlyn! Is that you? Yes, I thought that was you!"

Caitlyn froze in her tracks not sure if she should just run like hell or acknowledge her presence.

The woman was Mary Ann Murphy, as a child she had been Caitlyn's arch nemesis. Mary Ann was the worst kind of enemy; she was a frenemy, someone who acted like your friend but who was really your enemy.

What the hell was she doing here thousands of miles away from Ireland? Well no matter now, here she was.

Mary Ann approached her with a man in tow; the tall, lanky Englishman was every bit of 6'6" and 175 lbs with the way she had her arm wrapped around his and gripped on tight she was making it obvious to the world this was her man, and everyone else needed to back off.

"Oh yes Caitlyn, I thought that was you! How have you been?"

Mary Ann asked in her usual cheery, bubbly condescending tone.

"I am well, how are you?"

Was the only thing Caitlyn could think to say.

"I am so glad you asked, I would like to introduce you to someone, this is my Fiancé Robert!"

Mary Ann gloated with a twinkle in her eye that just made Caitlyn want to claw them out but trying to be the lady she smiled and shook his hand as he extended it as her mother had made her do so many times before.

"Hello, how do you do?"

Caitlyn said as she smiled her best fake smile.

"Very pleased to meet you."

Robert responded in perfect proper English.

"Robert is a Lieutenant in Her Majesty's Royal Navy!"

Mary Ann pronounced.

"Really? Well, congratulations to you both."

Caitlyn smiled as she wondered how long she would have to endure this horribly uncomfortable conversation.

"Are you here for the cruise?"

Mary Ann queried.

"Um no, I am here working on a research paper for college."

"College? Where are you attending, not the community college I presume?"

Mary Ann smirked. Caitlyn smiled her first real smile of the conversation as she casually said:

"Um no, University of Hawaii."

As the words came out of her mouth, Caitlyn could see Mary Ann's expression start to go cold.

"Oh, then what are you doing all the way up here?"

Mary Ann Quipped.

"Well you see I am studying Marine Biology and I am writing my thesis on whales."

Caitlyn replied dreading the obvious verbal daggers she knew were about to come.

"But how did you wind up here from Hawaii?"

Mary Ann again queried.

"Well you see I hired a boat to bring me up here so I could see them first hand and photograph them."

Caitlyn replied, hoping not to have to reveal anything of her ordeal with the captain that had ripped her off.

"Isn't that expensive? That sounds very expensive to me. I know Robert's parents were was so gracious to buy us these tickets for our holiday, and that was very expensive, I can't even imagine how you afforded to charter a whole boat."

Mary Ann smirked feeling any moment she would be able to deliver the Coup De Gras to Caitlyn's self-esteem.

> "Well actually it is a sailboat, and well, I, I got him to bring me for free."

Caitlyn Blurted not knowing what else to say.

At this Mary Ann smiled and leaned in close and whispered:

> "Are you fucking him, is that how you got him to bring you up here?"

> "I, I've done nothing of the sort!"

Caitlyn bellowed in her thick Irish accent, Mary Ann set back on her heels and then smiled before saying:

> "Oh, poor dear, you fancy him, but he doesn't want you."

Mary Ann replied shooting an evil grin right through Caitlyn.

This was all it took, yes Caitlyn wanted him, yes she was hot for him, and it made her crazy that he was showing no signs of reciprocation now this bitch was rubbing it in her face!

Caitlyn boiled over, she exploded and leaped at Mary Ann in a fit of rage swinging at her with everything she had her Irish temper getting the better of her as they went crashing through a display case they sent trinkets flying everywhere!

⚓ SEVEN ⚓

Water beaded down from the twilight sky as Mike trudged up the steps of the Ketchikan Police station, he grabbed the door, and it squeaked as it opened, allowing entrance to the hall where flickering fluorescent lighting flooded the space with cold, ugly light.

There on the hard wooden bench in the hallway sat a tall, lanky man who despite his ripped jacket and messed up hair and the claw marks on his cheek sat composed with perfect posture waiting to be called upon.

Mike took a seat next to the man. They exchanged glances Mike looked him up and down one more time and spoke:

> "Well, I suspect you would be part of what is going on here, care to fill me in?"

The man looked to Mike, shook his head and started speaking in his perfect Queens English.

> "Well you see, earlier today I was with my fiancée, we were here to take a cruise for our holiday, and we were out shopping, and then she spotted an old friend they began chatting, and the next thing you know they were fighting!
>
> I just couldn't believe it!"
>
> "Your fiancée knows Caitlyn?"

Mike asked.

> "Yes apparently, they are old friends going back to primary school. Or at least they used to be."

Robert replied shaking his head in disbelief.

Mike felt for him; he could see from his expression that Robert was finding out that the woman whom he had betrothed wasn't quite who she advertised herself to be.

About then the door in the hallway swung open, and a police sergeant stepped out.

> "You Mike Black?"

He asked.

> "I am."

Mike responded standing up to shake his hand.

With the introductions out of the way, the Sargent explained to the men that if the bill for the glassware the women destroyed in their brawl was paid in full that the charges would be dropped and the women would be released.

The two agreed to split the bill between them; it came out to $750.00 each.

As he put his wallet away, Mike reached out to shake Robert's hand and spoke:

> "Sorry for your troubles, I hope you have a better time on the trip from here out."

Robert smiled warmly and shook his hand then sighed as he spoke.

> "Thank you so much, but I am afraid there will be no cruise, we will be flying directly back to England, I am not going to marry her."

Mike frowned paused for a moment and then spoke.

> "Well that is unfortunate, I wish you the best."

Robert smiled and laughed a cheeky British laugh.

"Oh it's alright my good man, I'd have rather found out now that she was no good then after we had been married for some years.

I should be thanking your young lady for exposing her to me!"

That broke the tension, and Mike laughed and said:

"Well, I will say I do have my hands full with that one."

Robert smiled and said:

"You have a special girl in that one, I can see it in the way she reacted she has feelings for you. When this whole thing started, it was because Mary Ann was speaking badly of you."

Mike paused for a moment, unsure of what to say next and he didn't have to say anything, the door to the hall swung open again, and the Sargent lead the two men back to where Mary Ann and Caitlyn sat handcuffed at opposite ends of a bench.

The Sargent un-cuffed Caitlyn first, she stood up, hugged Mike, and the only thing she could say was:

"I'm so sorry!"

Mike just patted her on the back and said:

"Let's get out of here!"

Then he turned to Robert and extended his hand one more time speaking as they shook.

"Nice to meet you, Robert, I wish it had been under better circumstances."

Robert ever the gentleman shook Mike's hand, told him it was a pleasure to have met him and in true sailors fashion wished him "Fair winds and following seas."

They exited the room back into the hallway, and as they reached the door they could hear Mary Ann pipe up yelling inside of the room:

"No, no, darling please no!"

Mike shook his head knowing that Robert had delivered the bad news.

Caitlyn stopped and looked back, with a puzzled expression she looked to Mike all he said was:

"The wedding is off."

Caitlyn's heart sunk and she felt horrible.

Back at the harbor, they walked in silence, Caitlyn had her hands stuffed deep into her pockets, and her head down as they walked, all of the sudden Mike chuckled to himself.

"What's so funny?"

Caitlyn asked.

"Oh, I was just thinking to myself, this is the second time this week I've seen you in handcuffs, I'm beginning to think you like it."

Mike said with a deep hearty chuckle.

Caitlyn didn't know what to she could feel her face turning bright bright red, not knowing what to do she panicked and sprinted back to the boat trying to hide her embarrassment.

She hopped over the side, down the Companionway and locked herself inside of the Vee Birth before collapsing into her bed.

Mike completely unphased just laughed to himself as he walked calmly back to the boat.

⚓ EIGHT ⚓

The wiring of the Diesel Engine sputtering and coughing to life woke Caitlyn from a deep sleep, the light burned her eyes, and she was disoriented.

Her body ached and the previous day seemed like a bad dream, she was still sticky and sweaty and nasty from having been in the fight then sleeping fully clothed. She had spent most of the last night wondering if this morning Mike would tell her she was too much trouble and kick her off the boat.

She knew he had spent a lot of money on her last night; she knew what a big deal it was because she was down to her last three hundred dollars and if she had to pay the seven hundred fifty up front she would have been in real trouble.

She wondered what would become of Mary Ann, on the one hand, it felt good to finally have beaten the crap out of her after so many years of torment.

On the other, however, she felt horrible for taking part in ending her marriage. The fear that Mike would deliver the same news to her this morning that she was off the boat choked her up inside.

Timidly she reached for the handle to open the door to go and face the music and then jumped suddenly when the quiet tension of the cabin was interrupted by her phone ringing.

She pulled it from her pocket.

"Shit!"

She exclaimed when she saw it was Professor Ames.

"Hello Professor!"

She said trying to sound cheery and awake.

"Well hello Caitlyn, I hear we are having a bit too much fun in Ketchikan, are you alright?"

He queried her through the phone.

"Yes, everything is fine now, everything is ok."

She grimaced through the phone.

"I just wanted to check on you; the police had to contact me to find Mike so he could come get you out of Jail."

The professor said matter of fact.

Caitlyn's heart sunk at that word, Jail, she had been in Jail, and it was horrible.

Jail.

Big fat tears began to stream down her face; she said the only thing she could say:

"I'm sorry, I have to go, I will call you."

With that she hung up the phone and slumped back down on the bed, burying her face in the tattered ends of the sleeves on her hoodie.

She sobbed long and hard into them.

A bit later Caitlyn emerged from the cabin, her clothes were ripe, her hair was a mess, and her cheeks were stained black from mascara tears being wiped away.

She could feel the boat moving; they were under way.

As she made her way aft, she could hear the familiar sound of the main sheet as it was hoisted up the mast and the footsteps back to the cockpit then the engine cut off.

Caitlyn paused seeing her reflection, she looked like hell, and she couldn't let Mike see her this way.

She darted back forward into the head, washed her face and brushed her hair and her teeth, pulled off her tattered hoodie and found another one from her bag then she worked up all of her courage, it was time to face the music.

The climb the companionway steps felt like she was climbing the Swiss Alps, it was only four steps, but it took everything she had.

Caitlyn paused as her hand touched the hatch to slide it open. Finally, she swallowed hard, pulled it back and pulled out the board and stepped into the cockpit.

Mike sat in his usual place propped up against the edge of the cockpit with a book. He looked up as though nothing was wrong and greeted her with a big smile.

"Good morning."

Caitlyn nodded not yet ready to speak.

She sat down across from Mike in the cockpit. Leaning forward her chest against her knees, wrapping her arms around the front of her legs. She felt completely timid and childish.

An uncomfortable silence filled the air Caitlyn just couldn't find the words.

Finally, Mike looked up over his book and spoke.

> "Kid, I will give you this, you've got a lot of spirit, and you've got a lot of heart and a lot of passion."

Oh great here we go! Caitlyn thought to herself figuring next he was fixing to tell her she was off the boat.

"I don't know what went on between you and that woman growing up but I suspect you have your reasons.

I would just advise that in the future you think a little bit more about the ramifications before you start throwing punches."

Mike said in a somber, thoughtful tone; then he continued after a brief pause.

"I'm not mad at you; I'm not going to lecture you because I can see you're already doing enough of a job beating up on yourself over your decisions last night, you don't need my help."

DAMNIT! Caitlyn thought, she could tell that Mike could see right through her, she grimaced waiting for what was going to come. Next, she was sure this was the part where he was about to say he couldn't have her on his boat.

Then he totally shocked her, all he said was:

"You hungry? I'm going to make breakfast. Keep a watch out for me."

With that, he got up and stepped down the companionway into the kitchen and started rummaging through the cupboards.

Caitlyn still in disbelief sat back and ran her fingers through her hair, tears beaded up at the corners of her eyes and she wiped them away. Her adventure wasn't over… yet!

NINE

That night at dinner Caitlyn sat across from Mike at the table in their usual places, but there was still an ever-present tension that lingered in the air.

Mike calmly and quietly ate his dinner, Caitlyn, however, picked at her own, more concerned with her thoughts than her food.

Finally, she looked at Mike and asked:

> "So Mike, I have to ask you something?"

> "Yes?"

Mike replied looking up from his meal.

> "Why am I still here, why didn't you kick me off the boat? I've done nothing but cause you trouble."

Mike set his knife and fork down and sat back in his seat with the way his posture changed Caitlyn could tell he was preparing to deliver a very serious response then he spoke.

> "Well, you see it is because we are Shipmates."

> "Shipmates?" Caitlyn wondered aloud.

> "Yes, Shipmates."

Mike said again in his same serious tone, but sensing she didn't fully understand he elaborated:

> "You see there is an unwritten law of the sea and that is you watch out for your shipmates."

Seeing she didn't fully understand Mike continued

> "I'm sure you had your reasons for not liking that woman, getting into a fist fight in the middle of a crowded public market in the middle of the day is not something someone just goes and does when they are

completely sober, so I figure you must have had your reasons.

When you signed on for this voyage here with me, I promised you Seattle to Anchorage as long as you held up your end.

That made us shipmates. You're a part of my crew, and a good captain doesn't leave his crew behind.

That and I trust that in good time you will pay me back."

With that, Mike picked up his fork and knife and began eating again.

Caitlyn was totally flabbergasted, and with this, she understood something while relatively young, Mike had the heart of an old man of the sea.

His time in the Navy had beaten a code of ethics and honor into him that was unbreakable, and she was now beginning to understand many of his actions throughout this entire adventure were based on that simple, strong moral code that was centuries old.

That was what made this man so different, that is what drove her so wild about him he wasn't like so many other men of the day who were rude crass and selfish.

All of the things that had made her turn her affections and attentions to women in the first place.

Then she realized, she had not called her girlfriend since Seattle. She had been so enamored with this trip from the get go she had totally forgotten to call her.

"Shit!" She thought to herself.

Then she excused herself from the table, retrieved her phone from the charger in the vee birth, but it was no use now, they had sailed outside of cell service.

Caitlyn's heart sank, she felt like a horrible person.

She felt like she was just becoming a problem to anyone and everyone around her.

Now she wondered when this was over, would she have a girlfriend to go back to, would she have an apartment to go back to?

She could tell things in her life were changing and pondering these questions kept her awake late into the night.

The next few days things about the boat returned to normal. Caitlyn snapped photos of whales and took turns sailing with Mike.

They caught quite a few fish and even saw dolphins.

For Caitlyn, it was all so surreal heading up the inside passage the steep mountain faces covered in trees plunging skyward right out of the water in most places having little to no beach.

This land was beautiful, and it was deadly. That is always the way with Mother Nature; she is always her most beautiful when she is trying to kill you.

And soon the storms would come.

⚓ TEN ⚓

Through the end of June, they pushed north from Ketchikan up the passages that wound between the islands that plunged from the water thrusting skyward.

Some nights they would take shifts and keep sailing, others they would find a place to anchor.

Caitlyn got plenty of time at the wheel and at trimming the sails, soon she was sailing like a pro.

Mike found that she knew what to do before he could tell her to do it, and in him, a sense of pride was growing seeing how she was adapting to life on the sea.

Soon they had arrived in the sleepy little fishing village of Wrangell, as they pulled in to anchor on shore fireworks shot into the air and burst from different locations.

The sun had dropped below the horizon, leaving the sky with a beautiful iridescent deep blue glow, which set an amazing backdrop for the pink, red and orange fireworks as they whizzed up and popped in the air.

Once they had anchored, Caitlyn and Mike just stood there in the cockpit looking out at the spectacular scene of the fireworks and the massive mountains lumbering in the distance.

As the fireworks ashore went off with flashes and bang a feeling overtook Caitlyn, a sense of belonging, she looked over at Mike who was standing next to her looking out at the display; she wanted to reach out and hold his hand she started to reach but turned back afraid.

Feeling silly she turned and went below to start making dinner.

A couple of moments later after checking the anchor, Mike came down.

"Not feeling the fourth of July?"

He asked sitting down in his usual spot.

"Oh no, I have celebrated the 4th before, remember my dad is American."

Caitlyn replied in her thick Irish accent as she tried to get dinner together.

"Oh, you came down here kind of suddenly, everything alright?"

"I'm fine."

"You sure about that."

"Yes yes, I'm fine."

Caitlyn snapped back twisting and obviously frustrated.

Mike took that as his cue to step back topside. He sat down where he could see the town and the random fireworks that popped off in the distance.

The sky began to pierce through with the dusting of stars; the night was calm and peaceful except for the occasional distant pop.

A bit later Caitlyn stepped topside with a plate of food and handed it to Mike.

"I'm sorry I snapped at you, I am just feeling a little homesick."

She lied hoping he would buy it; the truth was she had hardly thought of home since she had been here.

Mike didn't say anything, he just took his plate and sat back and quietly ate.

Caitlyn stepped back below and ate her food.

As she sat picking through the last of it the excuse she had given started to work through her mind, home.

She was very far from home in Hawaii, she had hardly spoken to her girlfriend since she had been here, and now she was conflicted, she really liked Mike, but Anne was sweet too. It wasn't very serious, in fact, their relationship was rather casual.

She still felt guilty, and the guilt started eating her up.

The next day after a walk-through town they weighed anchor and headed back north, more whales, more amazing scenery, more wildlife.

The beauty of the place was so amazing that at times it was overwhelming!

The evening of the July 3rd they crept up to Juneau, a light breeze pushing them over almost flat calm water. Finally, they reached the Marina and grabbed a slip after radioing the office.

As they paid for the slip the clerk behind the counter told them they should check out the 4th of July parade in the morning that it was only two blocks away., Mike said that they would.

The night was uneventful, Caitlyn tried calling Anne before she went to bed, but got no answer, she started to feel alone and confused.

This trip had already had so many ups and downs, she began to feel like she would have been better off to just not come at all.

She wanted to fly back home but her ticket was for Anchorage, they were still many miles away. She didn't have the money to change it.

Nothing was going the way she hoped, and the bad feelings about being arrested welled up inside of her, it didn't help that Mike had been so easy going about it, in fact, it would have been better if he were upset then she wouldn't have felt so guilty.

The feelings all were starting to gnaw at her insides; she lay in bed just thinking everything over unable to quiet her brain she kept checking the time on her phone, 1:38, 2:27, 3:14, 4:40

Suddenly she was stirred awake by Mike knocking on the cabin door.

> "Hey wake up, get your camera, you don't want to miss this!"

He shouted through the door, Caitlyn grabbed her clothes, skipped her shoes and came topside camera in hand.

Mike pointed to a Bald Eagle resting on a light pole towards the end of the pier.

Caitlyn lifted her camera and started taking pictures, the bird just sat there though preening its feathers then stayed, soon it lifted off and simply flew away.

It was anti-climactic, to say the least.

Caitlyn cleaned herself up and skipped breakfast; she was feeling pretty haggard from the night before.

This morning her mood had only improved marginally.

They walked up town, and each got a beer from a vendor selling them from a tent, and they found a place to stand and watch.

Soon the parade began to roll by, Caitlyn was a bit surprised when the Veterans at the front of the parade passed carrying the flag, Mike popped to attention and saluted the flag.

It reminded her of something, a happy thought, the way her father had done the same many years ago when she was just a girl on one of her first trips to the US to visit him.

He had taken her to the 4th of July parade in San Diego because he wanted her to understand what the day was all about. He wanted her to understand what freedom was all about.

She had asked him why he did that, his response was

> "Honey, it is because many brave men have died carrying that flag so we can be free."

Caitlyn slipped her phone from her pocket and punched out a text message.

Caitlyn: 10:46pm
I love you dad, happy 4th of July from Juneau Alaska!

Then a sound gripped her ears, a sound that ripped her back to the land of her birth.

Bagpipes marching up the street! They were playing Scotland the brave, and even though she was Irish, it made Caitlyn smile just the same because she remembered her grandfather taking her to see the pipers play when she was just a girl.

The warm memory faded back into reality, and she stood with Mike and watched the floats pass, then it dawned on her, he was so much like her father and her grandfather.

She began to think of them, and then a dreadful thought entered her mind, what would they think of her where she was at in life now, getting arrested, being a problem, being taken advantage of?

The thought made her feel horrible because she felt like they would be terribly disappointed. She had sworn her mother to secrecy, but in her gut, she knew her mother was terrible at keeping secrets. Especially ones about her.

That night they rode the dinghy over to the other shore and made a camp fire on the beach, and sat down on folding chairs they brought along with a cooler between them full of cold beer.

From there they could see the big city fireworks display in all of its glory thumping flashing and booming across the water.

They had not spoken much all day, Caitlyn seemed to kill whatever conversation Mike tried to start with short one word answers.

Eventually, he just let her be.

After sitting in silence for a bit out of the blue Mike just started talking.

"You know when I was just a boy my grandpa, and I sailed up here on his boat, it was the first long distance passage I had made in my lifetime, I remember it like yesterday, but it was so long ago.

No auto pilot we had to hand steer the whole way, his boat was old school, a tiller no wheel. Made of wood with a manual bilge pump you had to check several times a day to be sure it was dry.

If the boat had been out of the water for any period of time, the wood would dry out and when you put it back in it would leak until it swelled back up.

I spent a lot of time working that bilge pump as a kid, spent a lot of time on that boat polishing brass and sanding and varnishing.

That first trip was so special to me.

We wound up sitting not too far from here watching the fireworks just as we are doing now.

One night a few years later sitting at the dock a vagrant broke into the boat trying to stay warm. He took one of the pots off of the stove and lit a fire in it, but the heat caused the paint to combust under the pot and set the boat ablaze.

Before they could get it put out she had burned down to the waterline.

I had never seen grandpa so upset.

He had built that boat himself from a set of plans.

He eventually built another boat, and I helped him with that while I was stationed in Bremerton, but the new boat was a steel hull motor yacht, he never got another sailboat.

When I got out of the Navy and bought My Way, it was the first time he and I had been sailing since then.

The man was so happy he cried, I will never forget the look on his face.

He was supposed to come on this trip, but he is 95 and hasn't been feeling well."

Without saying anything, Caitlyn reached over and took Mikes hand, and he clutched hers back.

It was a sweet moment of solidarity and understanding as the fireworks boomed off in the distance.

⚓ ELEVEN ⚓

After another two weeks of good sailing, they found themselves becalmed 20 nautical miles south of Yakutat.

Finally, having had enough of sitting around Mike fired up the motor and pushed forth hoping to make the pier in Yakutat before nightfall.

A sailboat with no breeze is like a fat duckling trying to swim. In the swells that quartered the bow, she would bob and roll as they came through making the ride very uncomfortable.

Caitlyn found herself curled up below on the settee wishing the conditions would improve.

Soon they rounded the point, and the swells let down once inside the protected anchorage.

Caitlyn emerged from the cabin to find Mike standing at the helm, he greeted her with his usual smile and pointed towards town.

She turned to find a small town emerging before them.

The City of Yakutat was quaint, nothing more than a village really, long piers lined with fishing boats sat adjacent to the public dock where they moored for the night.

At dinner, Mike sat at his usual place, and Caitlyn sat at hers, Mike talked of all of the preparations they would have to make before leaving on the next leg of the voyage to Kodiak Island.

Caitlyn, however, was distracted and restless; she longed to get off the boat and to have some fun. It had been so long since she had a night out the desire was burning inside of her to get out and mingle.

"Mike.."

She said catching his attention before continuing:

"I want to go into town."

"I don't think anything is open at this hour; it's almost Midnight."

Mike responded with a tone that just seemed to say 'That's not happening.'

Frustrated Caitlyn snapped back.

"They have bar's don't they?"

"They do, but Yakutat is not a town to play around in, it's a tough town, a fishing town. The fleet is in, and they don't play nice here."

Mike responded with the same somber authoritarian tone.

Not wanting to be told what to do Caitlyn stood up and dawned her jacket.

"We'll I'm going. Are you coming with?"

Mike just shook his head and sat back in his seat giving her a look that seemed to say: 'Are you out of your mind?'

"Fine, I will go by myself."

Caitlyn Quipped.

"Suit yourself."

Mike said this time without any feeling in his words.

This pissed Caitlyn off, as she stepped off the boat and stormed up the pier towards town she said to herself over and over that it wasn't fair for him to tell her not to go to town.

She was a grown woman; she could take care of herself, she didn't need Mike telling her what to do.

Up the street and into the first bar she came to, and when Caitlyn stepped through the door, it was like all of the sudden everyone just stopped talking and looked at her.

Here she was 5' tall red haired freckled faced Caitlyn Campbell all the way from Cork Ireland now standing in a bar in Yakutat Alaska, literally on the other side of the world with a bunch of fishermen who looked and smelled as though they had been on the boat for weeks.

Caitlyn tried to act as though nothing was wrong, after a moment the talking started again and she made her way to the bar trying to maintain her composure and not break out blushing as she was so prone to doing.

She sat at the bar and the bartender the only other woman in the place asked her what she wanted.

"Do you have Guinness?"

Caitlyn responded trying to sound as American as possible not wanting to draw any more attention to herself.

The bartender looked her up and down and halfway snorted before saying nothing and stepping off to get her drink.

She returned and placed the bottle down in front of Caitlyn on a little bar napkin.

As soon as the bartender turned and walked away there he was, the stench of this man about made her eyes water, he had obviously not bathed in a long while, he was dirty, grimy and covered in fish guts and engine oil.

The man pushed a stool out of the way and leaned up to the bar next to her, Caitlyn just froze in place half disgusted, half mortified.

The man looked her up and down wriggling his pockmarked nose, below it an unfiltered cigarette dangled from his lips that were as weathered as the rest of his face.

Not removing the cigarette from his mouth he managed to retain it while it flipped up and down as he spoke.

"Haven't seen you round here before."

Caitlyn remained silent hoping he would just go away.

"I'm Earl. What's your name?"

The man queried after a moment of silence, and a few hard drags on his cigarette.

Caitlyn finally looked half way at him realizing she had made a mistake she hopped off the stool said she was sorry that she had to go and made her way for the door.

Outside Caitlyn walked quickly her arms wrapped around herself pulling her coat in tight as though that would keep her safer.

As she walked, she kept feeling as though she was being followed, but the town was too poorly lit for her to see.

Now and then she would turn about and look back, but nothing other than the creeping feeling she was not alone.

Then she realized, she wasn't entirely sure where the boat was, where Mike was, where safety was.

Panic started to set in, Caitlyn walked faster finding the piers she started looking for the boat, but she didn't see it. Finally, she spotted her sitting tied to the dock, Down the pier she walked, then she felt it, a hand reached out and grabbed her arm!

"Hey, I wasn't done with you yet!"

Earl's voice bellowed through the night.

Caitlyn let out a shrieking scream with everything she had as the big drunk pawed at her and drug her back up the pier towards an old wooden fishing trawler.

She twisted and convulsed, and the man slapped her making her ears ring, she fell to the ground, then a kick to her ribs left her wheezing and breathless, all she could do is curl up in a ball and try to protect herself as she gasped for air.

Wheez! Wheez! Wheez! The man shouted, but she could not hear.

Wheez! Wheez! Wheez! The big drunk reached down and grabbed a hand full of her hair and started to lift her by it.

Then she heard it, heavy footsteps running on the pier and with a sudden collision of two bodies slamming into each other like football players slamming into each other headlong the man was gone and she was all alone!

Then she heard it, the splash violent and sudden it sprayed water back up onto her wetting her face.

Wheez! Wheez! Wheez!

She rolled over to see down into the black water, below the surface there was a mass of twisted men foaming and frothing, but she could not see what was happening.

Wheez! Wheez! Wheez!

She tried to call out, but the pain in her chest stopped her.

Wheez! Wheez! Wheez!

Caitlyn lie helpless reaching an outstretched twisted hand towards the water watching the bubbles slowly fade leaving nothing but black water below.

As she wheezed and gasped for air Caitlyn started to sob heavy tears running down her face, she rolled onto her side and curled back into the ball.

Then a splash below, more splashes, a man gasping for air, Caitlyn tried to sit up but the pain was unbearable, she tried to move, but every time she did another sucking wheeze put her back down.

More splashes this time louder down on the dock below on the other side of the pier.

Then heavy footsteps clanking up the aluminum gangway mixed with the sound of water dripping from a body.

Caitlyn! Mike yelled out as he reached the top of the ramp half out of breath.

Trying to speak all she got out was Wheez! Wheez! Wheez!

Mike ran to her, as he touched her the coldness of his body was shocking. Everything was wet; his skin had begun to lose its color, he shivered uncontrollably.

Despite this, he managed to help her to her feet which helped, but the water from his clothing soaked into hers and the cold bit into her flesh his body felt like ice not a man of flesh and bone.

Back down the gangway they clamored, Caitlyn blurted out a small "I'm so sorry" as her wheezing slowed, so did Mike, the last steps back to the boat were labored and heavy and his body shook uncontrollably she could hear his teeth begin to chatter.

Over the gunnel and down into the cockpit, he forced the hatch open but could barely move, Caitlyn grabbed a hand hold and helped herself down the steps the best she could collapsing in a pile on the floor in the galley.

Mike collapsed just outside of the companionway staring down at her.

Caitlyn coaxed him:

> "Please come on, don't die on me, please I need you!"

It was as though Mike got her back to the boat and once she was safely inside he just gave up.

> "Please Mike, please don't quit! Please!"

Tears renewed streamed down her face, and she mouthed the words:

> "Please no, I love you."

Mike lay against the hatch frame and shivered staring at her.

> "Please please please!"

She sobbed.

With a final push, Mike rallied his strength, swung himself down into the cabin pushing his way forward to the shower, his curled frozen hands struggled to start the water but soon the hot water was flowing.

Caitlyn still lying heaped on the galley deck just went limp and listened, then a blood-curdling scream bit through the night as the warm water pierced into Mike's nearly frozen flesh.

The sound made Caitlyn wince; the tears streamed, then more screams, all at once the feeling consumed her as she murmured:

> "My god, what have I done?"

⚓ TWELVE ⚓

After what seemed like an eternity Mike emerged from the bathroom, a towel wrapped around his waist, his skin was red and blotchy.

All at once he dropped his mass onto the settee still labored in his breathing.

Caitlyn still sitting piled on the galley deck still sobbed more softly now, the wheezing had been replaced by a stinging burning in her side, but she was in too much pain to do anything about it.

Mike sat up and stoked the fire in the little stainless steel fireplace then laid back obviously in a great deal of pain.

"You still alive?"

He called out to Caitlyn.

"Yes."

She squeaked and sniffed.

Pulling himself to his feet, Mike helped her up off the cabin sole and back over to the seatee. Caitlyn winced with pain as he helped her sit down pulling her arm to her side like a chicken wing.

"Here let me have a look at you."

Mike demanded as he turned her slowly helping her remove her coat, then he lifted her shirt revealing a single kick mark about the size of a hockey puck on the back-right side of her ribs.

"He got you good didn't he."

Mike remarked, Caitlyn could do nothing but nod as she winced then Mike gently prodded at the wound with his fingertips,

Caitlyn tried to scream, but only a muffled wrenching noise came out as he whole body went tense and the pain exploded.

"Easy."

Mike said softly then added.

"I don't think your ribs are broken, just badly bruised."

With that, the prodding stopped, and Mike let her shirt fall back down.

Caitlyn looked up to him with tears in her eyes and asked:

"The man, where is he?"

Mike replied in a matter of fact way:

"He's dead."

Caitlyn went stoic and slumped into the corner. Dead? The man was dead. Mike had almost died. The sudden realization gripped her that this was all her fault.

Mike stood up and walked over to the NAV station firing up the radio he picked up the mic.

"Coast Guard"
"Coast Guard"
"Coast Guard"
"This is sailing Vessel My way Over?"

The static crackled through the radio as it came alive

"This is US Coast Guard, Vessel hailing please Identify yourself over."

"This is the sailing vessel My Way, repeat My Way over."

"This is US Coast Guard, go ahead My Way."

"Coast Guard this is My Way, We're at the pier in Yakutat, there has been an incident there is a body in the water, we need assistance, can you call local law enforcement? Over."

"My Way this is Coast Guard, you are at the pier, and there is a body in the water? Over."

Soon the pier was flooded with a cacophony of life and activity; a patrol boat ran through the harbor panning a light back and forth, the sheriff and several deputies arrived.

Soon Caitlyn was answering questions reliving the whole ordeal over and over; then it came time for Mike to tell his story:

"I was down in the boat reading a book, I heard a blood-curdling scream, as I opened the hatch I could see the man throw her to the ground, so I charged up the pier at him.

We tripped over the top of her and went into the water, he kept trying to drag me down, he had pulled my shirt over my head, I was able to get to my knife and stabbed him several times until he let go.

Then it was all I could do to get back to my boat and into the shower to warm myself back up."

The sheriff looked at Mike unsure whether to believe his story. Then his radio crackled to life: "Sheriff, you had better get over here, we found the body."

The sheriff walked up the dock to the patrol boat that was just tying off.

Laying in the back was the hulk of what had once been Earl, his mouth agape, slash marks covered his forearms where the now grey flesh opened up in places down to the bone; a piece of

Mike's tee shirt still wretched in his fingers, Mike's knife still rested plunged into the man's eye up to the hilt.

> "Earl Earl Earl, I guess you met your match this time didn't you."

The sheriff remarked with a twisted grin.

> "Alright, boy's bag him and tag him."

The Sheriff ordered as she stood up wiping the grit from the deck from his knee.

He stepped back aboard My Way to find Mike and Caitlyn sitting there talking to a paramedic that was examining Caitlyn.

> "Yeah ole Earl, he had a bad habit of thinking he could do whatever he wanted when he got drunk, I guess he finally met up with someone meaner than he was.
>
> If you can do that when you're sober, I'd hate to see you drunk. You cut that boy to ribbons."

The Sheriff said as he rested against the cabinet in the galley.

Caitlyn puzzled looked to Mike and then back to the Sheriff.

Mike leaned back in his seat and smirked then retorted:

> "Play stupid games win stupid prizes!"

The Sheriff chuckled then responded.

> "Ole Earl, he had a reputation and a record to go with it around here, there are a lot of folks who won't shed any tears over seeing him go.
>
> But his brother is just about as much as a son of a bitch as he is, and when he finds out, you killed him there is no telling what he will do.

I am going to suggest you folks get under way tonight and get some good distance between you and here to let things calm down."

Mike more serious replied.

"I think that is a really good idea, that is what we will do."

After completing a police report and getting the go ahead from the Sheriff Mike untied the lines and pushed off the dock while Caitlyn hauled herself forward into the vee birth collapsing into bed.

Mike rounded the breakwater and motored out towards the open ocean.

They slipped away quietly into the night.

⚓ THIRTEEN ⚓

Caitlyn awoke to bright sunlight pouring in through the portlights; the engine was off they were under sail. The sea was choppy.

She pulled off her clothes which now had begun to stink and pulled on fresh ones before making her way topside.

Mike was sitting in his usual place in the cockpit, but no book in hand and his normally fresh-faced smile was absent replaced by a man who was cold somber and tired.

Just as Caitlyn appeared, he stood.

"You alright?"

He asked.

Caitlyn merely nodded, her vocal cords still wrecked from the night before.

"I've already got the plotter set; we're heading across the Gulf to Kodiak Island, I want to get as much distance between them and us as we can.

If his brother comes looking for us he is likely to watch along the coast up to Anchorage; we're going to shoot well south of that across the gulf. Then we can backtrack to Anchorage."

Caitlyn again nodded taking up her usual seat in the cockpit.

"Can you take it, I need to get some sleep."

Mike asked running his hand over his weary face.

"Yes... yes, I will be ok, you sleep."

Caitlyn replied timidly.

Mike nodded, and as he made his way down the companionway he said over his shoulder:

"Don't forget to clip in."

Before sliding the hatch shut.

Caitlyn reached down and grabbed the carabiner on the life line and clipped it into her life jacket.

She sat stoically scanning the horizon land was completely out of sight, off to the north a storm system was building, and a thick gray haze covered the sky.

The boat bobbed over the swells; the wind was light with the occasional gust, it was miserable sailing.

Even more miserable was Caitlyn's mood, she sat perched in her seat, shifting her weight to work with the swells, each time she did the pain in her back would flare.

With this the events of the night before replayed over and over again in her head. She kept thinking how stupid she had been not to heed Mike's advice.

Why did she always have to be so stubborn? Why did she always let her temper get the better of herself then get humiliated?

It all began to manifest its self into a giant ball of frustration and guilt growing inside of her.

The following days came and went, the sea state was never favorable, the passage as a whole was miserable, running away from something was never a pleasant experience, doing it across the Gulf of Alaska in crap weather was even worse.

 Mike and Caitlyn hardly spoke. It was clear the events had now strained their friendship to the frayed ends.

Caitlyn was consumed with a sinking feeling that she had fucked everything up. That it was all her fault and had it not been for her being there, Mike would have been enjoying his trip to Alaska, not dealing with her problems.

They had been sailing for days when one morning Caitlyn awoke to her phone ringing. She had not heard it ring in so long the sensation startled her, she leaped out of bed and fumbled with it, but the call ended before she could answer.

Pulling up the caller ID she saw it was Professor Ames, quickly she redialed him.

> "Hello Professor?"

> "Caitlyn, yes how are you, you never called me back I was beginning to worry about you. Is everything ok."

Sniffing Caitlyn began to sob.

> "No, no it is not ok, everything is wrong, I ruined everything."

> "What do you mean?"

The professor queried in a concerned voice.

> "I wrecked Mikes summer, he doesn't even want to speak to me, I made so many mistakes. He hates me now. No matter what I do he won't talk to me, it is like he has shut me out!"

> "Oh, it's probably not all you."

> "What do you mean?"

Caitlyn asked confused, from the pause she could tell the professor was about to tell her something deep and personal.

> "Mike and I served together, he was married and had a son."

"He is married?"

"Not anymore, you see, well... we were on deployment off the east coast of Africa on an anti-piracy mission.

Mike's wife and son were back in Hawaii.

She had got to feeling sorry for herself and started drinking and partying.

And... well, one night she couldn't find a babysitter, so she loaded their son up in the car and went to the bar leaving him inside.

She got drunk and hooked up with a stranger; they went back to his place forgetting that their son was still in the car.

By the time the police found him the next morning the hot sun had roasted him."

"Oh my god that is terrible."

"That isn't all of it."

"It's not?"

"No, when he got back to Hawaii, she blamed him, she took no accountability for her actions, she claimed he had abandoned her with the child in Hawaii while he was out playing hero and she was stuck there taking care of his problems.

They charged her with the homicide, and she went to prison for 15 years, that is where she is today."

"Oh my god that is horrible. But what does that have to do with me."

"If you want him to warm up to you, you're going to have to be accountable. You are going to have to swallow your pride. Otherwise, he is just going to shut you out.

That is how he has been since it happened, he got out of the Navy, bought that boat, sold their house, sold their cars, sold everything they owned, he just sailed off and disappeared."

"That is horrible."

"Like I said, if you want him to warm back up to you, you're going to have to take accountability. That is the key to his heart."

Caitlyn thanked the professor and updated him on her project, compared to everything that had happened it all seemed so unimportant now.

Stepping from the cabin, she found Mike in his usual repose of the last several days, quiet and cold towards her.

She was hit by the sweet smell of land dancing on the breeze, off to starboard she could see the faint outline of Kodiak Island looming in the distance.

She sat down across from him in her usual position and muttered.

"Mike I am so sorry."

Mike cut her short holding up his hand in a gesture revealing that he didn't want to hear it.

Dismayed Caitlyn pulled her jacket up tight sat and stewed, they were close to landfall now, she expected when they got there, Mike would kick her off the boat.

If she was going to fix this, she was going to have to think of something fast but what to do, what would make this right?

Her head raced and the time flew by before she knew it they were dropping anchor in the harbor out away from where the rest of the boats were.

"We're not going to the dock?"

Caitlyn Asked.

"If we don't go to the dock, you can't go ashore, which means I can finally get a good night's sleep!"

Mike quipped back at her.

"I deserve that."

Caitlyn replied eyes down.

Trying to keep things civil Caitlyn made dinner, the selection was pretty sparse, the fish had run out days ago, and they were into canned goods with no fresh vegetables on the boat.

It was corn and chili, but it was warm, and the taste wasn't bad.

They sat and ate in silence as the last bit of sunlight drained out of the cold gray sky. Finally, the silence became too much for Caitlyn to bear.

"Mike, I am sorry."

She began to speak before he stopped her with the hand gesture again.

She swallowed hard.

"No I mean, it, I fucked up, I should have listened, I am sorry."

Mike cut her cold again.

"I don't think it matters anymore."

The tears began to stream.

"Please Mike."

Mike set his fork down in his bowl and leaned back and stared at her not showing any sign of emotion.

This was too much, Caitlyn got up and walked into the vee birth, Mike thinking she was simply going to bed returned to his meal but was surprised when she returned with the handcuffs in hand.

Awkwardly Caitlyn dropped to her knees slow and unsure of herself holding the handcuffs up to him in her outstretched hands.

She swallowed hard and finally spoke

>"I don't want you to forgive me; I want you to punish me!"

She said with more conviction than she had said anything for weeks!

FOURTEEN

Mike set his spoon down in his bowl with a clank.

Sitting up straight Mike turned to face her she could feel his presence shift from his calm demeanor to something more commanding and foreboding, and it made her nervous and excited all at once.

Then he looked directly into Caitlyn's eyes as he spoke:

"This is what you want?"

he asked?

"Yes... Please."

She pleaded.

"Take your clothes off."

Mike commanded taking the cuffs from her hands.

Caitlyn stood and began undressing slowly.

"Faster!"

Mike barked, the military man in him coming to the surface.

Caitlyn rapidly unbuckled her jeans and pushed them to her ankles stepping out of them.

As she stood there naked, she held her hands together in front of herself wriggling under the pressure and embarrassment of being fully exposed to him.

Mike handed the cuffs back to her.

"Cuff yourself, hands in front."

He said quickly as he stood up. Caitlyn did as she was told the cuffs locking closed with a heavy click click click.

With the sensation of the cuffs closing her sense of vulnerability heightened and the anticipation reached a new level, was she ready for this?

It was too late to turn back now!

Mike pulled a piece of rope from the locker under the pilot berth, he grabbed her by the cuffs and looped the strand of rope around them, then had her face the mast in the center of the cabin, he lashed her cuffs just above her head fast to the mast.

Then he pulled out an old tee shirt, ripped it in two and tied a large knot in the middle; it was painfully obvious to Caitlyn this was not his first time doing this.

With the piece of the tee shirt in hand, Mike stepped to her side and stuck his face close to her ear.

> "Are you sure this is what you want, you want to be punished?"

Mike asked in a low forceful tone that made the hair on her neck stand up.

> "I deserve this."

Caitlyn softly replied.

With that, he took the tee shirt and shoved the knot into her mouth and tied the ends behind her head forcing the knot deep into her face causing her to chomp and drool.

Then he pulled a wooden dowel about 3 feet long from the same locker with more rope, spread Caitlyn's legs apart just past shoulder width, and lashed the dowel to her ankles forcing her feet apart.

Caitlyn felt a fuzziness begin to form in her head; her chest grew warm, beads of saliva poured over her lip, down her chin and landed on her chest.

Mike started with a soft caress of her back and behind; the soft sensation made her get goosebumps and a tingling sensation all over her body, then wham!

Caitlyn shook and shuddered with the first crack of his hand, she felt the tears well up in the corner of her eyes and let out a long "OWWWWWWW" through the gag.

Then crack, Another! Again! Again!

Caitlyn began to dance with the movements of his hands, trying to anticipate, being tripped up every time she thought he was going to strike but then met her back side with a soft caress causing her wiring in her head to go crossed.

The tickles hurt and the pain felt good, not in a pleasurable way but in the sense that she now had a reason for all of the hurt she carried inside, it was as though all of the sudden the world made sense.

With the pain came a release, and the feelings of guilt slowly faded away with each stroke of Mike's hands until Caitlyn was overwhelmed with it all and began to cry and sob and whimper uncontrollably.

As her body started to go limp Mike could see that Caitlyn had had enough, he loosened her ankles, and as he did, she did a little dance readjusting to her feet being free.

Then he uncuffed her hands and removed the gag. He sat on the settee next to the fireplace and pulled her into his lap, so her legs straddled his, wrapping his arms around her he let her head fall onto his shoulder, then he began to hug her and rub her back.

This caused the waterworks to start up again.

The softness of his touch made her feel things she wasn't willing to, and all of the hurt and anger and pain just came pouring out of her in heavy long sobs and a trail of tears that streamed down her face wetting out the shoulder of Mike's shirt.

⚓ FIFTEEN ⚓

After what seemed like an eternity of sobbing into Mikes' shoulder Caitlyn sat up and used both hands to pull all her curly red locks back. Then she tried to wipe the tears from her eyes, but all she managed to do was wipe mascara all over her face.

"Here."

Mike said as he stood her up so he could get up then set her back where he was sitting.

Mike handed her a roll of paper towels and poured her a glass of water, her mouth had run dry, and the water was cool and refreshing.

Mike stood in front of her and reached out with his hand pulling her hair back behind her ear, Caitlyn buried her cheek in the palm of his hand as it was offered cupping it with hers, she nuzzled his hand and felt the warmth.

Then standing up she wrapped her arms around his neck.

"Thank you."

She murmured soft and sweet.

Then she squeaked:

"Please... please love me."

Mike smiled and brushed her hair back again leaning in to kiss her Caitlyn raised up on her tiptoes to meet him half way.

His hands traced down her sides; then he grabbed a hand full of her behind pulling her up into him kissing her long and hard.

As he let her go Caitlyn reeled back, her head was swimming, and the burning between her legs could no longer be ignored.

She slid her fingertips up under Mike's shirt peeling it upwards revealing his chest before he pulled it the rest of the way off flinging it away.

Caitlyn's hands lingered on his chest, then she leaned in and began to gently kiss his body working her way down to his belt buckle, then she grabbed the buckle and popped it open along with his pants.

Mike stepped from his jeans a big hard knot in the middle of his underwear painfully obvious.

Caitlyn placed her palms flat against his stomach again sliding her hands down using her fingertips to snag the elastic band pulling his skivvies away to reveal his manhood.

Mike took her hand and pulled her to her feet pushing her back down on the seatee; he lifted her ankles high in the air pushing her crotch up into the air.

The anticipation for what came next filled Caitlyn with desire, she wanted this so badly, she could see Mike wanted it too.

She had spent the entire summer watching him, wanting this and now it was time. She reached down, grabbed ahold of him as he pulled back and as he came forward she shoved him inside of her and let out a moan as she felt him push in until he could go no deeper.

Mike smiled and held it there looking down peering into Caitlyn's eyes.

Then he began to pump and push his weight into her with each thrust forward.

Caitlyn began to moan; her hands roamed over her body from her chest to her fingertips in her mouth which she sucked between moans.

Soon she could feel it building, and her body let loose with a hard, powerful screaming orgasm.

As she came down from coming, Mike pulled out of her and took a step back letting her legs down, then without hesitation Caitlyn followed him back dropping to her knees; once again taking him in her mouth, she began to lick and suck until she felt his whole body go tense and he began to pulse pushing the hot stream of salty liquid into her mouth.

She held it there and continued to suck just the tip looking up at him wide-eyed, Mike looked back at her with the biggest smile she had ever seen from him.

He pulled himself from her mouth, and she swallowed everything down and smile back up at him.

Mike leaned forward caressed her face kissed her on the forehead smiled and said two little words that would make her glow on the inside:

~ Good Girl ~

⚓ SIXTEEN ⚓

The next morning Caitlyn awoke as Mike tried to slip out of bed quietly.

"where are you going?"

She murmured still half asleep.

"I'm starving."

Mike replied with a smile.

"Don't you remember we skipped dinner?"

"How could I forget?"

Caitlyn beamed.

Soon the aroma of freshly brewed coffee wafted through the cabin it brought Caitlyn around she worked her way to the end of the bed. As she stood up, the cold cabin sole took her by surprise letting out a peep as it did.

She stepped naked from the vee birth into the saloon and held her hands over the fire.

"Good morning."

Mike said smiling at her from the kitchen where he was cooking up some canned ham and potatoes.

Caitlyn smiled and gave a little curtsey.

Soon the temperature was back up, and the boat became warm again.

Caitlyn slid into the dinette but this time next to where Mike sat instead of across from him. Noticing this he smiled and handed her some silverware, and a plate of food then sat down next to her.

Without missing a beat, Caitlyn wrapped her arm under his and rested her head on his shoulder looking up at him with a playful smile.

"Thanks for breakfast, but please can we go into town and get some fresh food!"

She asked as she batted her eyes at him.

Mike with his mouth full of food just smiled and lifted his glass as if toasting her sentiment.

"I was just thinking the same thing."

He said as he swallowed down his last mouthful.

Mike couldn't help but notice all through breakfast that where a once quiet reserved and cold woman had been there was now a woman who was happy, even behaving girlish, friendly and alive!

A while later they weighed anchor and motored from the bay at the north-east end of the island then south between near Island and Crooked Island then back north to Kodiak.

Along the waterfront, Caitlyn was amazed to see all the piers ready to receive fishing boats and can their catches then ship them to market.

This was the interesting thing about Alaska, some of the buildings were modern and new, and some were of a bygone era that still seemed to linger in this place.

It's what gave Alaska its own kind of magic, a new old land where civilization barely had a toehold in the wilderness, where nature reigned the supreme overlord of the land.

After tying off to the pier and getting provisions onboard, Caitlyn was startled to hear another couple yelling at each other.

She followed Mike up the companionway, looking around she saw a boat attempting to pull into a slip, but they just couldn't get their angle right and instead of communicating they were yelling at each other.

Mike having realized they were having issues stepped over onto the dock, seeing what he was doing Caitlyn followed his lead.

After a few tense moments with the couple a bit slightly embarrassed at the scene they had caused now being a bit humbler they got them into the dock and tied off.

Mike reached out and Shook the man's hand who introduced himself as Ernie Taylor and then introduced his wife Edith to both Mike and Caitlyn.

Their boat a much larger 75-footer was a beautiful boat. Twin masts in a ketch rig, the hull was painted silver but had quite a bit of dock rash.

Ernie tried to explain his maneuvering antics saying "the bow thruster is broken." but it was obvious to both Mike and Caitlyn that his boat was a bit more machine than he was capable of handling.

After the usual where are you going? Where are you headed? Conversations cruisers get into it was discovered that both boats were headed back north to Anchorage.

Even though they were both headed the same way, Caitlyn was surprised when Mike gave a different departure date when discussing leaving even though he had told her earlier they would be leaving on the same day.

After saying goodbye to the couple and perhaps we will cross paths again Mike and Caitlyn went back to My Way, once out of earshot, Caitlyn asked:

"Why did you tell him a different date than you told me we were leaving?"

"It's because he is the type of boater with more money than sense."

Mike said then paused for a second.

"He is the type with a big mouth and small ears."

Caitlyn grinned at the analogy understanding that Mike didn't want to get stuck buddy boating with a know it all the entire trip up to Anchorage.

They would let the other boat slip out of the harbor; then they would leave a few hours later.

⚓ SEVENTEEN ⚓

After a couple of days exploring around Kodiak, it became time to head back towards Anchorage to be sure Caitlyn could make her flight back to San Diego.

As they set out on the final leg she could not help but feel a sense of dread about her summer coming to an end, her time on the boat coming to an end, and yes, her time with Mike coming to an end.

She was so conflicted on so many things, she hadn't been working as hard as she should have on her thesis, she had plenty of photos from the trip along the way, but the words just wouldn't come out of her.

"The weather is going to be iffy."

Mike said breaking her thought.

"What is going on?"

Caitlyn asked.

"There is a front slipping by to the northwest of us if it drops any further south and east we could be in for a rough ride."

Mike replied neither knew how prophetic these words would be in the coming days.

It was then Mike's phone buzzed to life, he answered it and stepped below. When he came back above decks, he had a very different expression on his face.

"What is wrong?"

Caitlyn asked the concern showing in her voice.

"That was my sister; My grandfather is not doing well."

Mike replied not trying to show his emotions.

"I'm sorry to hear that, you've never spoken of your family much. What is he like?"

Caitlyn replied hoping he would divulge a bit more.

"When I was a kid he taught me to sail, just a little 30' sloop he built in his garage back in the 60's, but to me, as a kid, it was my whole world. We spent a lot of time together."

"That is great you had that time with him, I never knew my grandparents."

"He is the reason I went into the Navy, he was on destroyers in WWII, had two ships sunk out from under him, one at Pearl Harbor, one at Guadalcanal, Kept going back for more.

He did his 20 and then some, they finally made him retire as a Master Chief.

He was a gunner's mate; I became a gunner's mate."

"Aww, that is so sweet! How long has it been since you have seen him?"

"Just before we left, he was doing pretty good; he has been going through a lot of treatments for cancer. He still lives down in Bremerton in an old house he built there in the late 50's after the war.

He's 95 and still kicking. We had to take his truck away because he is getting too blind to drive, that was on hell of a fight."

"He sounds a lot like someone I know!"

Caitlyn teased with a big smile.

"He is a better man than I am."

Mike replied somber looking down resting his elbows on his knees placing his weight upon them.

"Why do you say that?"

Caitlyn asked puzzled as to why Mike would put himself down.

"I was married years ago; I was dumb, nineteen, she was twenty-one, she saw me coming a mile away and took me for a sucker.

Grandpa never liked her, he told me I could do better, and he was right, but we married anyways.

He told me a story about how he had met a woman before shipping off to the war, and he was afraid it would be his last chance to get married, but then his friends talked him out of it.

He told me if he had married her he would have never met my grandmother, they had been married 54 years when she died.

But I didn't listen, Sarah and I got married, we had a son, I named him Stephen after grandpa hoping it would make him warm up to her a bit.

He never did warm up to her, but little Stephen was his pride and joy, a great kid. Smart, strong.

But..."

Mike just trailed off.

"It's ok!"

Caitlyn coaxed as she moved next to Mike and wrapped her arm around him rubbing his back trying to comfort him. She could see his eyes well up.

"He was the best thing that ever happened to me; he wanted to be just like his dad. The last time our ship pulled in he met me at the pier dressed in a little sailor uniform with the same Chief Petty Officer Gunners mate crow I had on mine.

We used to build Legos together on all of my days off, or I would take him to the base marina and take him sailing.

But Sarah had a problem, she was a good for nothing drunk, and she blamed my being in the Navy, and being frequently deployed for all her woes.

One night she went out and got shit faced, left Stevie in the back of her car, she went home with a stranger.

The next morning by the time they found him Stevie was in really bad shape, a passerby saw him and knocked the window out of the car, they called an ambulance.

He lingered on life support for three months, the heat fried his organs and his brain, but he was such a fighter, he kept trying to fight, trying to live.

When I got the red cross message we were off the coast of Somalia, my CO arranged for me to catch a helo to shore then a flight home. But there was nothing I could do but sit there and hold his hand.

I went back to our house and found his little sailor hat and brought it to him hoping somehow it would make a difference but it didn't.

They had arrested her and taken her to jail, somehow, she was able to make bail, and she showed up at the hospital.

She walked in as though she had done nothing wrong and I lost it, I used her face to open the door as I ejected her from the building.

I got arrested, out of spite she signed the paperwork to have the plug pulled.

By the time I got out of jail, Stevie was gone, she had left his body there at the hospital, didn't even have the decency to do anything with it.

Sarah disappeared, the last time I ever saw her was at her trial, I testified against her.

When the judge found out what she had done he gave her the maximum sentence for negligent homicide; he said his only regret was that he could not give her more time.

She is still in Hawaii serving out that sentence."

The tears that had welled in Mikes' eyes were now falling freely. Caitlyn wrapped herself around his arm and held on clutching his hand with both of hers.

She now understood why he was so hard. Why he didn't let people close to him, she felt so badly knowing there was nothing she could do to take that kind of pain away.

⚓ EIGHTEEN ⚓

A violent rocking swell brought Caitlyn suddenly to consciousness, the boat creaked, and it was obvious the sea had gotten rough.

She dawned her clothes and slipped out of the vee birth.

"Is everything ok?"

she asked Mike who was at the Nav station looking at the weather on his laptop.

"No, it's all gone to shit. That front is pushing in on us, and the sea is angry. It's going to be a rough ride."

Mike replied.

About three hours later Mike was topside trimming the sails, Caitlyn was trying to make some lunch when the radio crackled and roared to life.

"Hello? Can anyone hear me? Hello? Hello?"

The voice at the other end cried out, Caitlyn immediately recognized the voice as Edit the woman from the Ketch.

She grabbed up the Microphone and replied.

"Vessel hailing, this is My Way, My Way, My Way, is that you Edith?"

The static crackled then Edith's voice came back on the line.

"Yes, I need help, my husband has had a heart attack!"

Caitlyn burst through the companionway hatch.

"Mike! you better get down here!!!"

She yelled, seeing it was an emergency Mike moved quickly down inside slamming the hatch shut.

"It's Edith, Ernie had a heart attack."

Mike grabbed the mic.

"Edith, this is Mike Black, are you there?"

"Yes Mike, Ernie had a heart attack."

"Is he still breathing?"

"No, this was an hour ago, he is turning cold! I don't know what to do; I can't sail this boat!"

"Edith, what is your position?"

"I'm somewhere between Kodiak and Anchorage."

With this Mike had to rest his forehead in both of his hands. Then he muttered.

"That's only about a million square miles to cover."

"Edith, are you near the chart plotter?"

"Yes, It's right here. There is an alarm, it says off course, it looks like we're just going around in big circles."

"Ok, I want you to look around the edges of the screen, you're looking for a latitude and longitude, I need you to give that to me."

"It says 58 degrees 30'38.69" North, 151 degrees 8'37.43" West. the heading thing says one-two-one."

"Great she is headed out to sea."

Mike exclaimed.

"Can't we do something?"

Caitlyn asked.

Mike punched the coordinates into the chart plotter and discovered they were only about four miles away.

> "Edit, this is Mike, we are coming to you. You are only twenty-four miles away; I need you to stay below, put on your foul weather gear, stay by the radio. Can you do that?"

> "Yes, just please get her quick!"

Edith's voice sounded shaken, as though she were about ready to give up.

> "We're on our way, Edith."

Mike hung up the microphone and looked to Caitlyn.

> "This is going to suck! Can you get your foulies on please?"

> "Yes I can do that, is there anything else?"

> "Yeah, be ready for a wild ride!"

Mike darted back up the companionway and pointed the boat towards the coordinates Edith had given him, soon Caitlyn joined him, she was amazed at how the wind whistled through the rigging on the boat, the sea was short and choppy, just enough to make the ride really uncomfortable.

Soon they were closing in on the coordinates, and Mike fired up the big searchlight on the bow of the boat, he swung it back and forth through the blackness searching for the Ketch.

Soon there was a gray flicker, and he spotted the boat, in irons bobbing helplessly on the waves.

He maneuvered My Way up closer then stepped back in and grabbed the mic again.

> "Edith, we are off of your port side, do you see us."

"I'm afraid to come up!"

A frantic Edith replied through the radio.

"Fuck me!"

Mike muttered.

"Edith, I need you to get ready to get picked up, do you have an exposure suit?"

"What's that?"

"It's a neoprene suit that protects you if you go in the water."

"I'm not going in the water are you crazy!!!"

"I'm not asking you to come in the water Edith; I am asking you to put it on in case you fall in when we pick you up."

"I'm scared, can you come get me?"

Mike rested his elbows on the chart table and leaned down trying to formulate a plan.

"She is fucking losing it."

He said to Caitlyn.

"Is there anything we can do?"

"The only thing we could do is if I drive her boat back into port, I don't think she is leaving it."

"I can handle My Way if you can drive her boat."

"Are you sure about that?"

"I have already docked her several times, I've sailed her plenty, I can do this."

Mike groaned knowing he was about to leave his boat in the hands of a still very green sailor. He breathed deep and looked to Caitlyn.

"Ok, I trust you."

Caitlyn smiled and hugged him but there was no time for playing around, Mike pulled out his exposure suit and slid into the big red garment. Then he put his PFD on over the top of it.

"Here is what we will do, her sails keep filling then she goes a little way and then winds up in irons again.

We are going to come up with our sails still up but under the motor, right into the wind, so when we get next to her you can cut the throttle, and I can step aboard.

Then as soon as I am off, you gun it again and pull straight away, don't steer away because you'll likely smack the stern into the side of her and knock me back into the sea."

"I can do that."

"If I go in the water put the transmission in neutral, and drop the swim ladder. If I go in, I will try to dive deep, so I don't get smashed between the boats which means I will likely come up behind us. Be ready for that."

"OK"

"Are you ready?"

Caitlyn thought for a second then nodded.

"Alright, let's do this."

"Wait!"

Caitlyn sprung forward and hugged Mike.

"Please be safe!"

Moments later Mike had directed Caitlyn at the wheel on a course that was running them directly into the wind to come up along the port side of the drifting boat.

As they grew near Mike clipped onto the lifeline that ran forward and stepped out onto the deck taking a seat on top of the cabin, he motioned to Caitlyn which way to steer and then yelled "CUT IT!" as they pulled alongside.

He unclipped from the life line, stood up as they drifted forward then he jumped to the deck of the other boat falling forward over its rails onto its roof, he scrambled to his knees, grabbed the handrail and shouted to Caitlyn:

"GO! GO! GO!"

She gunned the throttle and My Way slipped forward and then moved off to port making a large circle to come around and rejoin up behind them.

Mike made his way back and pushed open the doors on the companionway, as he stepped down inside he saw Edith sitting stoic at the chart table, Earnie's body lie blue and cold on the floor.

"We're going to get you to shore Edith."

"Thank you!"

She exclaimed.

"I just want to go back to Fontana to see my grandchildren. I just want to go home."

"We'll get you there don't worry."

Mike called in their predicament to the coast guard, and made arrangements to meet an ambulance at Port Graham, then went topside.

To his surprise everything on the Ketch was automated, all he had to do to trim the sails was hit switches, and the electric winches did all the work, soon he had her out of Irons, and they were making way beating into the head wind.

Through the night, Mike and Caitlyn talked on the radio, assuring each other everything was fine.

Mike couldn't help but notice how smartly Caitlyn sailed, through the tacks she laid the boat over like a pro swinging it through the dead zone then back onto the other tack, pulling in the jib sheet cranking the winch.

She worked her tail off sailing the boat by herself through the night.

As they entered the Port Graham waterway it was just past four in the morning; the wind slowed as they worked their way up to the town where they were able to anchor each vessel about 1/8 of a mile from a group of fishing boats that lay tugging at their anchors.

The chop was ugly but not terrible because the terrain sheltered the waterway from the current angle of the wind.

Mike lowered the Ketch's dinghy into the water and sped over to My Way to retrieve Caitlyn, then together they raised the anchor and brought the Ketch into the dock.

About the time the paramedics arrived the sun was just beginning to backlight the clouds that hung gray and low over the mountains, soon the winds had shifted and then it happened.

⚓ NINETEEN ⚓

As the winds shifted the boats at anchor, all shifted, on one boat the anchor chain old rusty and neglected snapped and the boat began to drift across the bay lazily.

The dock was a cacophony of people, an Alaska state trooper, the local Sheriff, the paramedics and curious locals as well as Mike, Caitlyn and Edith all stood on the pier.

By the time anyone noticed the drifting boat it was already too late, it was making a B-line for My Way, Mike ran up the dock and screamed "HEY! HEY! HEY" but it was too late, and no one on the trawler could hear him anyways.

Within seconds the big heavy wooden hull boat slammed into My Way the upper works of the fishing boat tangled in the mast dragging it backward ripping the roof of the cabin open before snapping the mast off laying it down neatly over the back of the boat.

The collision brought a wellspring of activity to the decks of the trawler; men emerged in various states of undress, lots of shouting occurred. They fired the engine up and turned towards open water not realizing a state trooper and the local sheriff were standing right there.

Everyone piled into the Sheriff's boat and took off after the trawler, 30 minutes later it was tied off at the pier, the vessel's captain in handcuffs.

Then they went to assess the damage to My Way, the side of the hull had been ripped open for 12 feet above the waterline, she still floated, but it was obvious she was totaled.

They cut the mast, and rigging loose with bolt cutters and pulled them fully aboard. Then fired up her engine and made their way to the pier.

Once there they were met with a teary-eyed Edith.

"I am so sorry..."

She exclaimed over and over.

Mike tried to assure her that his boat was insured, that everything would be ok.

"I just want to go home to Fontana."

Was the line Edith repeated over and over.

Finally, Mike broke in.

"How about we sail your boat up to Anchorage and you can catch a flight from there, then you can pay someone to come get it for you."

Edith hesitated, it was clear she did not want to get back on the boat.

"I don't think I can."

Edith exclaimed.

Then Caitlyn piped up

"I have to be there in 10 hours if I am going to catch my flight."

The Sheriff then interjected.

"There is a flying service here mam, if you need to get to Anchorage, they will take you, but with this weather, it probably will not be for a couple of days."

"That would be fine; I would rather fly."

Edith replied with much more enthusiasm in her voice, then she paused, thought for a moment then looked to Mike.

"My boat, I want you to have it."

"You don't have to do that."

Mike explained completely shocked, this was a million and a half dollar sailing yacht, not a fifty thousand dollar thirty-six footer like My Way.

> "No I want you to have it, I can see that you two are sailors, you were meant for the sea. And I never want to step foot on a boat again!"

With this Edith started to sob, Caitlyn moved in to comfort her.

They made arrangements for Mike to meet Edith in Anchorage and they would find an attorney and do the paperwork on the boat.

After digging through My Way and pulling out all of his gear and dragging it onto the Ketch, Mike took some plywood and boarded up the gash in the hull to keep water from shipping in as she was towed to Anchorage.

As they prepared to depart, he looked around, and sadness overtook him.

> "She was good to me, we sailed a lot of miles together, Seattle to Alaska twice, Mexico, Panama, Colombia, she saw some miles under her keel, never let me down."

> "She was a good boat; I will miss her."

Caitlyn replied hugging Mike's arm.

Mike bumped the bottom of his fist on the companionway hatch frame one last time, sighed hard and motioned for Caitlyn to step out.

> "Goodbye old friend."

He said in a somber low voice. Then he stepped up placed the boards in, and closed the hatch for the last time.

⚓ TWENTY ⚓

The big Ketch slipped out of port, Mike at the helm grinning like a kid with a brand-new toy.

She had some bumps and bruises to iron out, but she was a beautiful boat, an aluminum hull, teak decks, carbon sails, the best of the best, a no expense spared kind of boat.

The interior was huge; the saloon had its own lounge and a separate dining area.

There was a massive stateroom in the rear which he would move into once Edith had collected her belongings, in the front there were three more cabins, a large guest cabin with a private bath, and two smaller crew cabins with bunk beds in each.

There was a storage locker forward with large work bench.

The boat was everything a sailor could dream of.

"So, what do you think I should name her?"

Mike asked Caitlyn with a huge grin on his face.

"How about the 'Stephen Black'?"

The corners of Mikes' mouth curled up even more, and his eyes welled up.

"The Stephen Black!"

Caitlyn got up from her seat and gave Mike a big hug, and held on to his side as he stood at the wheel pushing the big boat up the straight to Anchorage.

Sadly, as they arrived Caitlyn's flight was already off the ground. She called the airline and did the dance of requesting another ticket.

She would have to wait three days before she could leave. After making all of the necessary calls, she settled into the dinette across from Mike who was IM'ing with his sister about his Grandpa.

"How is he doing?"

"The old fart wants to go sailing, says to get my ass back down there!"

"Boy is he in for a surprise!"

"I'd say so, haven't told anyone about the accident yet."

"Don't want them to worry?"

"I'm worried he will have one of his Navy buddy's fly him up here and he will go demand payment from the captain right there on the spot with a .45 in his hand!"

Caitlyn broke out in laughter. Then when a new thought crossed her mind, she spoke up more somber this time.

"Mike, what happened out there, why did Edith just lock up like that? Couldn't she sail this boat, could I sail this boat?"

"This boat is easy to sail; everything is automated. The problem with Edith is Ernie never taught her how to do anything.

She didn't know port from starboard; she was a passenger, a non-participating on at that when things got bad, all she could do was panic, she was helpless."

He paused for a moment as he reminisced about the rescue.

And by the way, I was really proud of you out there yesterday."

With those words "really proud" Caitlyn smiled and got shy, her cheeks went red, and she twisted her hands in her lap like a nervous little girl.

Before long the conversation dwindled, and the fatigue of the all-night sailing adventure took over as the sun set.

Caitlyn put fresh sheets on the bed in the master's stateroom, she and Mike settled in for the night together, but it was somber, and they fell asleep quickly.

The next morning when they awoke the sky was clear. Caitlyn rummaged through the galley and made breakfast.

At breakfast the mood changed, it was as though they knew they were parting ways and Mike and Caitlyn stopped being all love dovey towards each other.

By noon Edith had arrived complaining about the crazy bush pilot that flew her back to civilization, she now had her daughter and son in law in tow who had flown up the night before when they got the news.

They rummaged through the boat and cleared out everything she cared to take, then her attorney fresh off of another flight arrived paperwork in hand.

She signed the boat over to Mike, asked nothing in return. It was obvious she was grateful for his giant leap from ship to ship to save her life, and a bit embarrassed at her failure.

Her daughter hugged Mike and Caitlyn thanking them for "Returning her mom to her."

Then it was Edith's turn to say goodbye, she hugged Caitlyn with tears in her eyes and told her she was:

> "so brave and a beautiful sailor girl."

Then she turned to Mike:

> "Young man, you did a great thing for me, I'd have been lost without you, take this boat and live out your

dreams, make her yours, whatever you do, please don't squander your life being unhappy."

He assured her he would, and she hugged him, then everyone piled into the car and drove off, then it was just Mike and Caitlyn.

They spent some time rummaging through the boat, Caitlyn found some clothes Edith had left that she decided to keep, much of the rest was loaded into big black garbage bags and hauled topside.

On one of the trips to the top Caitlyn was greeted by a trio of backpackers, two women, and a man.

"G-Day mam, is the captain aboard?"

The man rattled off in a thick Australian accent.

"He is."

"I'd like to speak with him please if you don't mind."

"Please come aboard."

Caitlyn replied leading the man and his companions down into the saloon.

"Mike, there is someone here to see you."

"G-Day Captain, are you headed to the lower 48 by chance?"

"Direct to Seattle."

"Awesome, I'm Jim Coates, this is my lady Mary, and her sister Tania."

Mike stepped forward shaking each of their hands.

"What can I do for you guys?"

"Myself and Mary are experienced sailors; we're looking for passage to the lower 48. And possibly further if you keep on going."

"I had been thinking about going back down to Bogotá for the winter."

Mike replied with a grin.

"Outstanding Mate!"

Jim cried out with his thick Australian.

"Welcome to the Stephen Black!"

Mike replied shaking their hands once more.

After assigning cabins to each of them and making sure they had fresh linens everyone borrowed a van and rode into town to get provisions, back aboard the boat they enjoyed a night of drinking and storytelling.

It turned out the trio were quite the travelers having sailed up from New Zealand with another boat in the spring; they had backpacked all through Alaska in the summer, now they were looking to head south before the weather went bad.

All through dinner though Caitlyn was fairly quiet. Here she was amongst new friends, but she was somber and reminded of the fact that she had a flight to catch the next day.

That night she and Mike slept in the same bed but apart. She lay awake with the feelings gnawing at her insides.

It was clear she didn't want to go.

⚓ TWENTYONE ⚓

Caitlyn awoke to the sounds of laughter coming from the saloon, thick Australian accents coupled with Mikes' voice carried up the passageway.

Caitlyn rose and stuffed her things in her bag, brushed her teeth and then emerged from the stateroom.

She was met with good mornings and the usual how did you sleep questions.

When asked if she wanted breakfast she merely shook her head and replied that she need to get to the airport.

Twenty minutes later she was hugging Mike goodbye. She could see the sadness in his eyes. She could tell he was going to miss her.

Then a short trip in a cab to the airport and she found herself four hours early for her flight.

Sitting in the terminal surrounded by the smells of civilization, the cleaners, the rubber, the carpet the tile, the people and all of that noise and the hustle and bustle.

Caitlyn sat staring out the window mindlessly at the ground crews then something in her snapped.

She jumped from her seat, hoisted her bag over her shoulder and grabbed her wheelie bag and raced for the curb; she grabbed the first taxi she could find and had her race back to the dock.

The car pulled in, and she flung the door open and went running down the gangway only to find an empty dock where the Stephen Black had been moored three hours before.

Caitlyn rammed her hand into her pocket and dug out her phone, she dialed Mikes number but all she got was the voicemail, she hung it up before it would record her call.

Everything welled up inside of Caitlyn she dropped to her knees and began to cry. She knew now that she really loved him and wanted to be with him, but he was gone.

After a few moments, the cab driver emerged from her car and approached Caitlyn.

She asked with a thick Inuit accent.

"Mam are you ok?"

Caitlyn just cried and nodded, and finally forced herself to ask the woman to take her back to the airport.

Two hours later she sat in her seat staring out the window watching the green light on the tip of the wing flash out over the endless wastes of the Pacific that stretched out before her.

Broken clouds covered the horizon and the moon shown through casting shadows on the water that glimmered below.

Mike was out there somewhere; she wondered if he felt the same way, she wondered if he looked back if she would ever see him again.

She wondered had he turned back towards the pier or did he just keep going. Did he even care?

She was so stupid! She lived in Hawaii, she had school to go back to, she had to make things right with her girlfriend, yet here she was pining for Mike!

The next morning Caitlyn awoke to the sound of wheels screeching on blacktop as her flight from Seattle to San Diego touched down.

As she strolled from the concourse bag in tow, her mother was there with open arms waiting to greet her.

"Honey, have you been crying?"

"Mom, I messed everything up."

"Here tell me about it in the car on our way home."

The two loaded her bags into the car and drove off into the urban stucco sprawl that is San Diego.

"So honey what happened? Was he bad to you? I heard you got arrested?"

"Oh my god no mother! He was very good to me, and he is the one who came and got me after a fight."

"What have I told you about fighting, you know you have your grandfather's temper!

But you have to stop doing that!"

"Everything is fine mom; no charges were pressed!"

Caitlyn whined.

"Well maybe they should have, would have taught you a lesson!"

"Mom, just. Please don't."

Caitlyn went silent and just stared out the window, memories of her childhood in San Diego flooded back in.

After two weeks spending time with her dad and mom and patching things up with her girlfriend over the phone she flew back to Hawaii.

She went back to work, school started, and life just went back to the way it had always been.

⚓ TWENTYTWO ⚓

Stephen Black, Monica, and Abbey stood at the dock in Bremerton as the big Ketch slipped into view.

As the boat pulled in and they realized it was Mike they helped tie her off.

Mike dropped the boarding ladder and climbed down with his newfound Aussie friends grinning ear to ear. His grandpa looking baffled pointed to his name on the boat.

"Yeah! I named her after you, you old curmudgeon!"

"Well, will wonders never cease, how did you land this beauty?"

"Rescued her former owner after her husband had died of a heart attack, she gave me the boat as a thank you for saving her life."

"Where is My Way?"

Grandpa Stephen asked with a concerned look on his face.

"Fishing trawler broke her anchor chain, drifted across the harbor in heavy wind and smashed her up really bad; she will never sail again."

"I am sorry to hear that, she was a good ole boat, took you a lot of places and never let you down, I hope this one treats you just as well.

Let's take her out!"

The old man beamed with a Cheshire cat grin from ear to ear, then Monica stepped forward.

"Grandpa, you still have your doctor's appointment this afternoon!"

"Oh they won't miss me, I want to go sailing!"

"Tell you what I will take you tomorrow Grandpa."

Mike replied with a grin while laughing and shaking his head.

95 years old and the old man was still trying to be twenty-one.

That night at dinner everyone sat around a table at a nice bistro enjoying a meal, they laughed they joked, Grandpa wowed the Australians with stories of Aussie Diggers he met during the war.

Mike sat quiet, he laughed at the jokes but he didn't tell any, he kept looking at a photo of him and Caitlyn that he had snapped on My Way after their first night being intimate together.

It seemed so long ago and so distant now.

As everyone chatted amongst themselves, Grandpa Steven noticed Mike looking at the picture.

>"Pretty lady, is she what's got you all glum?"

>"What?"

>"Don't what me Michael, I can see that woman's got you all tied up in knots."

>"Ah! I'll be fine. Just some memories."

Grandpa Steven replied with a Harrumph and went back to his dinner.

Mike put his phone away and tried to join back in.

The next few weeks were a blur, several times Mike took his grandpa sailing, he loved every second of it and couldn't stop remarking what an amazing boat the Ketch was.

They made short trips across the sound to Seattle for dinner a couple of times, met some of his grandpa's buddies who were still kicking around.

Then the day came for the departure southbound to Colombia with a stop off in San Francisco at Grandpa's boat yard there to get the new boat ship shape before heading further south.

As everyone stood at the dock getting ready for the departure Grandpa Steven took Mike aside.

> "You love this girl; I can see it written all over you."

> "Nah, I will be fine, it wouldn't work. She has a life all planned out."

> "Son, plans change, your heart won't, your grandma has been gone seven years now this fall, and I miss her every day, I'd hate to see you spend the rest of your life missing this one."

> "Ah, I will be fine Grandpa, she didn't try to stay, she didn't even ask, I don't think she feels the same way."

> "God help you, Michael, you're as god damn stubborn as I am!"

> "You bet I am old man!"

Mike replied with a hearty laugh.

Finally, it was time to shove off, Grandpa Stephen stood and watched the boat disappear out of sight leaning on his cane.

As they went to take him home, he had a small coughing fit, and neither Monica or Abbey realized when he spit into the water it was full of blood.

The next morning when he stepped out to check his mail Grandpa Stephen found a letter addressed to Mike from a Caitlyn Campbell, he pulled out his pocket knife and found a thousand dollars cash inside and a note that read:

> Dear Mike,

I hope you are enjoying the new boat and the times with your new crew, here is the seven hundred fifty dollars I owe you from Ketchikan. Plus a little interest.

I hope you are doing well, say hello to your grandpa for me, I hope he liked the new boat.

Sincerely, Caitlyn

Putting the note down, he muttered to himself "Well to hell with this!" then he marched back up the steps into the house and over to the telephone looking up a number from an old tattered address book he punched the numbers in on the old green telephone.

"Hey Smitty, no I'm not calling about the reunion, that is months away, I'm coming to Hawaii, I need a favor."

⚓ TWENTYTHREE ⚓

Caitlyn pushed the key into the lock of the little Kalihi Valley home she shared with Anne.

As she pushed the door open the house was dark and vacant, she pulled her bags inside and dropped them next to the door; then she plopped down on the couch sinking back into it staring up at the ceiling fan whirring in the center of the room.

The past two weeks in San Diego had been mentally taxing, it was nice to see her mom and dad, but her mom told her dad everything about her getting arrested, she wasn't going to live it down anytime soon.

It cast a shadow over her time with them, and because of this she was relieved to be back home, but everything felt off, she had been away so long that the house just felt different.

Being aboard My Way with Mike had begun to feel like home to her, now that she was home it had a bit of a sticky alien feeling she couldn't quite shake.

After a while of lying there, Anne came home from work, she hugged Caitlyn, but when she went to kiss her, Caitlyn felt weird and turned away.

> "Is everything alright?"

Anne asked

> "It's ok, I just, well I've been away so long."

Caitlyn replied.

> "Oh."

Anne exclaimed disappointed now realizing that Caitlyn's feelings towards her had faded.

Then she offered:

"Well, it's good to have you back."

"Thanks."

Was all Caitlyn could come up with to say and an uncomfortable silence filled the room.

As it did Anne stepped back, Caitlyn slumped back into the couch everything felt so strange.

This feeling would slowly dissipate for the next few days, Caitlyn and Anne started spending more time together, and Caitlyn began to feel like everything would be ok.

That is until one afternoon there came a knock at the door.

Caitlyn startled because she wasn't expecting anyone peered through the peephole, it was an elderly man and just beyond him in the drive she could see another elderly man in an old tan and white Ford pickup waiting in the driveway.

She unlocked the door and popped it open not knowing what to expect.

The man in his left hand held a cane, and a familiar-looking envelope, atop his head he wore a navy-blue hat adorned with several ribbons and big gold print that said "WWII, Korea, Vietnam Veteran."

Below the hat was a weather-beaten face old and wrinkled, but without a doubt, he had the same eyes as Mike.

Caitlyn's heart stopped in her chest when he reached out his hand and said:

"Caitlyn Campbell I presume?"

"Yes?"

She replied feebly and totally shocked.

"Stephen Black, mind if I come in?"

"Um, yes, please do."

Caitlyn replied shaking his hand then opening the door further.

Caitlyn gestured towards the couch and offered him a seat.

Steven grunted a little bit as he sat down and looked at her with a serious look on his face.

"So, you're the young lady got my grandson's heart all tied up in knots eh?"

Shocked, Caitlin didn't know what to do, she felt like darting, her hands began to fidget, her eyes darted towards the floor, she was not ready for this full on confrontation.

"Well, he could have picked a lot worse from the looks of you."

Stephen replied breaking out into a big toothy grin.

"I didn't mean to."

Caitlin said softly as she offered a small smile.

"Do you love him?"

Stephen queried in a serious gruff tone.

"You certainly don't waste any time do you Mister Black!

But yes, to be totally honest with you I think I do."

She said ending with a smile realizing she had just said it out loud.

"Honey, I'm ninety-five years old, I'm dying of cancer, I don't have time to beat around the bush.

I just want to know that you love him because I can see he loves you.

Would you be good to him? Would you stand by him? Thick and thin no excuses?"

Stephen asked in a still forceful authoritarian tone that military men use when speaking to their subordinates.

Caitlyn paused, bit her lip closed her eyes and thought about it, visions of the journey and Mike flashed through her head.

When she opened her eyes there was only one answer she could give:

"Yes, I love him more than anything."

She said tears welling up in her eyes.

"I am happy to hear that, that young man has been through a lot, he got burned really bad.

He deserves to have someone who will love him and stand by him, however, He isn't going to chase you. You're going to have to go to him."

Caitlyn nodded as she cried digging a tissue out of the box on the end table.

Stephen continued:

"You've got a choice to make, you can sit here, cry it out, or you can pack your things, and we can get going."

"Going where?"

Caitlyn asked with a puzzled expression figuring Mike was somewhere off shore where no one could reach him.

"Mike is in San Francisco doing a refit on the new boat, he is painting the sides and the bottom, apparently, the old owner couldn't drive her very well, so he is getting all that fixed before heading further south, those Aussie kids are helping him. You know how he is; everything has to be shipshape!"

Stephen replied with obvious pride in his voice.

"Oh yes I do!"

Caitlyn said with a big laugh and smile.

"Well, what are you waiting for, Let's GO!"

Stephen shot back.

"I don't know if I can. I have work; I have school... I have other responsibilities here."

Caitlyn looked down as she finished speaking.

Stephen rocked forward and pushed himself to his feet using his cane. He reached out his hand to shake Caitlyn's.

"Well, then I wish you the best."

Caitlin stood up, shook his hand and didn't say anything, the old man then just turned and started to make his way to the door, Caitlyn not knowing what to do simply followed and held the door for him.

As he walked out, Stephen turned and looked her over once more.

"You know it's too bad; he could have done a lot worse."

Then he tipped his hat and started making his way back towards the truck waiting in the drive.

As soon as he turned his back Caitlyn closed the door and collapsed on the floor, she began to sob and as she did she pulled out her phone and looked at a picture of Mike she had taken aboard the new boat as they sailed towards Anchorage.

In the photo he was standing at the helm in his foul weather jacket, grinning from ear to ear like a big kid with a new toy.

The feeling began to well up inside of her and then she snapped, she sprung to her feet, ripped the door open only to see the taillights of the truck backing out of the driveway.

She charged out the door down the drive catching the truck as it began to pull away slapping her hands on the side of it yelling out:

"Wait wait! Please wait!"

The brakes squeaked as the truck came to a stop and Caitlyn ran to the driver's window

"Five minutes, please just give me five minutes. Let me get my things."

Stephen nodded and said:

"We'll wait, hurry up!"

Smitty put the truck in park and Caitlyn darted back into the house.

She grabbed her backpack and suitcase and started frantically stuffing them with everything she could grab, she slammed the suitcase closed and fought the zipper shut.

Then she drug everything out to the door, then she grabbed a junk mail envelope that lie there, ripped it open and wrote on the inside:

"Anne,

I am sorry I had to go, I just can't do this. Please don't hate me."

- Caitlyn

With that, she ran out the door and flung her bags into the back of the waiting pickup truck, and the three headed off towards the airport.

⚓ TWENTYFOUR ⚓

The big jet shuddered and rocked, the noises of electrical and hydraulic components reverberated through the aircraft.

Caitlyn sat perched in a window seat staring out the window as the plane began to nose over on its final accent into San Francisco.

Out of the soup in the sky the city dropped into view, the big orange bridge spanning the Golden Gate came into view off in the distance and Caitlyn could have sworn she saw Mike's boat leaving under it.

Then she convinced herself how silly the thought was after all, Stephen was escorting her to where Mike was, but for some reason, she couldn't escape the feeling that the other shoe was about to drop.

She continued to look out the window as the city grew larger, soon automobiles looked like ants scurrying about the streets, then people clearly came into view; and finally they touched down at San Francisco International.

Stepping out of the airport there was an old 1980's Cadillac waiting at the curb, as the driver saw them coming he stepped from the vehicle.

The man was elderly, probably in his seventies, he wore a ball cap that read "Alameda Marine and Fabrication" and in the center of the hat was a service ribbon, a gold bar with green ends and three vertical red stripes indicating the man had served in Vietnam.

Caitlyn instantly recognized this because her father had the same ribbon on a hat he wore.

"Hey, Allen! How the heck are you?"

Stephen called out to the man as they approached.

"Master Chief! Been a long time! You look like shit!"

Allen replied with a big grin.

"Yeah yeah, how's that grandson of mine, he getting that boat ready to go?"

As they met the two men shook hands.

"He has put in a lot of long hours on that boat, stripped every last bit of paint off of her, fixed all the damage, and now he is working on fairing her, looks like she will be better than new!"

Stephen smiled with a grin that was full of pride, memories of when Mike was young teaching him to work on his boat flashed through his head.

"That's my boy he replied."

Allen Turned to Caitlin and reached out his hand to shake hers.

"Hello, who would you be?"

Caitlin smiled and stuck out her hand speaking in her thick Irish.

"Hello, I'm Caitlin."

"Pleased to meet you, you must be the young lady everyone keeps going on about?"

Blushing Caitlyn replied:

"Apparently so."

"Well, we had better not keep you two love birds waiting."

Allen said with a smile throwing a wink at Caitlin.

With that, he opened the car door for her threw her bags in the trunk and they were off to Alameda.

Sitting in the back of the Cadillac listening to the two men banter back and forth like a couple of old salts Caitlyn began to grow more nervous.

The thoughts began to pound her, what if this didn't work, had she just thrown everything all away?

What would she do, how would it be?

By the time the car turned into the driveway of the boatyard Caitlyn's stomach was in knots.

The car pulled up to a big long building covered in aging galvanized tin, Allen turned around and informed her that Mike was just inside working on his boat.

Caitlyn bit her lip and then asked:

> "Will you wait here before you go?"

Allen laughed and replied:

> "Young lady, we own the place, we're am not going anywhere!"

Caitlyn smiled and thanked him, she pulled the car door open and began to walk slowly towards the door of the building, stopping several times hands fidgeting rehearsing what she would say.

She rounded the corner through the door, and the building was full of the echoing sound of an orbital sander grinding away at the aluminum hull of the boat.

The boat looked so strange to her, all of the silver paint was gone. Instead, it was covered in red colored fairing compound that had been sanded through to the aluminum below in places.

The masts were off; the lifelines were removed, the portlights and windows had all been pulled out and were closed off from the inside with clear plastic taped in the openings.

Caitlyn walked around the boat until she came up on Mike covered head to toe in a white painter's suit grinding away at the hull with the sander.

He stopped and pulled the respirator from his face and pulled the painter's suit open after shaking the dust off, it was then he saw her standing there, he smiled big, and that is when it happened, another woman emerged from behind him.

Seeing Caitlyn, she wrapped her arm through Mike's in a possessive "He's mine" kind of way, then she asked:

"Mike, who is this?"

Caitlyn could see the look of regret spread across Mike's face as he blurted out.

"Oh shit."

It was the last thing Caitlyn heard; it's as though her ears began to ring, she stood there dumbstruck for a minute the other shoe had just fallen, and she was in shock.

After a moment of standing there paralyzed Caitlyn did the only thing she could do, she turned, and she ran from the building, she ran out the gate, she ran down the sea wall.

She just kept running until her legs gave out beneath her, and she fell down right there in the middle of the sidewalk and began to cry.

She felt so stupid, so silly, she had just thrown everything away for him, she loved him, and now he was with someone else; and she was very very far from home!

As Caitlyn charged from the building, Mike shook his arm loose of the woman and pushed her away glaring at her as he spoke.

> "Tiffany, I told you no! There is no us, get fuckin lost!"

Mike took off after Caitlyn but not as fast, as he exited the building he found his Grandpa and Allen sitting in the Cadillac looking puzzled he yelled out:

> "What the hell are you doing here Grandpa, Monica's been searching all over hell for you!"

Stephen just smiled and yelled out:

> "Go get her Michael; she got one hell of a head start on you!"

Mike took off towards the street; he didn't see her anywhere. He looked back to the car, and Grandpa simply pointed his cane in the direction she ran from his spot in the passenger seat.

Mike headed up the street and kept walking, and walking and walking, he kept looking, but Caitlyn was nowhere to be found.

Finally, he walked back to the boat yard, he got his phone from where he had left it in the shop, he tried calling her, but she had left her phone in the back seat of Allen's car.

Everyone held a meeting, Allen and Grandpa Stephen would take his car, Mike would take the Marina pickup, and the Australians would take the rental car they had been using to see the sights, and they would go search for her.

Mike set out in the old beat up Chevy heading in the direction Caitlyn had run off, he kept going and going, but she was nowhere to be found.

He searched all along the sea wall, all through downtown, but no luck.

Each time he saw a woman with red hair, he would jolt looking at her, but it always turned out to be someone else.

Soon the sun was setting in the sky, the wispy clouds turned hues of red, orange and purple, and slowly the buildings off in the distance turned into shadows on the horizon before night descended upon the town.

Mike extended his search further out; he just kept going and going finally having to stop to put gas in the truck.

Finally, he resorted to pulling out his cell phone, getting out of the truck and asking random people if they had seen her when he showed them her picture.

He was met with a sea of no's and bewildered faces some people didn't respond and just hurried off on their way.

Mike began to feel a sinking feeling that something may have happened to Caitlyn.

Where could she be?

Finally, he found himself back in the truck driving around scouring the town to no avail.

The hours drew on and the hot August night made the old truck very uncomfortable, the air conditioning didn't work, Mike had the windows down, but it was so hot outside it didn't do any good.

Soon the old Indian blanket seat cover was soaked through with sweat as were Mikes clothes, but he just kept on driving and driving until the sun began to show again on the far western horizon.

Finally, Mike turned around and headed back to the boatyard.

As he pulled into the gate he could see the rental car and the Cadillac, he pulled up to the office and walked inside and was met with somber faces.

Everyone was worried what had happened to her; no one had seen anything, no one knew where she had gone, it was just as though Caitlyn had disappeared.

Jim the Australian was the first to speak up.

> "Mate she is out there somewhere, from the sounds of things she is no weakling, I'm sure she will be fine, you had best get some rest, and we can start again in a few hours. You look like hell; you need it."

Mike nodded and fought the urge to close his eyes.

Then Grandpa Stephen spoke up.

> "Mike, I know you love that girl, but you need to get some rest, you're no good to anyone if you don't get some sleep.
>
> Allen and I turned in early; we will go take another look around."

Then Allen joined in:

> "I have a friend who is the prosecuting attorney here. I will give him a call and see if he can put out any feelers through the PD, see if they have heard anything."

Mike just nodded and mouthed thank you. Then he rubbed his chin and considered his options.

> "I am going to grab a shower and get some rest. Jim, Mary, Tania, thank you for all your efforts out there today, Please don't worry about this, enjoy your time here in the Bay, I know you wanted to see it."

"No worries mate! This is the most excitement we've had in a while!"

Jim replied with a big grin in his deep rich Australian accent.

Mike nodded to everyone and walked back out to the boat and climbed aboard.

He pulled off his sweat soaked clothes, poured a bucket full of water out of the sink stepped into the shower and dumped it over his head repeating a couple of times before wiping himself down with a wash cloth.

He dried himself and crawled into bed, the next thing he knew his phone was ringing, it was Allen calling.

"Hello?"

Mike practically choked on his words being so tired.

"Mike, we found her, she's in the Alameda jail."

Allen reported then continued

"Apparently last night a female officer stopped to help her as she sat crying on the sidewalk and she assaulted her."

Mike Grimaced mumbling to himself

"Oh fuck me."

"Alright Allen, thank you I will head down that way."

"Wait there is more, I will be over to the yard in about fifteen minutes, I will tell you when I get there."

"Ok, see you when you get here."

Mike replied before hanging up the phone, then he threw his feet over the side of the bed rubbed his tired eyes realizing he had only been asleep for about three hours.

Twenty minutes later he was standing in front of the office, Allen pulled in in his Cadillac with Grandpa Stephen sitting in the passenger seat.

The two men emerged and sat on the hood of the car.

"Well, what's the deal?"

Mike asked waiting to hear what she had done this time.

"Well here is what happened, a female cop found her crying on the sidewalk, she reached out to see if she was ok and Caitlyn snapped at her, the cop arrested her for assaulting an officer."

Allen started in.

"Oh great. So what now?"

Mike responded rolling his eyes.

"Well, you see that boat over there?"

Allen asked pointing to a 40' Beneteau sitting on stands by the building.

"Yeah, what about it?"

Mike asked a bit puzzled.

"It belongs to the prosecuting attorney, I just traded a bottom job on that boat for your girl's freedom, although the arresting officer was none too happy about it."

"I can imagine not, they don't like having their decisions overturned. Let me know what the bottom job costs, I will pay you for it."

"I will do no such thing when you get back with your young lady you bring her to talk to me, she Tiffany and I are going to have a bit of a sit-down."

Mike smiled realizing the old salty bastard had something up his sleeve.

"Alright, I'll do that! Who do I need to talk to when I get there?"

"Ask for Officer Morris. And Mike, whatever you do make sure Caitlin keeps her mouth shut, the officer isn't happy."

Mike nodded in agreement then hopped in the pickup and headed out to the police station.

He parked the truck on the street and fed the meter with the maximum amount of coins just to be safe; then he walked up the steps into the police station.

At the reception desk, he asked for Officer Morris, within a few minutes a short slightly fat policewoman emerged.

At one time she had probably been fairly attractive but now in her 30's it was obvious she was letting herself go, and her face was taking on a semi-permanent scowl.

"Mister Black I presume?"

She asked with obvious disgust in her voice.

"Yes, that is me."

Mike replied acting unphased by her attitude.

"Come with me; she is in here."

The officer motioned for him to follow.

Mike did, they walked back up through the security door back to a room with hard wooden benches with rings screwed into them.

Caitlyn sat at one of the benches cuffed to one of the rings.

The officer opened the door for Mike, and he walked in as Caitlyn looked up he blurted out.

"You know, we got to stop meeting like this!"

Caitlyn began to sob all over again, all she could do was mouth the words "I'm so sorry" over and over.

Mike came to her and hugged her, she took her free hand and hugged him back.

A moment later when she had calmed down, enough the officer approached.

"I'm going to uncuff your hand, DO NOT TRY TO HIT ME AGAIN! UNDERSTAND?"

Caitlyn nodded in agreement.

The officer uncuffed her hand, and once she had stepped back, Caitlyn stood up and hugged Mike.

"Well come on I haven't got all day!"

The officer blurted out.

Mike turned to her and offered a few words:

"Thank you for your time, and thank you for finding her, everyone was very worried about her."

Caitlyn's eyes flashed, she wanted to speak, but Mike Elbowed her in the ribs before she could and began to lead her from the building half walking half dragging her.

As they stepped outside the bright light burned Caitlyn's eyes, she looked like hell, she had been awake all night. She had cried until she could cry no more, rehydrated and then cried some more.

The steps from the front of the building up the sidewalk to the truck were easily the worst walk of shame she had ever endured.

As Mike pulled the door open, she couldn't climb in fast enough, sliding all the way over to the other side. Mike then climbed in and shoved the keys in the ignition, but he didn't start the truck.

> "Well, you want to tell me what happened?"

> "Tell you what happened? Tell you what happened? You found someone else that is what happened!"

Caitlyn shot back with obvious anger in her voice.

> "Tiffany is not my girlfriend, she is Allen's grandniece, she has been all over me the whole time I had been here working on the boat, she wants me in the worst way, but I don't want a damn thing to do with her, she is a little trailer trash druggie.

> I tried to tell you, but you just turn around and ran."

Caitlin, all of the sudden, felt so incredibly stupid when she saw the woman she had just frozen in her tracks, then she remembered it was when Mike pulled his arm from Tiffany's and began to walk towards her that she bolted.

Her instinct had just told her to run, so that is what she did.

It was as though all of her fears had just come true at once so she ran and ran far away as she could go.

She still couldn't bring herself to explain this to Mike, however, and thus all her pride would let her say was:

"I'm sorry ok, I fucked up, I'm a fuck up."

Mike unamused turned back to the wheel, fired the truck up, and they drove back to the Marina without saying another word.

They pulled in and parked in front of the office, Mike got out of the truck and began to walk to the door Caitlyn stayed seated in the truck a stoic look on her face.

It was obvious the events of the last 48 hours were running through her brain like a freight train at 3 am.

Mike turned around and opened the door for her, obviously annoyed as he gestured for her to get out and walk inside.

Up the steps, they went Caitlin again paused at the office door. Mike held it open and gestured for her to enter which she did trying to compose herself.

As she walked in she was greeted by Tiffany sitting at the receptionist's desk.

"Well hi, nice to see you again."

Tiffany blurted out in her most condescending Cali girl voice.

As she did Caitlyn looked at her, and her eyes flashed fire, but her lips remained sealed, Mike grabbed her by the arm and pushed her along into the sitting area where everyone was waiting.

Mike directed Caitlyn into a chair by her arm, and she plopped back into it with a look of defiance on her face.

Allen spoke up

"Tiffany get in here."

"Coming."

Tiffany replied almost singing the words.

Allen then gestured towards the seat next to Caitlyn and told her to sit down.

Tiffany looked at him, looked at Caitlyn and looked at the Chair; it was only then she realized she was in deep shit too.

She made her way to the chair and sat down crossing her arms turning her whole body as far away from Caitlyn as she could.

"I don't see why you need me here!"

She exclaimed.

"Because you started all this shit, how many times did I tell you to stay away from Mike, that he wasn't interested in you?"

Allen asked her with a very stern voice and disappointed, frustrated look on his face.

"I didn't think you were serious."

Tiffany lied through her teeth and smacked her gum flipping her blonde hair wiggling in the chair like nothing mattered to her as if magically the rules didn't apply.

"Oh I never!"

Caitlyn blurted out realizing this woman had duped her into behaving foolish, but before she could finish the sentence, Mike reached over and grabbed her hand cutting her short holding his other hand up to his lips telling her to shush.

Caitlin clamped her jaw shut, but the fire in her eyes caused Tiffany to get a bit nervous, Tiffany was five foot nine inches, but what Caitlyn lacked in size, she obviously made up for in pure venom and spite.

Finally, Allen continued.

> "You girls caused a lot of problems down here in the last 24 hours, Tiffany you're already on probation, and because of what you two did I had to go back to the DA for another favor."

Tiffany scoffed and broke in:

> "It's not my fault this bitch is crazy!"

Caitlin opened her mouth to speak, but Mike squeezed her hand hard stopping her.

Allen shot back to Tiffany:

> "She is not crazy she is in love stupid, and if you ever cared about anyone other than yourself you could see that!"

Tiffany just rolled her eyes and smacked her gum.

Allen continued:

> "I had to pull in a big favor; we're going to have to paint the bottom of that boat out there that belongs to the Attorney, you girls are going to do the work."

Simultaneously both of their mouths dropped, and they began to protest, but before the words could come up, Mike butted in.

> "Allen I think that sounds like an awesome idea, I think they both need to learn consequences have actions."

Hearing this from Mike stopped Caitlyn in her tracks, she began to flash back to the man Mike had killed in Yakutat protecting her.

All of the sudden all her anger and indignation melted away into guilt, she had screwed up again, not so bad this time no one died, but he was right, her actions did have consequences.

Allen then broke the silence:

> "Well ladies, tomorrow morning seven am sharp, be
> here, meet Manny out in the yard, he will get you all
> setup. You're going to work on that boat until it's
> finished. Manny will show you what to do."

Tiffany still with a bad attitude spoke up in a sarcastic voice.

> "I'm not doing it; you can't make me!"

Allen leaned forward in his chair and stared her down.

> "Young lady, you're on probation, a condition of your
> probation is that you keep your job here, either you
> come here to sand the boat tomorrow, or I call the DA,
> he pulls your probation, and you go to jail.
>
> Understood?"

Tiffany nodded, got up and bolted from the room obviously
beaten. Then Allen turned to Caitlyn and spoke:

> "That goes for you as well young lady, do you
> understand."

Caitlyn not skipping a beat knowing what to do to earn his favor
instantly blurted out:

> "Yes sir, I will be here, seven am to sand the boat. I
> won't stop until its done."

Allen smiled and said:

> "I am glad we understand each other, now you folks go
> get some sleep."

Everyone stood up, Mike shook Allen's hand and thanked him,
shook Grandpa's hand, then escorted Caitlyn back out through
the office door, across the parking lot back to the boat shed
where his boat sat waiting for him to finish her.

He didn't let go of her hand until he reached the ladder then he pushed her up it following close behind. When they got on board, he pulled the ladder up, pulled his handcuffs from his pocket and locked the ladder to the rail effectively trapping her onboard.

"What's that for?"

Caitlyn queried.

"It's so you can't get down, and she can't get up, I am not taking any chances, I need a good night's sleep I have way too much to do on this boat to have another night like I did last night."

Caitlyn, not understanding how hard Mike had looked crossed her arms in disgust as though she wasn't trusted, in fact, she knew she wasn't and that hurt.

She had wanted this to be a happy time, a happy trip, they were reunited; and instead of it feeling so good it had all turned to shit.

Mike walked below not waiting for her, after a moment she followed, but stopped short in the salon, instead of going to bed with him she elected to lay down on the seatee as a way of punishing him for not trusting her.

She lay down and curled up, pulling her jacket over her like a blanket.

As she lay there in the dimly lit salon, she started to run the events of the last few days through her head. But before she could come to any conclusions she had nodded off to sleep.

With the sounding of three bells signifying 5:30 am the ship's clock started Caitlyn's day.

She sat up groggy with a pounding head, her mouth was dry, and her tummy ached, she now realized the last food she had eaten was on the airplane now almost 48 hours ago.

She stood up and needed to pee, but had to hold it because she was unsure if the head worked with the boat out of the water.

So she sat back down and waited in the dark.

Soon four bells rang, and then five telling her it was now 6:30, soon Mike was stirring, he drug himself from the captain's quarters obviously tired and feeling like hell.

He pulled a bottle of water from the fridge and kicked the lights on. The light burned Caitlyn's eyes, and she had to hold her hand up to block it out.

"Good morning."

Mike said, eyeing her up and down.

"You may want to get cleaned up before you go out, are you hungry?"

"Starving!"

Caitlyn responded.

"You can use the sink just don't use the shower, we only have so much water onboard, and the toilet is ok just don't use it a lot."

"Ok."

Caitlin responded then she carried herself down into the guest head when she flicked on the lights.

Instantly she was shocked by the face she saw in the mi*rror, she barely recognized herself! Her hair was a mess; her cheeks were smudged with eyeliner that had been cried out and wiped away over and over, her eyes were dark and heavy.

After cleaning herself up, Caitlyn emerged from the head to find that Mike had made bacon, eggs, and toast. She sat down and scarfed the food down without saying a word.

Then the clock struck six bells Caitlyn looked up to see it was now 7 am, she grabbed her plate and her glass, rinsed them in the sink and ran topside to find the ladder still cuffed to the rail.

Mike emerged a moment later, uncuffed the ladder and set it down for her.

Caitlyn turned to take the ladder paused then turned back to Mike, she hugged him and said she was sorry, then climbed down and scurried out the door.

In the yard she found Manny, the first words out of his mouth were "You're late!"

Caitlyn apologized, then looked around not seeing Tiffany anywhere.

Manny got her a painter's suit and an orbital sander.

Then he showed her how to take the bottom paint down, and instructed her not to sand any further once the paint was gone.

He showed her the motions to take, then handed her a respirator and turned her loose.

Caitlyn started sanding away, about 30 minutes later she turned around to see Tiffany getting out of a car that had just pulled in.

The car sped off, and Manny met her and directed her to the boat, Caitlyn was a bit disappointed he didn't read her the riot act. Apparently, Manny knew it would go in one ear out the other.

He set Tiffany up on the other side of the boat telling her each woman would have their own side to do, and that whoever finished last got to do the transom as well.

Hearing this Caitlyn dug in, there was no way she was going to let Tiffany beat her, she worked the sander up and down back and forth until her arms were practically falling off.

Soon it was lunch time, and the two women stowed their tools and began walking back towards the office, Tiffany had stopped working several minutes before, so she had a head start back to the building.

As Caitlyn approached, she realized she had an audience all morning that Grandpa Stephen had been sitting in a chair watching her work.

> "I will give you this kid; you've got spirit, you're a hard worker."

> "Thanks!"

Caitlyn smiled for the first time in a while.

> "What do you say we all go grab some lunch?"

> "What about Mike?"

> "Mike had to run across town to get some parts for the boat. He won't be back for a couple of hours."

Allen and Tiffany emerged from the office; everyone piled into Allen's Cadillac, Tiffany sitting behind Allen, Caitlyn sitting behind Grandpa Stephen.

Each woman refusing to look at the other but despite this, they managed to have a nice lunch before returning to the boatyard.

As they pulled back in Caitlyn looked for Mike's truck, but it was nowhere to be found.

She wanted to see him, to talk to him, but he wasn't here now, so she walked back to the boat, pulled her painter's suit on, picked up the sander and went back to sanding.

By the time four pm had rolled around Caitlyn was spent, her arms ached, she hurt all over, the noise of the sander reverberated in her ears.

Every bit of her face that wasn't covered by the respirator or painters suit was covered in sanding dust.

She made her way to the office and cleaned herself off, as she stepped from the building she found Grandpa Stephen sitting where he was earlier in the day.

> "You worked hard out there today."

He said with his big toothy grin.

> "You've got almost a third of that boat all sanded down."

> "It's taking forever! I am so sore and tired!"

Caitlyn complained.

Then she sat down with a bottle of water next to him.

> "Does Mike hate me now?"

> "Hate you?"

Grandpa asked with a quizzical look on his face.

> "He hardly said anything to me today or yesterday; I think he hates me now."

> "I seriously doubt that I think just the opposite is true."

Grandpa replied then he continued.

> "You know when he couldn't find you on foot, he came back here, organized us all into a search party, Allen and I gave up around 9 pm, you know us old farts we can't stay up late.
>
> The Aussies made it until 2 am.
>
> But Mike, he didn't stop, he kept going and going, he stayed out all night long, he never stopped looking for you.
>
> I could see it in his eyes when he came back in the morning; we had to force him to get some sleep, he wasn't giving up on you, he would have gone until he found you.
>
> That doesn't sound like something someone who hates you would do now does it.
>
> Sure, he is a bit sore at you right now, you scared the hell out of him, I could see it in his face he feared the worst had happened to you, can't say I blame him for being upset you put him through that."

Caitlyn swallowed hard as tears welled up in her eyes, she didn't know Mike had been out all night scouring the town for her.

She didn't know he had been in the truck, on foot, everywhere else and had burned up a couple of tanks of gas looking for her.

All the sudden all of her anger turned to guilt, she felt so stupid, while she was sitting in jail she got mad at him for not being there, for not being the one who found her.

She had done a very dumb thing running out into the middle of a strange city, she should have stayed where she was, she should have asked what was going on, but instead, she jumped to conclusions, and now she was paying for her mistake.

She made up her mind then and there to see this through, to make things right.

The next morning Caitlyn arose early, by the time Manny rolled into the yard at 6:30 Caitlyn was already hard at sanding on her side of the boat.

Tiffany didn't roll in until almost noon, it was almost one before she started doing any work, and even then, it was sporadic.

Towards the end of the day, Caitlyn had a rhythm going; she was two-thirds done with her side of the boat when all the sudden her sander lost power.

She followed the cord back to the bank of outlets on the wall and found out that it had come loose and fallen out of the plug.

She picked it up and plugged it back in when she got back to the boat her sander was gone.

Caitlyn looked around; Tiffany was gone, it was then Caitlyn saw that her side of the boat was less than halfway finished.

She saw Manny walking by and told him that both Tiffany and the sanders had disappeared. Manny just shook his head and said he would bring her another one in the morning.

That night Caitlyn was too tired to think about anything, as soon as she laid down on the seatee, she was fast asleep.

The next morning at six thirty Manny rolled in, Caitlyn was there waiting for him. To her surprise so was Tiffany.

Manny had stopped by her place to pick her up on the way there.

Somehow the sanders had magically reappeared, but Caitlyn didn't ask any questions, she just put her painter's suit on, grabbed her sander and set to work.

The morning went by quickly, soon it was ten am, but as Caitlyn quit working a sight greeted her she didn't want to see, two cop cars pulling into the lot.

A large male cop stepped from one car, from the other stepped good ole Officer Morris.

Caitlyn thought to herself:

> "Oh no, they are here for me, they changed their minds!"

But this was not the case, a few moments later Allen rolled in with a strange man in his car.

As they stepped from the car the man directed the officers towards Tiffany, she resisted at first and cried out, but soon enough she was subdued sitting in the back of the cop car.

The man turned out to be the district attorney, he introduced himself to Caitlyn and asked Officer Morris to join him.

Officer Morris obviously still had hard feelings about having her arrest overturned; but when the DA explained to her that Caitlyn had agreed to work on the boat instead as punishment and that she had been hard at it for three days now.

Officer Morris seemed to change in tone realizing that with the overcrowding in California's jails that Caitlyn would have only served a day or two if convicted anyways.

It seemed to her standing in the hot sun sanding bottom paint off a boat was a far worse punishment than the legal system would have dealt her.

The DA remarked that she was doing a good job, but lamented that now the other half wasn't getting done with Tiffany going back to Jail.

Allen stepped in and said he would have the guys from the yard finish it, but Caitlyn cut him short.

> "No, I want to finish this myself. I need to finish this."

> "It's alright; you're almost done with your side, the deal was whoever finishes last has to do the transom, you're obviously going to be done first."

Allen insisted, but Caitlyn didn't have it.

> "No, I need to finish this, I need to see this through!"

> "Suit yourself!"

Allen said with a smile, Caitlyn then looked to Officer Morris, and spoke:

> "I'm sorry for what happened, I was very upset, very emotional, I shouldn't have done what I did. I know you were just trying to help, trying to do your job. I acted very badly towards you."

Saying this it was like someone pulled a string in Officer Morris's back and all of the sudden her face came to life with a brilliant smile that she had obviously not used in quite some time, she sprung forward at Caitlyn saying.

> "Honey, it's ok!"

As she gave her a big hug.

As she stepped back, it was obvious that a bunch of the dust from her painter's suit wound up all over her uniform.

Everyone laughed as Caitlyn tried to apologize for the dust, a quick shot with the air hose and the uniform was right as rain again.

The officers climbed back into their patrol cars and whisked Tiffany off to jail, the DA turned to Caitlyn and shook her hand telling her once more she was doing a fantastic job and that she had his respect.

This made her feel really good although she wished Mike had been there to see it.

That brought her thoughts back to Mike, the two of them had hardly spoken in days, he had been so busy working on his boat.

She resolved to get cleaned up and talk to him.

That night at dinner, she climbed up in the boat, got her bag and made her way to the showers in the back of the office.

She got herself cleaned up, did her hair and makeup, not too fancy, she was still in a tee shirt and jeans, but she wanted to look nice for him when she saw him at dinner.

As she exited the building, her plans were shattered as a car load of Australians pulled back in and piled into the boat shed where Mike had been working all day.

Soon sounds of laughter were pouring from the building, Caitlyn just slumped into the chair on the porch of the office for a bit before mustering the courage to face them.

She climbed on board about the time dinner was ready, Mike said good evening and handed her a plate of food, but through dinner, she was silent occasionally listening to the stories the Aussies were telling about their travels through the city.

The next day they were heading back up to Wine Country in Napa, then would be back after Mike had the boat painted to help him re-step the masts and to help fit all the rigging.

Caitlyn hearing this hatched her plan, she would work as hard as she could sanding the other boat then try to catch Mike before the Aussies came back.

Something deep inside of her was stirring like it was just before the reached Kodiak, but this time she knew what she needed to make things right between them.

⚓ TWENTY-SEVEN ⚓

For the next three days, Caitlyn worked like a beast sanding on the hull every minute of the day she could bear.

She finished stripping her side, cleaned up Tiffany's half ass work and then finished stripping her side of the boat and the transom.

When she was finished, she called upon Allen to inspect the boat; he was followed out by Grandpa Stephen who was grinning ear to ear watching her work over the last few days.

The two men wandered around the boat giving their accolades. Finally, Allen told her that if marine biology didn't work out for her, she had a future in the marine industry considering she had done a better job than some of his employees.

This made her smile for the first time in days.

After the men had finished admiring her work Caitlyn stripped off her painter's suit and dumped it in the trash, she got the tools back to Manny and grabbed her shower bag to go clean up.

When she stepped out of the shower Caitlyn noticed her body, the week of hard work and little food had taken her already shapely body and caused muscles to push out everywhere, her arms were ripped, her abs were ripped, and her legs were solid.

This was probably the best she had ever looked in her life.

She took great care to prepare her body; she shaved everything from the neck down, she fretted over every detail doing her makeup. She put her hair up into a braid then wound the braid into a bun securing it with elastic bands.

She slipped back into her clothes then headed out back to Mikes boat to hatch her plan.

Mike was still working on prepping, scrutinizing every detail, Caitlyn knew he planned to prime the hull in the morning.

Soon he showed up inside grabbing his bag to head over to the shower, as soon as she heard him clanging down the ladder Caitlyn sprung her plan into gear.

She went into the bedroom where she knew Mike kept the handcuffs. She found some rope, one of his belts, and brought it all back to the salon.

On the dinette table, she laid out both pairs of handcuffs, coiled the rope neatly as Mike had taught her to do on deck. Then she shed her clothing and kneeled on the cabin sole holding the belt palms up in her hands and waited for Mike.

It seemed like forever before he returned, his footsteps up the ladder and across the deck were heavy and tired, he entered down the companionway steps, and as his face dropped below the combing, he saw her kneeling there waiting for him.

He dropped his bag and asked:

"What's this?"

With a quizzical look. He was genuinely surprised to find Caitlyn kneeling naked on the floor.

"I hurt you, and I am sorry. I should have waited, I should have remained calm, I should have found out what was going on but instead I ran away, and I ruined everyone's day.

I lost my temper and let my emotions get the better of me, I made a fool of myself, I made everyone here stressed out and concerned for my wellbeing, and I made you look bad in front of your friends.

I also distracted you from working on your boat, from the things you needed to do to get it back in the water, I know how much you love being on the water, and for that I am sorry.

I feel like I deserve to be punished like you did in Kodiak, Please forgive me!"

Mike was shocked by the gesture; he had completely not expected it. But he rubbed his chin; then he smiled the first smile he had smiled in a long time at her.

Caitlyn felt her head begin to go light, a tingling sensation inside of herself start to build, all of the sudden she found herself hyper focused on Mike, it was like the rest of the world for that moment ceased to exist.

Mike slid the companionway shut; then he locked it shut.

He walked to Caitlyn and instructed her to stand, then he cuffed her hands behind her back using a pair of cuffs at her wrists, and the other above her elbows.

Then he took a piece of the rope and tied one end to the cuffs, running the other end through one of the handrails on the ceiling pulling her arms up and behind forcing her to lean forward.

Then Mike grabbed the belt; he held the end of it in his hand slowly tracing the tip up and down the backs of her legs and insides of her thighs, Caitlyn squirmed at the sensation that made her head rush with endorphins then WHACK!

The first blow landed on her left cheek and caused her to pull her left leg to her chest as she moaned out in pain, then WHACK! On the other side, she began to dance.

Mike began working the belt back and forth causing Caitlyn to cry out with various noises that were a mixture of pain and ecstasy.

As the pain set in she began to find relief for the emotional grief, she felt inside.

Soon she began to cry, and the blows began to hurt more, the muscles in her legs ached, her arms ached from being pulled back, but she took every blow he was willing to muster.

Finally, Caitlyn was a big sobbing mess, tears streamed freely down her cheeks, her backside and the backs of her legs had turned bright red her knees began to shake uncontrollably, but she did not cry out for mercy.

Mike was tired too; he could feel the burn of the weeks work through his body, his hands and arms felt the burn of working the belt, he was sweating again and breathing hard.

He stopped with the belt and reached his hand out around Caitlyn's side; this caused her to jump at first, but then she realized he was steadying her.

Mike let the rope loose and stood her up. Then he let the cuffs go.

Caitlyn collapsed into his chest repeating over and over:

> "I'm so sorry, please forgive me!"

Mike told her to shush, then he picked her up and carried her back to his stateroom. He toweled the sweat off of her body and dried her tears.

Then he set her on the bed and climbed in with her.

Mike gently stroked Caitlyn's face with his hand then rubbed her back causing her to bury herself into his chest.

As Mike caressed her, Caitlyn began to kiss his chest softly before working her way up to kissing him on the lips.

Mike then rolled Caitlyn onto her back spreading her legs apart he climbed between them and pushed himself inside of her as he continued to kiss her.

They would go on like this late into the night.

The next morning Mike and Caitlyn emerged from the boatshed together and much later than the usual arm in arm they walked to the office, Caitlyn looked like a different person smiling and bubbly.

As they approached the office, they met Grandpa Stephen there sitting in the chair on the porch of the building as he usually did.

He smiled and greeted them.

> "Well, it looks like you two did some making up last night! Glad to see it!"

With this, Caitlyn turned bright red and buried her face in Mikes' arm to hide her embarrassment.

Mike just laughed, and so did Grandpa.

It was the start of a great new day.

⚓ TWENTY-EIGHT ⚓

Caitlyn and Mike spent the day prepping the hull; they wiped it down several times with solvents and clean rags, Mike locked the doors to the boat shed shut so no one could come in and stir up the dust.

Then they took the hose, sprayed down the floor to keep any dust from getting up, turned on the fans and Mike began spraying.

After the second coat had set Mike and Caitlyn went out for dinner, but both were tired and turned in early although sleeping in the same bed again now.

The following day was much the same, get up, clean like crazy, then paint.

They buried the hull in 4 coats of the same royal blue My Way had been painted in. The topsides were painted white and to do so all of the freshly stained teak had to be masked.

After the bottom had been painted and cured they installed the zincs and the vinyl lettering.

Soon it was time to kick the barn doors open, and the big travel lift entered the building and brought the massive sailboat back out into the sunlight.

Everyone watched as the big blue vessel emerged from the boat shed, its blue hull glistening in the sun.

Grandpa Stephen whistled and proclaimed what a beautiful boat she was.

Soon she had splashed into the water, and Mike and Caitlyn climbed aboard, they checked the bilge for leaks, once sure there were none they maneuvered her around to the pier where they would step the masts the following day.

At dinner, everyone was there, Mike, Caitlyn, Grandpa Stephen, Allen, the Australians: Jim, Mary, and Tania.

Grandpa Stephen stood up and got everyone's attention banging his spoon against his glass.

Once everyone was paying attention he spoke:

> "Michael, I just wanted to say how proud I am of you, you've done some amazing things in your lifetime from serving our country to your adventures on the high seas.

> This new boat you have, she is something special, and I have something for you."

Grandpa Stephen dug into his pocket and pulled out a plastic coin case that had a real silver dollar in it from 1921 in it which he held up for all to see.

> "Back in 1957 when Allen and I bought the property and built the first boat yard here in Alameda when we got our first check from the first job the yard had completed I was still on active duty, Allen sent me a silver dollar which was the first Dollar the company had made me.

> I kept that dollar all these years, and as is Navy tradition after I retired from the Navy in 1964 I built the sailboat Michael grew up on at the boat yard when it came time to step the mast I stepped it on this coin.

> Back in the ninety's some bum came aboard the boat and caught her on fire trying to stay warm, she burnt down, but this coin survived so I saved it.

> All the years I have had it, it's brought me luck, now Michael I want you to have it so tomorrow when you step the mast on your new boat, you will have a piece of me aboard with you always."

As he finished speaking Grandpa Stephen was almost teary-eyed as he handed to coin to Mike who had to stand up and give him a big hug, then he passed the coin around the table for all to see.

It was obvious he was very proud of Mike, and everyone understood what a big deal the coin was considering it was tradition to step your mast on a coin, one with such meaning was considered to be very good luck.

The next morning around nine am the big yellow crane entered the yard and the crew began to set up. Mike, Caitlyn, and the Aussies had spent the evening installing all the new rigging to the masts before they all went out to dinner.

The crane lifted the mainmast slowly and gently into the air, Mike and Jim guided the mast down into the deck hole and set it on the old silver dollar Grandpa had given them that had been secured to the top of the mast step with double sided tape. The aluminum mast fit down over it snugly into the shoe.

Soon Jim and Mike had all of the stays pinned in place and the rigging partially tensioned enough to keep the mast up; then they repeated the process for the second mast.

Eventually, the Crane rolled up and rolled out, and they set to work tuning the rig, tightening the shrouds and stays checking the bow of the masts hooking up the radar, wind instruments and lights.

It was a late evening, but by the end of the day, the boat was close to being ready to sail.

As the sun was setting Grandpa Stephen grabbed Caitlyn and asked her to walk with him which she did, they walked down towards the water and had a seat on a couple of old plastic chairs that were sitting there overlooking the bay.

It was a beautiful evening the sun painted the sky, the glass of the buildings across the bay shimmered with its reflection. It was a beautiful evening.

"So young lady I have a question for you?"

"Yes?"

Caitlyn replied with a look of puzzlement.

"I am going to share a bit of a secret. I am dying; there is cancer in my lungs, its slowly eating away at me. Eventually, it's going to end me. Nothing the doctors can do about it. "

"That is horrible; I'm so sorry."

Caitlyn said tearing up a bit; she had grown quite fond of the old salty sailor and his antics.

"Before I go, I have one last bit of business I need to tend to, and that is I am figuring out how I am going to divide up my estate.

All I have left are Michael and his sister, his sister has said all she wants is her grandmother's old paintings and some of her Jewelry which I happily gave to her, but that leaves me wondering what to do with my stake in the boat yard.

I own half of this place, I own some other property here and in Seattle too, some of these places I have owned for forty or fifty years now and they are worth a lot of money.

Most of it is managed by a rental company that tends to the buildings, finds tenants, takes care of the money, all I have to do is collect a check, it's a good deal.

My plan is to leave it all to Michael, I trust him, I know he can manage it well, he has my sense for business, and he has done well for himself in his business ventures.

But that leaves me one question in mind, and that is can I trust you?"

"What do you mean?"

Caitlyn asked not understanding at all where he was going with this.

"It's obvious Michael loves you, he hasn't let a woman get this close to him in years. Not since… well, you know.

I suspect you two will be together for a long time, possibly even get married; I just want to know that you will look after him, that you will care for him. He needs a good woman in his life, and I think you are it."

Hearing this Caitlyn's face turned bright red.

"Why thank you!"

She beamed with a huge smile.

"After watching you take on that bottom job on that boat to make amends, to make things right.

You didn't have to do the whole thing, but when Tiffany didn't hold up her end, you stepped in and got things done because you understood the importance of that and because of this you earned the respect of everyone here."

Grandpa Stephen paused for a moment and rubbed his chin with his old bony weather-beaten hand.

"What I want from you is your assurance, I want you to promise me that you will be there for Michael, that you will be good to him, that you will help him in his time of need because when I go, I know it is going to be very hard on him."

Caitlyn leaned in and hugged him.

"You have my word; I will do whatever it takes."

As she leaned back, she could see the tears in the old man's eyes, and with this, she could see how much it meant to him knowing that she would be there for Mike after he was gone.

That night Caitlyn elected to cook for everyone, she had spent most of the day getting the galley aboard the big boat back in order. The previous three weeks in the boat yard had left it a bit of a wreck sitting up on the hard.

Even Grandpa Stephen climbed aboard for dinner, he told stories of his time in the Navy, about running from the MP's in Subic Bay after a bar fight, or of when he first visited Japan in 1948.

Then his stories turned to Mike when he was a boy learning how to sail; he talked about the little sailing dinghy they had built for him of wood and fiberglass that Mike had sailed around Puget Sound.

He talked about how after Mike's parents had died when he was 12 years old how he had jumped in the boat and sailed off, and four days later they found him at the Canadian border.

Like a pirate, he had eluded everyone looking for him in his little sailboat and had made it almost two hundred miles north.

When they asked him where he was going, he told them Alaska. It caused quite a stir; he was even on TV because of it.

Jim the Australian wound up laughing so hard at this story he howled, proclaiming Mike had apparently always been crazy and thus was worthy of becoming an honorary Australian.

Mike laughed at this and told him you have to be crazy to live on a continent that has spiders that can eat birds and snakes!

This caused everyone to break out into a fit of laughter.

As the night carried on and everyone told their stories and laughed out loud, Caitlyn found herself snuggled up to Mikes side, her arm wrapped around his holding his hand and eventually as the night dwindled she fell asleep on his shoulder.

The next morning Caitlyn awoke in bed with Mike, the last thing she remembered was sitting around the table getting sleepy, he must have carried her in there.

Mike was still passed out sleeping, but he deserved it, they both had worked so very hard over the last two weeks.

As she lay there cuddled up to him, her thoughts began to drift through the conversation she had with Grandpa Stephen the previous day.

She began to wonder how much time he had left, how long he would still be around and what it would take to get Mike to be ok again when he was gone.

The thought saddened her because she realized in the short time she had known him she had grown pretty fond of the crusty old fart.

*Soon Mike was stirring, and Caitlyn couldn't help put pounce on him.

After breakfast, everyone sat down to start getting a plan together; the boat still needed to be provisioned for the trip south, they had decided on port calls in L.A., San Diego, Bahia Tortugas, Puerto Vallarta, Puntarenas and Finally Panama City and the Pacific side of Colombia.

Today they would start working on stocking up on dry and canned goods, as well as enough fresh food for the trip to L.A. Then when they were in San Diego they would top off their supplies again before heading south.

As they emerged from the boat and made their way across the parking lot, a yellow cab pulled into the parking lot, and a woman with curly red hair stepped from the back seat and pulled a bag from the trunk.

As soon as Caitlyn saw her, she stopped dead in her tracks.

Mike looked at her, looked at the woman and then back at her, the woman saw Caitlyn and started heading their direction.

"Shit!"

Caitlyn muttered as the woman called out her name. Trying to paint on a smile she called out:

"Mom, what are you doing here?"

The woman called back in a thick Irish accent much stronger than Caitlyn's

"I just wanted to see you and see this young man and his boat you have been telling me all about."

At that point Mike took over, he stepped forward and shook her hand.

"Hello, you must be Melany, Caitlyn has told me so much about you."

Mike said with a big smile.

Then he introduced her to the Aussies; the whole-time Caitlyn nervously smiled hoping her mother wouldn't embarrass her too much.

Then Jim offered up that if they wanted to spend some time together, they could put off provisioning until tomorrow, that they could make a day trip over to the Golden Gate bridge, that they had wanted to walk across it.

Mike agreed that it would be a good idea, and then offered to take Caitlyn and her mom out for lunch but first they had to throw her bags onboard.

As they walked to where the boat lay moored they stopped as Caitlyn's mom gasped and proclaimed how beautiful the yacht was.

It did look good; the royal blue sides had been polished to a mirror-like reflection, the whole boat was covered in bits of stainless that had been polished to a high luster.

At seventy-five feet long she dwarfed the other boats in the area.

They Climbed aboard with her bags, and she marveled at all the wood work on the inside that had been epoxied, varnished and polished to a beautiful shine.

Caitlyn retold the story of how she had driven My Way while Mike Jumped from ship to ship in the middle of the night in the daring rescue that eventually landed him as the owner of the big boat.

When Mike butted in and told her how proud he was of Caitlyn for handing his boat with such skill, Caitlyn became full of a warm and fuzzy feeling; it felt so good to hear him tell her mother this.

After showing her the boat everyone loaded up in the truck and headed out to Lunch.

There Caitlyn and Mike got to tell her mother more stories of the sailing adventures, Mike left out any reference to her arrest but did tell her the story of killing the wayward fisherman who had attacked her daughter.

Caitlyn's mom was amazed at the story of all the adventures they had in just a short summer.

Then Mike Suggested that she come with them for the trip south back to San Diego.

She agreed never having been on a sailing trip before she thought it sounded fun and wanted to see what she had been missing out on.

The next day everyone pitched in getting the boat provisioned, they spent several hundred dollars on groceries and much of the evening packing it all onboard.

Labels had to be peeled from cans, items in cardboard boxes were transferred to plastic containers, no paper wrappers labels or cardboard were allowed aboard the boat.

This was because cockroaches liked to lay their eggs in cardboard and paper, especially on food products. By removing the labels, it kept the cockroaches off the boat.

This was an absolutely vital step of provisioning a boat because once you had roaches on your boat, they were almost impossible to get rid of.

That night Caitlyn and her mom cooked dinner together on board the boat, she hadn't done this in many years, and it reminded her of happy times during her childhood.

The next morning everyone got up early ate breakfast and started getting the boat cleaned up and ready to go.

Grandpa Stephen showed up around nine; he sat down on a pile of lumber overlooking the boat named in his honor, pride gripped him every time he stared at the big boat.

His thoughts were interrupted by a coughing and hacking fit that ended with him spitting blood out into the grass before recovering himself. He felt a bit dizzy and leaned on his cane for support.

After about fifteen minutes Caitlyn emerged from the boat with a bag of garbage in each hand, as she climbed the gangway to the pier she saw Grandpa Stephen sitting on the pile of lumber.

He stood and began to walk towards her, and that is when it happened. He began to cough hard, within a moment he had taken a knee leaning on his cane for support.

Next thing he was down on the ground semi-conscious blood coming from his mouth.

Caitlyn dropped the garbage bags and ran to him as fast as she could dropping to her knees next to him when she saw the blood she screamed for Mike to call an ambulance.

Mike came charging up out of the boat phone in hand, Grandpa kept trying to get up but he didn't have the strength, he kept coughing and hacking and spitting blood.

Soon sirens came, and paramedics with a stretcher rushed onto the scene, they loaded him up and whisked him away to the hospital, Mike and Caitlyn rode in the ambulance.

Everyone poured in and waited in the waiting room; the minutes seemed to tick by like hours.

Mike paced, Caitlyn fretted, Her mom sat quietly reading a magazine. Allen sat quietly contemplating his longtime friend's fate.

Soon a doctor appeared, and everyone gathered around. The physician explained that they had taken X-rays and that Grandpa Stephens lung cancer was getting very bad, and that he did not have long left.

There is nothing we can do here, so we are going to release him. The best thing you can do is keep him comfortable. Don't let him overdo it.

As the stream of somber faces entered the hospital room they were surprised to see him sitting up putting his shoes on.

He looked up and spoke with conviction.

"Michael, don't argue, get me the hell out of here!"

Mike didn't argue, he handed him his cane, the nurse came in with a wheelchair, but grandpa just took his cane and shoved the tip against the seat of the chair stopping her.

"Get that thing away from me; I'm walking out of here on my own two feet!"

He said with gritty determination in his voice.

Outside everyone piled into Allen's Cadillac. As they climbed in Grandpa Stephen spoke up again.

"Mike, will you take me back to your boat, I'd like to spend some time sitting on the water."

Mike just nodded to Allen, and they headed off towards the boat yard.

Back at the Boat Mike lowered the swim platform and helped Grandpa step aboard then stood behind him as he climbed the stairs, then set him up sitting in a comfortable spot in the cockpit where he could see out over the bay.

Everyone gathered around with somber faces before he waved his cane and yelled at them.

"Well god dammit don't stand around like it's my funeral! I'm not dead yet!"

Mike had to laugh at this; he called him an old stubborn pig headed curmudgeon and grandpa replied telling him he was damn proud of it!

Caitlyn asked if she could get him anything, Grandpa smiled and asked for a Bloody Mary which Caitlyn served up to him.

They all sat around for a bit before Jim the Australian made an appearance.

"Well Mate, I am guessing this changes plans?"

He asked fully understanding what was going on without having to be told.

"I'm afraid it does."

Mike responded unhappily coming to the realization that his sailing adventure was not going to happen.

"I reckon we had best be making other plans then, too bad because we were all looking forward to making this trip south with you."

Then Allen spoke up.

"Well, I might just have an idea. You three are all skilled sailors aren't you?"

"Sure am! Been sailing since I was just a boy!"

Jim said with pride.

"You see that 42-foot yacht up there on the hard?"

Allen asked pointing to an old 1960's sailing yacht that looked a bit dirty and ignored, but still a fine boat underneath.

"Yeah what about it?"

Jim asked not sure what he was getting at yet.

"That boat belonged to a friend of mine who died about a year ago, his family neglected to do anything with it, we wound up filing a lien against it and got the title if you kids want to sail it south for the winter she is all yours.

Just have her back up here to me in the spring so I can sell her."

Jim smiled at the prospect and jumped at the chance, he and Allen headed up on the hard to check the boat out with Mary and Tania in tow.

It was decided they could spend the next week cleaning her up and getting her ready to sail; Mike would let them fill her full of provisions from his boat since he would no longer be making the trip.

It set the Aussies off on a great adventure and allowed him to spend a bit more time with his Grandpa before he was gone.

⚓ THIRTY ⚓

The next week was spent getting the other boat cleaned up, and in the water, they changed the oil, impeller and checked out the electrical, a set of radios were stolen out of another boat that had been surrendered to the boat yard when the owner failed to pay.

After a few test sails, they were reasonably happy with the condition of the boat and started loading it down getting it ready to go.

Caitlyn's mom decided to fly back to San Diego instead of hanging around, with everything going on she began to feel as though she were in the way but it was nice for her to see her daughter in a good situation.

That evening the weather was beautiful, and everyone ate dinner on deck aboard the Stephen Black including Grandpa and Allen.

As they all sat around and everyone chatted Grandpa was stoic and silent, you could tell something was on his mind. Finally, he blurted out.

> "Pearl Harbor"

> "What?"

Mike asked quizzically as everyone else went silent.

> "I have been trying to decide where I want to be buried, Pearl Harbor, the 75th anniversary will be this year, I'd like to have my ashes spread there.

> When the attack happened I was on the USS Utah; She was my first ship, my mother was from Utah she came to Seattle looking for work during the first world war where she met my father.

When I was a teenager, and the Utah pulled into Seattle, she took me down to see the ship telling me stories of her childhood.

In 1940 my best friend growing up Stewart Callahan and I went down together and joined the Navy, we both became gunners mates.

Because my mother was from Utah and she had shown me the ship a few years earlier we asked to be stationed aboard her.

When December 7th rolled around, we were moored in Pearl Harbor at Pier F-11.

The Japanese hit us, and we scrambled for our battle stations, mine was in a 5" mount on the starboard side. Stewart worked a mount on the port side. He never made it to his battle station.

We lost a lot of good men that day, did a whole lot of hard fighting to avenge them.

I'd like to have my ashes spread there to be with them for eternity, and I'd like you to do it, Mike, I'd like all of you to do it."

Mike reached across the table and grabbed Stephen's hand, it was obvious he was holding back the tears.

"Grandpa, I would consider making that trip the highest honor."

Caitlyn then placed her hand atop Mike and Grandpa's both.

"It would be my honor as well she said with a teary eyed smile."

Then Jim the Australian spoke up.

"Mister Black, I've only known you a few short months now since we met in Washington, but I can tell you are one hell of a man, I know I speak for Mary and Tania, we would be honored to help with that trip this spring.

When we get back from our little adventure assuming you're not still kicking around by then."

Then it was Allen's turn.

"You know Steve when we first met it was onboard the USS Maddox in 1955.

I was just a kid scared out of his mind, I'd run away from home, and the Navy seemed like the place to be.

I showed up at the ship, and you took me under your wing, you showed me the way, taught me how to save my money, taught me how to conduct myself, and it was the start of a friendship that has lasted to this day.

I'm seventy-three, too old to be making open ocean voyages anymore, but you can count on me flying out there to meet up with these kids and helping them spread your ashes.

I wouldn't miss it for anything!"

With that, there wasn't a dry eye around.

It was such a strange feeling knowing they were planning for the death of a friend, a life that had seen so many adventures and touched the lives of so many others was coming to an end.

When that end would be none of them could be for sure, but they knew that it would not be long.

Finally, Grandpa Stephen broke the silence.

"When you kids get there I am going to have my attorney meet you in Hawaii; I don't want my will read until you have spread my ashes."

"That won't be a problem."

Mike replied not even really wanting to think about that part of things; he had resolved to spend as much time with Grandpa as he could.

Finally, Grandpa had one more request.

"Tomorrow, I want you to take me sailing, all of you; it's going to be the last time I get to go, and the last time you all will be in the same place at once, it will mean a lot to me."

Mike smiled a big toothy grin.

"We can definitely do that!"

Then Jim chimed in:

"I think we can push our departure back another day for that!

Besides, I'm going to miss sailing this big boat; she rides like a dream!"

Everyone spent the night carrying on and laughing; Grandpa told more sea stories, the Australians got to hear about Mike saving Caitlyn from the crazy fisherman.

Around nine Allen and Grandpa Stephen headed off for home.

Finally, as the clock struck eight bells Mike proclaimed it was time to get some shut-eye, the Australians headed back to their new boat, and Mike and Caitlyn headed back to their stateroom.

As they lay down, Caitlyn cuddled up to Mike.

"Today was so crazy; I just can't believe all of this is happening. I mean a month ago I was in Hawaii, I was going to school there, I was totally lost, then your grandpa shows up at my doorstep out of the blue, he drags me back to you, I make a fool out of myself but fall in love with you all over again.

Now he is dying, and it is all so surreal."

Then Caitlyn's face turned sour and sad. It was obvious something deep was troubling her.

"Mike?"

"Yeah?"

"Am I broken?"

Mike was totally caught off guard by the question.

"No, why would you say that?"

"Because I like the things I do... Why do I like to feel pain and be tied up?"

"It's because you care so much, you take things personally, you worry about everything and everyone."

Caitlyn giggled and replied:

"Well, that is very true!"

Then Mike thought for a moment and continued.

"You're a submissive and a people pleaser, you like to make people happy, and when you can't make people happy, it makes you sad."

Caitlyn bit her lip not knowing what to say; he had however really nailed it down. Then she asked:

"Is that a bad thing?"

Mikes eyes lit up as he responded:

> "Not at all, in fact in the right situation, it is a very good thing. People like you and I build relationships on it."

Puzzled Caitlyn asked:

> "How so?"

> "It's called a power exchange relationship, it's really just where one person is the leader, the other is a follower, but it's all about teamwork.

> You work together so you can have a better life than you could apart, it is as though you are two halves of a yin-yang, you complement each other and find balance."

Caitlyn smiled very big at Mikes response and said:

> "I like the sound of that!"

Mike smiled back and continued to speak:

> "I have seen your scars; I know you used to hurt yourself."

Caitlyn grew very uncomfortable with this; cutting was a part of her past she was not comfortable with or proud of at all.

When she remained silent Mike spoke again:

> "You don't have to be ashamed or try to hide them from me, I know why you did it, it is because the emotional pain you felt inside became so great you needed a physical reason for the pain to feel better."

Caitlyn was shocked by this.

> "How can you know this? I have never told anyone this!"

"Believe it or not it is normal for someone like you. That is why each time I have punished you, you have received so much relief from it.

Being punished let you let go of the pain and the guilt you felt inside and allowed you to be happy again."

Caitlyn was in awe of Mike's answer, she knew he was right but no one had understood this about her before, she had felt like a freak her whole life finding relief in experiencing physical pain.

It was something she hated about herself, something that made her feel broken and not worthy of being loved.

The fact that Mike understood it left her wanting to know more.

"Why do I enjoy being tied up then? Why does it make me feel so good?"

Mike smiled and chuckled a bit as he started to speak:

"You're a worrier, you worry all the time, you're worrying right now, and I can always tell when you are really worried because you start to fidget with your hands like crazy and you will pace back and forth!

For you being tied up takes away your ability to worry and stress out, each time it has happened haven't you noticed how calm you become?"

"Oh god yes, that is so great!"

She replied with a big smile that seemed to say the lightbulb in her head had just come on.

"For you being tied up is the only way you can be at peace otherwise you will worry obsessively."

Now everything was starting to make sense to Caitlyn, she had always felt these things, but Mike had just been able to put words to them and explain them in detail.

Now her curiosity was going into overdrive.

"Mike, how does it work, a relationship like this?"

He thought for a moment and replied:

"The way it is usually done is you would decide you want to belong to me, and I would put a collar on you."

"A collar? I have always liked them for some reason."

Caitlyn stated a bit embarrassed.

"It is just a physical symbol of the relationship you carry with you every day, and usually they lock in place.

For most submissives like yourself, they find wearing the collar gives them a sense of comfort and purpose."

Caitlyn's eyes lit up.

"I like that idea."

"There is more."

Mike said pausing to form his words carefully:

"In a power exchange or in this case D/s or Dom/Sub relationship, the sub usually calls the Dom Sir or Master. It is a sign of respect."

Caitlyn thought for a moment and asked.

"Can I call you that?"

Mike smiled a huge smile obvious the sentiment meant a lot to him.

"If I collar you."

Was his response.

"Why don't you?"

Caitlyn asked feeling like she might get rejected.

"It is something I have thought a lot about, I care about you a lot, but at the same time society doesn't approve of people like you and me when they find out.

They don't realize how many people like us there are around; many are just too scared of what people will think to accept that part of themselves, or at least to let people know they are into it.

I didn't know how you felt about it, I was thinking of discussing it with you as we sailed south to Colombia. I even bought a collar just in case."

Caitlyn smiled really big.

"Really can I see?"

She replied.

Mike got up and opened one of his closets and dug a small wooden box out from under some clothes where he had stashed it.

Inside of the box was a stainless-steel ring that was hinged on one side and had a security screw that held it together on the other.

It was about five inches in diameter, and the steel was three-eights of an inch round.

On the front of the collar, there was a polished stainless steel ring about an inch in diameter.

To the casual observer who did not know any better, they would simply think this was a necklace; most people had no idea the devices real meaning.

Caitlyn reached out and touched the collar; it was cold and smooth.

"Can I try it on?"

She asked that warm fuzzy feeling growing inside of her.

Mike smiled and unscrewed the security screw with the special key; then she held her hair up as he placed the collar around her neck and put the screw back in.

Caitlyn reached up and touched it; the cool steel felt good around her neck.

Mike was right; there was something very comforting about it.

Then Mike went to take it back off, and Caitlyn stopped him reaching out her hand cupping it over the top of his that held the key.

She looked him in the eyes and spoke.

"Please, make me yours, I want to belong to you!"

Mike smiled, then he reached out and grabbed the ring with his finger and used it to pull her to him and he kissed her very deeply.

As she pulled back, she gasped and murmured the words.

"Thank you, Sir!"

THIRTY-ONE

The next morning Grandpa and Allen showed up down at the boat bright and early.

The Aussies climbed aboard, and they cast off the lines and set off towards San Francisco.

They passed between Treasure Island and the city its self under the Oakland Bay Bridge, past the ferry terminal and all the piers that lined the waterfront.

Caitlyn sat watching Mike steer the boat grinning from ear to ear.

She kept reaching up to touch the collar she now wore locked around her neck; there was something so comforting about it to her, it just felt right, simply having it on gave her a sense of peace.

They sailed up past the Golden Gate Yacht Club up to the bridge its self, then turned north following the bridge across the channel.

As they did, the clanking noise of the cars overhead could be heard traveling along the bridge deck.

From his seat in the cockpit, Grandpa Stephen looked up and watched the bridge as they sailed by grinning from ear to ear like a little school boy.

In his lifetime, he had sailed under this bridge so many countless times, in the Navy and on his own boats; seeing it one more time meant the world to him.

As they turned back to the northeast towards Sausalito, he nudged Caitlyn pointed to the bridge and began to speak.

"You know the first time I went under this bridge was in 1940; I was just a seaman then, 18 years old, wide-eyed ready to go see the world.

They sent me by train from Seattle down to San Diego for boot camp, then back up here to meet the Utah.

When we sailed out under that bridge, I thought to myself "Well, I guess I am a real sailor now, I've sailed under the Golden Gate!"

It's kind of fitting my first and my last sailing trip would be under that bridge."

He said with a big smile.

Caitlyn reached over and grabbed his hand and gave it a big squeeze as she smiled at him.

Then she looked over at Mike who was standing at the port helm steering the big boat.

They pushed on to the northeast of Belvidere and Angel Island into the northern bay up towards San Quentin before turning back south.

As they headed south, they found themselves running downwind, and Mike yelled out to Jim asking him if he wanted to help him fly the spinnaker.

He had Caitlyn take the wheel, and he and Jim pulled the big sail out of the storage locker, set the pole and hoisted the big sail skyward as it filled and came to life the boat began to accelerate.

As he walked back to the cockpit, Mike asked Grandpa Stephen if he wanted to drive. A quick "Hell yes I do!" settled the issue and Mike Helped him to get behind the wheel without falling over.

He steered the whole way back taking the boat along the Berkley coastline Under the bridge between Treasure Island and Oakland back to the north end of Alameda Island, past the USS Hornet finally turning the boat back to Mike as the approached the boat yard.

Mike and Jim pulled the big spinnaker back in, and Mike fired up the engine to drive them the rest of the way into the slip.

As they approached the dock, however, they were met with a surprise visitor who did not look too happy to see them.

Mike's sister Monica stood at the dock, hand on her hip tapping her toe with an angry look on her face.

She yelled out across the water as they approached.

> "Sailing! You took him out sailing! Grandpa, you should be at home resting! Not out sailing!"

Mike seeing her and hearing her complaints smiled an evil grin, reached down and popped the boat into reverse.

With a bob, the vessel changed direction, and they began to back out of the moorings into the open water. As they did Monica began to run down the dock after him.

> "Michael Black, you get your butt back here this instant!"

She screamed out across the water, grandpa just pulled his ball cap off smiled and waved at her from where he sat in the cockpit.

As she reached the end of the dock, Monica stopped and stood with her arms crossed scowling at Mike who stood behind the wheel of his boat with a big shit eating grin on his face.

Finally, Grandpa told him it was enough and to take them in. He didn't want to get her too pissed off because he would have to hear it all night.

Mike started the boat back forward again and pulled into the slip, as they tied off Monica started in again.

> "Two days ago, I get the call you collapsed and had to be rushed to the hospital, today you are out sailing. I don't believe it! I just don't believe it!"

Grandpa slowly walked down the steps using his cane to balance him in one hand and the rail in the other. As he stepped from the swim platform onto the dock, he looked at Monica with a big smile.

> "She is a beautiful boat, the finest I've ever sailed, that brother of yours has done a mighty fine job with her."

> "But Grandpa!"

Monica exclaimed looking up at Mike and scowling at him.

> "Oh it will alright now give me a hug, and you can take me home and worry about me there!"

Grandpa said with a smile. Monica's anger seemed to melt as she hugged him. Jim stepped from the boat and reached out to shake his hand.

> "Mister Black, it has been an honor to get to know you we will be leaving bright and early in the morning if I don't see you again, fair winds and following seas sailor!"

Grandpa Stephen reached out and shook his hand and smiled thanking him. Then Mary and Tania climbed down and gave him a big hug.

After they had said their goodbyes Monica took his arm in hers, and they walked back up the gangway to the pier then back out to where her rental car was waiting, she helped him inside, and they headed off to Allen's house.

Back at the dock Mike and Caitlyn spent the evening helping the Aussies get ready to leave, they all enjoyed one last meal together and shared their wishes of a safe Journey.

As they left the Aussies boat, Jim stepped onto the pier behind them and extended his hand to Mike.

> "Mate it has been a pleasure getting to know you, you're fortunate to have some very amazing people in your life.
>
> That being said I don't envy what you will have to go through in the next few months. That grandfather of yours is one hell of a man; I'd say they don't make them like him anymore, but I reckon you're just like him, hell practically the spitting image!"

Mike just laughed and shook his hand.

> "It won't be easy, but it will not be unexpected when it comes, and he will go to his grave with nothing unfinished or unsaid between us.
>
> And by the way thank you for helping us take the boat out today, I can tell it meant the world to him."

> "I wouldn't have missed it for the world; he's a good man, and she is a beautiful boat."

Finally, Caitlyn hugged Jim and wished him and the girls a happy and safe voyage telling them how much she would miss them.

As she and Mike walked back to the boat, he took her hand in his and held it as they walked. The small gesture made her feel warm and fuzzy inside.

Back aboard they tidied up and settled in to watch some TV for a bit. Caitlyn snuggled up to Mike and just enjoyed being there with him.

Finally, some questions she had been pondering started to boil to the surface, and she had to ask them.

"Mike, how long do you think he has?"

"I don't know, but he is starting to go downhill fast. Up until a few months ago, he was still driving himself around, since he can't do that anymore he has started to deteriorate having to rely on everyone else.

It isn't easy for a man like him."

"Or a man like you."

Caitlyn replied with a smile.

"Or a man like me!"

Mike replied with a chuckle.

"Mike?"

Caitlyn asked in a small sweet, shy voice.

"Yeah?"

"I love you, Sir."

She replied burying her face into his arm. The statement totally caught him off guard, but when she looked back up at him, he reached over with his other hand, swept his fingers through her hair and replied.

"I love you too."

Then he leaned in and kissed her before pulling back to look her in the eyes that were staring back at him soft and dreamy.

Then Mike pulled her into him and began kissing more passionately. Soon they were wriggling out of their clothes using their hands to explore each other's bodies before retreating to their stateroom where they made love late into the night.

THIRTY-TWO

The next morning Mike and Caitlyn awoke early to see the Aussies off, both emerged from the boat looking tired and run down.

It was just before 5 am, everything was still dark, but the bay was lit up by the glow of the city lights.

As they approached Jim was already in the cockpit getting the boat woke up, he saw Mike and Caitlyn coming.

> "Good morning! It sounds like you two had quite the night last night."

He said with a cheeky grin, realizing what he was talking about Caitlyn became so shy and embarrassed, Mike and Jim just started laughing.

It took a few moments for the embarrassment to wear down. Apparently, they had not closed the hatch on the master suite, and Caitlyn had become very vocal, and the noise has carried all the way down to their boat.

Mike always quick on his feet changed the subject to the pending departure, soon Mary and Tania had appeared on deck, and everyone said their goodbyes before Mike and Caitlyn cast off their lines and helped push them off the dock.

They stood on the dock together with their arms around each other watching the boat disappear off into the night.

Then Mike asked Caitlyn "Want to go back to bed?"

She gave him a big nod and hugged him, and they climbed back aboard and into bed.

When Caitlyn awoke, bright sunlight burned in through the portholes; she was groggy and disoriented not knowing what time it was, she found her phone and looked at the time it was 1:33 pm. She had slept half the day away.

She came forward into the salon called out for Mike, but he didn't answer.

She texted him but found his phone was still sitting on the chart table, then she stuck her head above decks but didn't see him anywhere.

Finally realizing she was a hot mess, she jumped in the shower and got cleaned up but when she emerged still no Mike.

She got dressed and headed up towards the office but when she got there the door was locked with no one around, this was very strange for a Tuesday.

Then she went over to the boat shed, inside she found Manny, that is when he hit her with the bad news.

Earlier that morning everyone had been sitting around the office talking, Grandpa Stephen stood up to go to the bathroom and collapsed again.

He had been rushed to the hospital.

Caitlyn grabbed her phone out of her pocket and called for an UBER, twenty minutes later she found herself walking into the hospital waiting area but no one could be found.

She asked the receptionist if they were there, and she was directed where to go.

The ride up the elevator seemed to happen in slow motion; all her emotions welled up inside of her.

The bell dinged, and the doors slid open, she stepped out into the hall and tried to remember the directions the receptionist gave her; she didn't find the room, but she did find the vending machines where Mike and Monica were in a heated argument.

"I told you he needed to rest; I told you this was going to happen again! No one would listen, why wouldn't you listen!"

"Hey you know as well as I do Grandpa is his own man, he isn't going to let anyone tell him what to do."

"Well you could at least try, you just stand by and don't say anything, it's not like you're trying to help."

"What do you want me to do, cuff him to the bed?"

"Well, it would make him stay there wouldn't it!"

"You know I am not doing that! Look Monica, I know you're going to miss him, but when it's his time it's going to be his time, let him enjoy his last days, stop trying to force him into a box, you're not helping by trying to keep him fenced in, it just makes him miserable!"

"But what if he got his rest and he could live longer? What then?

"Monica, It's fucking terminal cancer, inoperable, it's in both of his lungs, there is nothing we can do about it other than to make sure his last days are filled with happy memories, this isn't helping!"

With this Monica's face turned sour into an extreme scowl, it was obvious she wasn't happy with Mike's stance on things, she turned and stormed out of the vending room glaring at Caitlyn as she stormed past.

Then Mike saw her standing there. She rushed to his tears in her eyes, hugged him as hard as she could then asked:

"Is he ok?"

Mike hugged her back and stroked her hair.

"He will be, for now, they are just running more tests, it sounds like a mix-up with the medicine he is on is making his blood pressure too low."

After a few moments, Caitlyn ducked into the lady's room and dried her eyes, then she joined Mike back in the hall, and they walked down to the room.

Grandpa was sitting in the bed, obviously annoyed at being in the hospital and having everyone fuss over him.

Caitlyn ran in and gave him a hug. It warmed up his mood a bit, and he looked at Mike with a smile on his face and spoke.

"You know Michael; you're lucky I am not 50 years younger, or I'd be all over this one.

Such a pretty young lady."

Mike and Caitlyn both laughed, Monica was obviously not having any of it. Then Mike shot back.

"Hell, you old curmudgeon, you would chase after her if you were twenty years younger!"

Grandpa got a good laugh at this and replied:

"Yeah, you're right about that. Speaking of young ladies, where is that doctor at, is she ready to let me get the hell out of here yet?

It looks like a beautiful day; I don't want to waste it sitting in here."

Monica hearing this got even madder and stormed out of the room, it was obvious she didn't find any humor in his words.

"I know that sister of yours means well Michael, but this pity party is starting to get to me, I'm the one who is dying here."

"It's just because she loves you, Grandpa!"

"Yeah, I know, but I wish she could show it without getting mad."

Grandpa Stephen smiled and put his hand on top of Caitlyn's who was now sitting next to his bed.

"She takes after her grandmother, always fretting over me, that woman was a good woman, but she fretted over me for years.

I remember when I took Michael on our first long distance trip up to Canada. We got caught in a storm and wound up anchoring in a little protected bay for three days.

When we didn't show up to Ketchikan in time she called the coast guard and had them out looking for us, it was quite the shock when we pulled into port, and the Sheriff came down to meet us, we didn't know we were missing!"

"I remember that you called her to let her know we were ok, all we had done was sit aboard the boat and play cards and read books, and you told me stories, it was a real non-event, just a bit of bobbing around with the wind and rain.

Then you call grandma, and she practically climbed through the phone at you."

"I think she had paced a hole in the carpet between the phone and front door by the time we got back!"

Grandpa said with a smile causing everyone in the room to chuckle.

Soon the nurse came in and stated the doctor would be releasing him shortly. Then the doctor paid a visit and had the new prescriptions.

This time they didn't even try to bother with the wheelchair as Grandpa went to leave he actually had quite a bit of pep in his step.

Once outside they realized that Monica had left in her rental car, Mike figured it was just as well because she needed to cool her heels.

They all piled into Allen's Cadillac and got his prescriptions on the way back to the office.

When they got there, Monica was nowhere to be found.

No one said anything, but it was obvious that it bothered Grandpa Stephen quite a bit.

As the car came to a stop, he muttered.

"I think it is time to go back to Washington."

Allen bumped his knuckles against the steering wheel and stated that he understood.

Within a couple of hours, Monica had shown up back at the office.

More calm now she was happy to hear the news that Grandpa was ready to go home.

She went over to Allen's with him and helped pack his things, for him it was a somber trip. He had long occupied the guest house whenever he was in town on business, so it was full of many things he had left there over the years.

The room was full of so many fond memories, on the walls hung pictures of the family, his wife now long since deceased, his brother, his son, employees past and present and their families, and shipmates from many years ago.

It was as if the room were a museum, the photos chronicling his life.

Mike and Caitlyn showed up with boxes, and everyone helped pack everything up. The room felt bare and empty by the time they were done.

Finally, Grandpa sat in the middle of the room on a wooden chair. The tearing down of all his things got under his skin.

"I don't want to be here anymore!"

He blurted out as he stared blankly at the floor.

"Come on grandpa; you can stay on the boat tonight."

Mike offered hoping it would lift his spirits.

"Mike, I appreciate that, but I want to go home.

I want you to call Ed over at Spartan Aviation and see if he can get a plane to fly me home."

As Mike made the call, Monica came over to comfort him.

Caitlyn could see just how bad he was hurting on the inside seeing a place that had been so very familiar to him for so many years torn apart.

The guest house had been built in the early 1960's, she guessed from the faded paint on the walls where some of the pictures had hung that many had been here the entire time as the wood paneling on the walls had faded except for where the pictures had hung.

It was obvious to her that Grandpa Stephen had called this guest room home for many years while he was in California and now with its destruction, a piece of his life was now gone forever.

Soon Mike got off the phone and informed Grandpa that the King Air 300 was standing by to take him home.

Forty-five minutes later they all found themselves standing on the tarmac at the airport as Grandpa and Monica were ready to board the plane.

Allen and Grandpa shook hands and looked each other in the eye; it was understood this was probably the last time each man would see the other alive after a friendship and business partnership that had now spanned the better part of five and a half decades.

Caitlyn gave him a hug and told him to be safe. Then it was Mike's turn, he shook his hand and gave him a hug and told him that he would see him in Washington in a few days.

Finally, Grandpa looked at Allen one more time and nodded before climbing the steps slowly but surely into the cabin of the aircraft followed closely behind by Monica.

The pilot pulled up the stairs and closed the door, soon the Aircraft roared by down the runway and climbed off into the sunset bound for home.

⚓ THIRTY-THREE ⚓

The next morning Mike and Caitlyn packed their personal belongings into the box truck they had rented for the trip back north.

Then they met up with Manny and the Boat Yard crew to pull the boat back out of the water. Once it was back up on the hard, they secured all the hatches, disconnected the batteries, removed all the food and shut off the fridge.

The massive boat now sat towering over the land in the corner of the boatyard; there she would wait until Mike and Caitlyn would return in the spring for her.

At the office, they met up with Allen to say their goodbyes; he offered his assurances that the yard would look after the boat.

It was a somber goodbye and Mike, and Caitlyn both could tell that for Allen he had enjoyed having them and Grandpa around, now things were going to be quiet and mundane slipping back into their usual routine.

Mike and Caitlyn jumped in the rental truck, and Mike stuck the new GPS he had purchased to the windshield and punched in the address.

The black box showed eight hundred seven miles to their destination in Bremerton.

Mike put the box truck in gear and set out waving goodbye to Allen who watched from the porch of the office.

They headed out onto the 880, then I-80, up through Berkley over through Vacaville where thy caught the 505 to I-5.

Something Caitlyn noticed is that people in California seemed to drive with a death wish!

No matter what the speed limit they always seemed to run twenty to thirty miles per hour faster, they changed lanes without signals; it was like watching the running of the bulls in Spain only played out with cars on the freeway.

Within a few hours, the fertile farmlands of north central California had faded away, and by the time they reached Redding, they found themselves in rolling hill country.

Further north the rolling hills turned into mountains barren at first, then slowly they turned covered in trees.

They stopped for fuel in Yreka and stuffed down some fast food. Then up over Siskiyou Pass, they entered Oregon about the time the sun was setting.

Somewhere around Roseburg Caitlyn fell asleep in the passenger seat; she woke up on the south side of Portland when Mike slammed on the brakes to avoid hitting a car that cut him off and braked suddenly to take an exit.

They passed through the labyrinth of roads making up the massive port city over the drawbridge and into Washington.

The rain dripped down from the sky with tiny little droplets; the thick heavy clouds made sure no moonlight would make it through to the ground.

The road appeared a black ribbon that just carried forward into the night disappearing in front of them as though the world just ended where the white and yellow lines disappeared.

Every once in a while, a car would pass them, and they could follow for a ways as its tail lights burned a hole into the night, but then they too would be gone, and they were once again charging forth into the blackness.

Driving at night in this kind of rain was a special kind of hell, as traffic approached from behind it would blind you and burn out your night vision making it very difficult to see forward, then once they passed you, they would then be blinded by your lights and frequently slow down.

This scenario played out repeatedly until finally they came upon the south end of Olympia where they stopped at a truck stop and fueled once more, and choked down some more fast food.

Mike had called Grandpa before they got back on the road and he informed them that he was in his boat waiting for them that he had the heat and the refrigerator turned on and that Monica had been nice enough to go to the store and get them some groceries.

Back on the road, Mike could feel the tiredness taking hold of him, the last ninety miles of the trip were going to seem like nine hundred.

They pushed north through Lakewood catching highway sixteen north to Bremerton. Finally, they found themselves at Grandpa's Boatyard.

The rain was cold and heavy now; Mike got soaked getting out of the truck to unlock the gate then relocking it behind him once they had pulled in.

The drove down to the pier and scurried down the gangway to where the big custom built trawler sat tied off to the dock; its cabin lights glowing out into the darkness portraying the warmth within, the sweet smell of the small ships wood stove burning permeated the night.

They climbed aboard through the transom gate off the swim/dinghy platform then entered through the big sliding glass door on the rear of the cabin.

Once inside Mike and Caitlyn both stomped their feet on the rug trying to shake the water that had blasted them off.

The wood stove sat adjacent to the door, and both found much comfort in holding their hands out to dry and be rewarmed.

Grandpa had been sitting up in the pilot house when they arrived he made his way down into the salon.

"How was your trip?"

He asked with a big grin happy to see them.

"It was long but uneventful other than the usual idiots, really made me appreciate how much I enjoy traveling by boat!"

Mike said as he stepped forward to shake his hand.

"So happy to see you, how are you feeling?"

Caitlyn asked as she stepped forward to hug him.

Grandpa jumped a little bit letting out an "OOOF" noise.

"Young lady your hands are cold, you had better go warm them up!"

About then another set of headlights appeared on the Pier, Mike grabbed a foul weather jacket from the locker and went up to give Monica and Abbey a hand with the groceries.

As he shut the door behind him, Grandpa turned to Caitlyn and asked:

"How is everything with you and Mike?"

Caitlyn paused and thought for a moment then replied with a big smile.

"Couldn't be better! The last few weeks for us have been really good."

"I am glad to hear that."

Grandpa responded with a big smile. Caitlyn could tell he was rooting for things with her and Mike to work out well.

Soon Monica Mike and Abbey returned with grocery bags, they had grabbed as many as they could each bear all at once to keep from having to make a second trip out into the storm.

They stowed the goods, and everyone chatted briefly, but it was clear everyone was very tired.

Finally, Monica stated she needed to get grandpa home; Mike walked him up the gangway holding an umbrella over him and on this particular night he didn't complain about being fretted over a bit.

He got the gate for them as they left locking it behind, then returned to Caitlyn aboard the boat.

They were both exhausted and retired to the stateroom that was amidships. Inside the stateroom, there was a large king size bed surrounded by finely finished wood.

When Mike turned on the switch, a series of lights under the bed and counter tops came on gently illuminating the room with a soft, pleasant warm light.

They shed their clothes and crawled into bed.

As they drifted off to sleep, Caitlyn wondered what this next chapter of their life would hold.

⚓ THIRTY-FOUR ⚓

The next morning Caitlyn awoke early, Mike was still passed out cold, the eight-hundred-mile drive that followed all the packing out had left him flat wore out.

Then she had an idea; she snuck out of the stateroom and up to the rental truck where she grabbed her suitcase and opened it, she pulled out the black frilly lingerie she had bought down in California along with some stockings and black high heels along with her ditty bag.

She crept back aboard the boat and up to the guest head, showered, did her hair and dawned the seductive outfit.

Then poking her head up out of the companionway into the pilot house she looked around to see that they were alone, it was a Saturday morning, so the yard was quiet.

Just to be safe, she checked the doors of the yacht to see that they were all locked. Then she crept back down into the stateroom where Mike lay sleeping tiptoeing like a cartoon character the whole way.

She checked her hair one last time in the mirror and poked her head around the corner, Mike was lying barely awake rubbing his eyes.

She stepped out in her most seductive pose leaned against the corner.

"Hey sailor! You gonna sleep all day?"

She said with a big smile in a sweet seductive, playful voice.

Mike lifted his head up and blinked a few times hard as though he were unsure if he was actually seeing what he was seeing.

Caitlyn looked amazing; she stood in the 6" black high heels with the fishnet stockings running up her legs to the garter belt that held them in place.

The black frilly bra and pantie set accentuated her pale skin covered in freckles, the ring in her belly button glinted in the center of her flat stomach.

On her face, she wore a big smile that was framed perfectly by her red curly hair that fell over her right eye and cascaded off of her shoulders.

Mike rubbed his head for a second and sat up not saying anything just admiring the view, then finally he spoke.

"Well, that is one hell of a way to wake a guy up!"

He said with a huge smile before motioning with his finger for her to come to him.

Caitlyn walked to him in a slow-motion prance rocking her hips back and forth until she stood between his legs looking down at him.

Mike reached up and grasped the sides of her hips with his hands and pushed her back just a little bit so he could clearly see her face.

"You're beautiful."

He said smiling from ear to ear. Then he reached up with his right hand swept her hair back and cradled her face with it.

Caitlyn responded by nuzzling his hand with her cheek lifting her hand to cradle his.

The Mike rose to his feet and pulled her in and kissed her long and deep before picking her up and laying her on the bed.

He sat down next to her once again brushed her hair aside smiled and said

"I love you!"

Then he leaned in and kissed her again.

"I love you too sir!"

She replied when he pulled back with a huge smile on her face and a warm and fuzzy feeling that filled her body.

Then Mike laid down next to her, and they began running their hands all over each other spending most of the morning enjoying each other's bodies.

Later as they lie together snuggled up in a tangle of sheets and each other they felt the boat rock as someone stepped aboard.

Then they could hear the door open and Monica's voice in the cabin.

"Mike, Caitlyn, Hello?"

"Hold on a minute!"

Mike yelled up to her crawling out of bed begrudgingly to find his clothes.

"Shit!"

Caitlyn blurted out.

"My clothes are in the forward head!"

"I will get them for you."

Mike promised.

He stepped up the companionway to the salon pulling his shirt over his head.

"Give me just a second!"

He said to Monica before stepping up through to the pilothouse and down into the forward head to retrieve Caitlyn's clothes.

Monica looked at him with a grin as he stepped back down into the salon then as he turned to go back down into the stateroom she yelled out:

"Looks like you two have been having fun!"

"Yeah yeah yeah…"

Mike replied in a begrudging tone making it known he wasn't thrilled about being disturbed.

"Grandpa is in the car waiting; he wants to go get lunch."

Caitlyn pulled on her clothes as quick as she could and followed Mike back up into the salon.

Monica looked her up and down and with a great deal of snark in her voice wished her a good afternoon.

Caitlyn just glared back.

Mike seeing Caitlyn could use a couple of more minutes asked Monica where they were going, if it was just up to the diner.

She replied that was the plan and he told her that he would take the pickup and meet them there in a few minutes.

"Ok, buh bye."

Monica replied as she turned and walked out the door.

"Mike, I know you love your sister, but she can be such a queen bee sometimes."

"Yeah, she can be a little bull-headed. But don't worry about it, why don't you go get ready and I will go get the truck fired up."

Mike headed up to find the keys for the pickup in the office and Caitlyn went up to the forward head and redid her makeup and tried to force her hair into something that looked respectable. Finally, she gave in and just braided it into a pair of braids.

When she walked out Mike was waiting in the old 1972 GMC 4x4 at the top of the pier, she climbed into the cab and slid over next to him, and they were off for lunch.

At lunch both Caitlyn and Mike noticed how glum Grandpa Stephen looked. He wasn't smiling; he wasn't talking. He just quietly sat and ate his food.

He didn't banter with the waitresses; he didn't take part in the conversation, he just sat there and picked through his food.

The whole experience was uncomfortable for everyone.

After lunch, they all got into their vehicles and headed out to the cemetery.

As they pulled through the gates Mike muttered:

"I'm not looking forward to this."

Caitlyn just squeezed his arm and kissed his shoulder trying to comfort him.

By the time they rolled to a stop, Monica was already helping grandpa get out of her SUV.

He walked out into the plots cane in hand moving slowly. Mike and Caitlyn caught up to him quickly but didn't say anything.

They just kept walking forward out into the rows of old weather-beaten headstones before stopping at large one that spanned two graves and had the name "Black" carved into it.

One side said "Father Wilhelm Stephen 1897-1965," the other said "Rose May of Moab Utah 1900-1993".

"These are my parents."

He said pointing with his cane, then continued:

I get my longevity from my mother's side of the family. My father was a hard man, he stressed out too much and died young, His heart just wouldn't take it.

He worked hard all his life, died broke!

Spent everything he ever made, never invested anything. After he had died, I was left caring for my mother which was ok, by then I was already a fairly wealthy man.

She was a good woman, she scraped and saved to see that I was taken care of, I think half the time she hardly ate anything so I could eat.

The depression, those were hard times.

I get my frugality from her, certainly not from my father, I remember when I bought my first investment property I was still living onboard the ship.

Dad, he got so mad at me telling me I was being foolish that I should buy a house, find a nice girl, get married, have a family of my own, I told him someday when I could afford it I would.

He told me to take my smart mouth and get out of his house; this was in 1948.

By 1963 when I invested in the shipyard with Allen I was already a millionaire, the business I started here machining the naval rifles had won me several lucrative contracts with the Navy, and it paid dividends!

We bought big lathes from the government out of military surplus, shipped them out here on the train, set them up in a government surplus Quonset hut on that first piece of investment property I had bought in 1948.

He always held that against me and that is why I always tried to encourage your father and you kids to go after your dreams."

Monica grew teary-eyed spread her arms out and gave him a big giant hug.

"Grandpa you never told us this before."

"It's not easy to talk about; I could never understand why someone who was supposed to love me and support me the most was always the one to try to hold me back.

He always told me my ideas were dumb, he always told me that I had no chance, and then when I started doing well, he took it as a personal affront to his pride.

In the time I knew the man he never told me how much he loved me, or that he was proud of me and that is why I wanted to bring you, kids, here today; I am so very proud of you both, you have grown into amazing young people with bright futures ahead of you.

You have done well for yourselves beyond my wildest expectations."

Then he turned to Caitlyn.

"And young lady that goes for you as well, I see greatness in you. I think you have much to offer this world and I think if you and Michael can work as a team you will be able to accomplish great things.

One day if he puts a ring on your finger and makes you a proper member of this family I would be proud to call you a part of it."

Caitlyn's eyes welled up with tears, and she dove in and gave him a big hug all she could say was:

"Thank you, Grandpa!"

Then after a few moments, she let go, and they kept walking, further down they found another two headstones, the first read "Edith Black 1932-2009" the one next to hers read "Stephen Black 2001-2009."

Caitlyn could feel Mike grow physically tense as they approached the headstone, she realized this was his son little Stevie.

Just thinking about what had happened her eyes welled up. Then grandpa began to speak.

"Michael, I know you've not been up here in a lot of years, I know this is hard for you.

I miss that boy like none other, the day you called me and told me I was a great grandpa I was so proud, and when you told me his name it was one of the happiest days of my life.

It was a horrible thing what that wretched woman did to you and him. I have paid an attorney to attend every probation hearing she will ever have to convey my wishes that she not be given leniency for the entire duration of her sentence.

You don't know this, but about two years ago, she came up eligible for early release due to good behavior, I flew out to Hawaii, I attended the hearing, and after hearing my testimony about what she had done, they denied her release.

I just wanted you to know that I had done that. I miss the little fella every day; he was such a good boy so full of promise. I would never have believed what happened to him could have.

I remember taking him out on my boat and letting him drive up on the flybridge with his little sailor's hat on. You would have thought he was ten feet tall standing there steering the wheel he was so proud."

Mike gulped hard tears rolling from his eyes.

"I remember that day; you had just launched her a few months before, he loved that boat so much."

Grandpa turned and set his hand on Mikes' shoulder.

"I hope that is how you can remember him, I hope that in time you can find peace to remember how he lived and not how he died, I worry for you for that Michael.

That is why he is buried in my grave; it is so your grandmother can always keep him company. She loved him just as much as we all did and I think seeing him die broke her heart because it was after that she just lost the will to keep living."

The two men just stood there silently after that for a few moments; then it started to rain again. The umbrellas went up, and Monica exclaimed that it was time to get Grandpa in out of the cold.

They sauntered back to the vehicles and loaded up.

Mike paused before leaving and hung his arms on the steering wheel and leaned against it looking towards the grave where his son was buried.

Caitlyn didn't say anything; she just sat there next to him hoping that her presence offered him some comfort.

Finally, he reached down and shoved the truck into gear, and they drove back to the yard and went back aboard the Utah Rose.

Once aboard Mike didn't say anything, he climbed the ladder onto the bridge, he sat down in the port side observers chair and just stared at the wheel.

Caitlyn followed him up, she came up behind him and set her hands on his shoulders and began to massage them, as she did she could feel the tension drain away.

Then suddenly Mike began to speak.

> "You know the last time I saw him alive was on this boat. We had flown up for the 4th of July, we motored out towards Seattle for the fireworks show and spent the night off a mooring over there.
>
> Grandpa let Stevie drive quite a bit; he loved every second of it.
>
> The next morning, they dropped me off in Seattle, and I caught the train to the airport, I had to fly back to meet my ship because my leave was up.
>
> I haven't been back there since he died. I had his body flown back here to be buried I did not attend the funeral as I was still facing the charges and could not leave Hawaii.

Grandpa made all the arrangements; today was only the 3rd time I have ever been here."

Caitlyn told him she was so sorry and hugged him then kissed the top of his head.

"I can't even imagine what that must have been like."

She said softly, her words full of empathy.

Mike just reached up and squeezed her hand for a moment, then he stood up and walked to the wheel standing behind it gripping the smooth stainless steel surface with his hands before gently wrapping his knuckles against it then turning away.

"Let's go get dinner and try to think happy thoughts; I have had enough sadness for one day."

THIRTY-FIVE

The next few weeks saw a myriad of emotions, Grandpa seemed to do better but had one more surprise trip to the hospital when he forgot to take his medication.

Mike and Caitlyn began to grow very close; she started going up to the yard office with him every day and taking notes on the meetings and helping him stay organized.

Soon she had evolved into a powerhouse in her own right even helping make phone calls and keep track of the properties that were now falling into Mikes care.

At first Grandpa would ride along with them, but eventually, he handed over the reins. His days were spent driving around seeing the few old remaining friends he had left.

Soon Thanksgiving was on the horizon, Caitlyn asked Mike if it would be ok to invite her mom and dad up.

He said he would look forward to it since he had not met her dad yet.

She made the calls and the arrangements booking them separate motel rooms at different hotels. She knew it was the best way to keep the peace between them.

Soon the day was upon them, Caitlyn had decorated the Utah Rose with some Thanksgiving affair.

Mike had bought a big deep frying pot and would make the Turkey, Caitlyn, and Monica would make the rest of the fixings.

Caitlyn's father was the first to arrive; Mike thought it was cute how nervous she was, having him up meant a lot to her because she had not got to spend a lot of time in her life with him between growing up in Ireland and his time in the Navy.

When he called to say he was on his way down Caitlyn began to pace at the door nervously, then she would check her hair and makeup then back to the door fidgeting with her hands the whole time.

Soon his rental car was at the top of the pier, and he walked down towards the boat Caitlyn was surprised to see he wore a suit and tie. In his hand, he carried a brown paper bag by its twine handles.

As he stepped aboard, she threw the door open and squealed "PAPA!" and lunged forward to hug him.

As she escorted him inside Mike met him there and reached out his hand to introduce himself.

Caitlyn started the introduction:

"Mike this is my father, Chief Daniel Campbell."

Mike shook his hand and as he did Caitlyn introduced him.

"And father this is Senior Chief Michael Black."

Her dad looked at her and said with surprise:

"Senior Chief? I guess you do have good taste in men after all!"

He said with a big smile before letting go of Mikes' hand. Then he held up the bag in his other hand.

"Here I brought you something, some wine to go with dinner."

He said holding out the bag.

Caitlyn took the bag and Mike offered him a beer which he gladly took, they began to swap stories about ships they had served on and places they had been.

It made Caitlyn smile to see them getting on so well.

Soon, Grandpa, Monica, and Abbey showed up. Caitlyn's father was again surprised to find out that Grandpa Stephen was an old salt and a retired Master Chief to boot.

Soon the stories were flying, and Caitlyn and Monica set to work around each other in the Kitchen getting the meal ready, yet she was daunted by the fact her mother was still nowhere to be seen.

She had a creeping feeling coming up the back of her spine that something was wrong.

About 4:30 Mike put in the turkey, Dan jumped in to help, and they seemed to really hit it off well, Grandpa beer in hand supervised while they set up the pot on the dock got it lit up and got the bird set to frying.

Still though, Caitlyn's mom was nowhere to be seen.

Finally, a yellow cab appeared at the top of the pier, and Melany Caitlyn's mom stepped out dragging a big purse over her shoulder.

She paid the driver and headed down the pier where she found Mike, Grandpa, and Dan working on the Turkey.

>"Hello, Melany."

Dan called out to her trying to be polite.

>"Hello Daniel, It's ok, you don't have to pretend to be happy to see me."

She snipped back at him as she walked past saying hello to Mike and Grandpa as she stepped aboard.

Once inside Caitlyn stepped out of the kitchen to greet her.

Caitlyn introduced her to Monica and Abbey then she took a seat at the bar and poured herself a drink while Caitlyn went back to work in the kitchen.

Abbey sat down with her, and they began to talk while Caitlyn and Monica worked. They had pumpkin pie in the oven along with stuffing, A huge pot of Mashed potatoes coming together, a green bean casserole they had prepared earlier, and all of the other fixings for a fine Thanksgiving feast.

Soon the boys came back in with a fully cooked turkey and set it up on the table covered with aluminum foil.

Eventually, everyone got a drink and got seated around the table, and Mike offered grandpa the honors of taking the first cut out of the turkey.

Then he took over carving the bird.

While he did everyone chatted politely, but Caitlyn's mom couldn't help but shoot daggers at her dad from time to time in her words. Nothing too overt but you could tell who her comments were directed at.

Finally, as the food was distributed and everyone was ready to eat Grandpa, Stephen stood up and tapped his glass with a spoon to get everyone's attention.

> "Everyone, this is probably going to be my last Thanksgiving. As you all are painfully aware of, I have cancer and... Well, it isn't going well.
>
> Dan and Melany, I just wanted to tell you that I am glad you could be here today and that over the last few months I have got to know your daughter very well, and she has never ceased to amaze me with what a fine young woman she is.

Down in San Francisco, she worked extremely hard with everything that was handed to her there and has continued to work hard and to great work ever since.

I am very proud of her for all she has done, and I hope that you would be as well for you have every reason to be.

She has proven herself around here with her ability to get things done such as this dinner she and Monica arranged and put on tonight.

Thank you for being here."

Caitlyn's eyes welled up with happy tears, and she got up and hugged Grandpa Stephen and her mom and dad before sitting back down next to Mike.

Mike reached under the table and squeezed her hand and gave her a big smile and it made her get all warm and fuzzy inside.

With that everyone dug into their meal and the conversation remained pleasant but it was painfully obvious by the time dinner was over that Caitlyn's mom had had too much to drink and it was starting to affect her mouth.

When everyone had finished eating they cleared the table, Mike quietly suggested that he would take Grandpa and Dan up onto the bridge and Caitlyn could keep her mom occupied in the Salon with Monica and Abbey.

Up on the bridge, each of the men found a cold drink and a chair, and they sat around trading more old sea stories.

Down in the salon, though things were not going so well, Caitlyn's mom was starting to get a bit obnoxious, she kept butting into the conversation. Finally, Caitlyn had had enough.

She stood up and grabbed her phone and pushed the button calling for an Uber putting the pickup location at the top of the pier.

Then she grabbed her coat and her mothers and handed it to her.

>"Come, mother, take a walk with me."

>"I don't want to walk anywhere."

>"You want me to go alone?"

Caitlyn replied hoping that it would spur her into action.

The redheaded woman stood up and took her coat and pulled it on, and they stepped out onto the dock, then up the gangway onto the pier.

>"Just what's the meaning of this?"

Melany asked her daughter with an indignant tone carried in a thick Irish brogue.

>"You're drunk mother; you're embarrassing me."

>"I'm embarrassing you? I'm not the one who needs a man to take care of me! Some prince charming to shuffle me off to some hoity-toity fancy lifestyle living on yachts playing hand servant to this man and his guests.

>You had a dream; you were going to college, you wanted to be a scientist.

>You dropped out in your senior year to come be some kind of a servant to a man."

Caitlyn's eyes flashed, and her temper reared.

"Now you listen to me mother, I love that man down there, he is the finest man I've ever met, and quite frankly I just think you're jealous that daddy never wanted to be with you for more than the night!"

Watching from the bridge, Mike could see what happened. Next, Melany hauled back and slapped Caitlyn in the face hard causing her to spin around.

With that Mike was off like a shot, he kicked the door of the pilot house open so hard it slammed back against the hull his feet never touched the railing as he went over landing on the dock and began charging for the gangway as hard as he could run.

Caitlyn spun back facing her mother blood running from her nose then suddenly she heard a noise behind her that sounded like a charging elephant coming up the aluminum gangway, she looked back and saw Mike charging headlong at them eyes wide and fingers stretched out like claws.

He reached the top of the gangway with such ferocity and noise that Melany started to run as fast as she could towards the gate but fell in the mud.

As Mike reached Caitlyn he slid to a stop he looked at her he saw the threat was gone and it was if all of the sudden all of the ferocity melted away and he became very soft towards her.

He briefly examined her face and saw the blood coming from her nose and the tears that were beginning to stream from her eyes; then he did something very unexpected, he swept Caitlyn off her feet picked her up and carried her back down to the boat.

With all of the commotion, everyone had come out to watch what would happen next.

They all parted and made way for Mike to carry her back on board, Caitlyn had curled up shoving her face into his chest. The stepped aboard, and she asked to go downstairs to their stateroom.

Mike carried her to the companionway and set her on her feet so she could climb down, the ladder being too narrow for Mike to carry her.

Down in the cabin, she asked him to please just give her a minute to clean up and then she would be back up and asked him to tell everyone she was sorry for causing a scene.

Mike didn't say a word; he gave her a hug then kissed her on the forehead.

As he stepped up into the cabin, Mike closed the doors to the stateroom behind him.

Dan and Melany were now in a heated discussion up on the pier.

Mike walked back out and as he did Monica tried to stop him by grabbing his arm, he pulled free and made it clear she wasn't stopping him. Then he walked back up to the top of the pier.

There Melany was cussing Dan for all he was worth, calling him a worthless son of a bitch, as she saw Mike coming she started in yelling at him.

> "And you, you male chauvinist pig, who do you think you are to run at me like that? I mean just who do you think you are, are you a man who beats women?"

> "Mam, I am going to say this, and one time only, it is time for you to go, your ride is here you can either leave in it, or you can leave in a cop car which is it going to be?"

"FUCK YOU BASTARD!"

She screamed, but Mike now refused to get emotional and didn't offer her the satisfaction of any kind of a response, he just maintained his rigid military bearing expressionless with cold eyes her insults didn't even make it through his skin to register.

He simply pulled out his phone, and dialed a 9, then she crossed her arms, he punched in the 1 and the 1, and held his finger over send.

At this point she had no more cards to play, Monica flipped him off and stormed off to the waiting car that would take her back to the Motel.

Mike and Dan watched the car drive off, and as Mike turned to walk back to the boat, Dan spoke up.

"I should probably be going to."

"Negative, I think your daughter needs you right now."

"Sure she is not mad at me? They always seem to be mad at me."

"I've never heard her say a bad word about you."

With this Dan's face changed, he nodded and turned back towards the boat.

Mike followed him back down the gangway onto the dock; then everyone went back inside where they found Caitlyn sitting in one of the lounge chairs with tears streaming down her cheeks and a piece of toilet paper stuffed up her nose to stop the bleeding.

She saw her dad, and she just broke down, she got up ran to him and hugged him.

"I'm sorry daddy, it's all my fault, I just wanted you both to be here for Thanksgiving, I hoped mom could get along with you, I begged and pleaded with her not to do this."

"Oh, it's not your fault, you didn't do this."

He hugged her and rubbed her back and the back of her head.

Then Monica stepped forward and offered that it was not her fault, that there was nothing she could do and helped console her.

It took about fifteen minutes for her to calm down finally.

Out of the blue, she stepped back, rubbed her eyes and asked.

"Who wants pie?"

Everyone laughed at the absurdity of the statement but it worked, it broke the mood, and everyone gathered around for fresh baked pumpkin pie, Caitlyn dried her eyes and the evening carried on with some sense of normalcy.

As Caitlyn was cleaning up the galley Dan asked Mike to step aside, Mike agreed, and they stepped up onto the bridge then out on deck.

"I saw something in you tonight. I know that I don't know you well, but I can see you love my little girl."

Mike nodded and waited to see what else Dan had to say.

"If it would have been anyone other than her mother had slapped her like that you and I would have been fighting to see who could have got out the door first.

Melany has been nothing but a problem since I've known her. It was a one night stand, I come back from a cruise three years later and find out I have this beautiful little girl.

We tried to make it work for a while, but I just can't deal with her, she hates men, hates me, blames me for all of her problems.

I'd have completely cut her out of my life if it wasn't for Caitlyn. But she has always been so special to me, and my biggest regret is not being able to spend more time with her over the years.

It's like one minute she is a little girl, you go out to sea a couple of times and the next thing you know she is a teenager.

Then you blink, and she is off to college.

Now my little girl is all grown up; I'm retired out of the Navy, I'm not sure what to do next.

Do you know what I mean?"

Mike scratched his chin for a moment thinking about what he had just been told.

"Personally, it sounds to me like you need to mend your relationship with Caitlyn so you can get on with life without feeling guilty about it."

"That thought has crossed my mind, but with her living in Hawaii and now here she is awful hard to spend time with."

Mike thought for a second more.

"I tell you what, this spring we are going to sail to Hawaii sometime, why don't I get ahold of you a few weeks out of our departure, and you can make the crossing with us, spend some time with your girl, maybe make things right."

Dan's eyes lit up, and he smiled a big toothy grin.

"I would like that very much. That would mean a lot to me."

Mike smiled and shook his hand and as Dan turned to step back inside Mike stopped him.

"There is something I need to ask you about?"

"What is that?"

"Well you see, I already bought a ring."

Dan smiled stuck out his hand, and as Mike reached out and shook it, Dan gave him a big hug then stepped back still holding his hand.

"I saw everything I needed to see tonight, my little girl is happy with you, she loves you, and I have no doubt you love her.

I wish you many years of happiness. You have a great family, and I think she will do well to be a part of it."

"Thank you!"

Mike replied with a big grin; then both men turned back inside to rejoin the party.

THIRTY-SIX

After all of the guests departed, Mike and Caitlyn got the boat back in order and by the time they finished they were both exhausted.

They peeled off their clothes and climbed into bed Mike pulled Caitlyn up tight in his arms after shutting the lights off and kissed the side of her head and told her goodnight.

Within ten minutes they were both out cold exhausted from the long hard day.

The next morning, they discovered Caitlyn's mom had moved her ticket up and was headed back to Ireland via a text message, Caitlyn tried to call her, but she didn't answer.

This upset Caitlyn, since she had been a teenager she had been at odds with her mother, they were just two people diametrically opposed in their thinking.

It was something that had left Caitlyn feeling very alone for much of her life, which was funny now that she thought about it because she hadn't felt alone in quite some time, not since she was in Hawaii that day Grandpa Stephen showed up at her door.

She smiled at this and started reminiscing, realizing all of the craziness her life had been enveloped in the last few months all starting with the old sea captain who had ripped her off.

Then she thought to herself "Best 2,500.00 dollars I ever spent!"

The next few days flew by, Caitlyn Mike, Dan, and Grandpa all spent time together driving around seeing the sights, meeting grandpa's friends in the area.

They took a tour of the machine shop grandpa started way back when then they saw the aircraft carriers all docked at the Navy Yard.

Currently, the Constellation, Kitty Hawk, Independence, and the Ranger all sat in mothballs at the southern end of the harbor, north of them the John C Stennis and the Ronald Reagan sat in drydock having repairs done.

It was a great time for all, happy memories were made, but the one thing that was apparent was that it was harder for Grandpa to breathe.

Soon the time came for Caitlyn's dad to fly back to San Diego, Mike and Caitlyn drove him to the airport in the old GMC.

Standing at the terminal Caitlyn and Dan both got misty-eyed they had bonded over the last few days, it was one of the best holidays they had ever spent together.

Then he was gone, and it was just back to Mike and Caitlyn aboard the Utah Rose.

The next few weeks they kept busy with Christmas shopping, Caitlyn decorated the inside of the boat, and Mike decorated the outside with lots of lights, he used the new fancy LED's and the shined with a bright, clean, pleasing light that just made the boat light up so pretty.

Christmas was fast approaching, and Mike prepared a little surprise, he booked Dan a plane ticket so he could see Caitlyn for Christmas, he had previously told her he could not afford to come.

Everything seemed fine until one day Grandpa Stephen showed up pulling an oxygen tank behind him.

When Mike saw him coming down the pier with the tank his heart sank. It didn't take a rocket scientist to see he was going downhill fast.

Mike started spending as much time as he could with him. Caitlyn as well, she could see it too that he didn't have much time left.

On December 7th Mike and Caitlyn took him down to the VFW where they had a memorial gathering. Being a Pearl Harbor Survivor Grandpa was treated like a guest of honor although he hated the attention and Mike could see he was miserable sucking oxygen from the mask.

It was the 75th anniversary, and because of this, there was more fanfare than usual.

When the ceremonies were over Grandpa went home and fell asleep the rest of the day in his favorite chair.

Mike and Monica chatted in the kitchen as they watched him sleep about how worried they were about him.

That was the horrible thing about cancer. It didn't kill you quickly; it was a long drawn out process, it would go away sometimes, then rear its ugly head again, it slowly consumed its victim, it robbed them of their strength.

This time Grandpa had made the decision not to undergo chemo because he knew it was the end.

He had cancer ten years before and beat it, this time around was another story, it had infected his lungs and was slowly suffocating him.

Mike, Monica, and Caitlyn were relegated to watching a man they loved and revered slip away into being a mere shadow of his former self.

It left them all with a black disgusting sticky feeling on the inside that nothing could wash away. There was no comfort, no joy, no release from the special brand of suffering cancer brings.

The only relief that comes is when the suffering ends, but even then, for those who remain there is the memory of the slow downward spiral of the one they love until the bitter end.

THIRTY-SEVEN

Quickly Christmas was upon them, Mike and Caitlyn got wrapped up in going to Christmas parties at several of the businesses Grandpa owned in his absence.

Caitlyn was a hit at the parties with her thick Irish accent, and in realizing this, she turned it up a bit because it gave people an easy icebreaker to talk to her.

There were a lot of Irish in the Pacific North West, poor Irishmen had joined on with the Northern Pacific Railroad from its construction onward and because of this many had flooded into the area seeking a new life with their newfound wealth from the railroad.

Finally, the family dinner on the 24th rolled around.

 Mike had a car pick up Dan from the Airport; they elected to do dinner at Grandpa Stephen's favorite steak house, when they showed up the table was ready, Monica and Abbey were there, when Mike told the hostess that they were a table of Six Caitlyn looked confused, then she saw him.

"DADDY!"

She squealed out loud like a little girl. She ran to him and hugged him. He was very happy to see her.

They all made their way in and sat down to dinner.

Through the night they all made small talk, Caitlyn's dad got to tell her about his new job working as a consultant to the Navy at twice the pay he was making as an enlisted man. He also mentioned that he had a month of vacation every year with holidays off. And in delivering this news, he winked subtly at Mike as they were going to surprise Caitlyn on the sailing trip.

Grandpa Stephen was more stoic, he went back and forth between eating and his oxygen mask; anyone could tell he was not having a good time with it as it made it difficult to talk let alone eat.

After dinner, everyone headed back to the Utah Rose for a few drinks and pie.

They were all gathered around in the salon with the fireplace roaring when Mike got everyone's attention as Grandpa Stephen had done so many times before by banging a spoon against his glass.

He stood up, stood Caitlyn up, then began to speak.

> "Everyone I wanted to thank you for being here this evening, You are all great people and you mean so much to me, which is why I want you to be a witness to what I do next."

With that, he dropped to a knee and pulled a ring from his pocket holding it up to her. Caitlyn realizing what was happening broke out into tears instantly and covered her mouth with her hands.

> "Caitlyn Marie Campbell, Over the last eight months I have grown very fond of you, I have watched you come from a landlubber who didn't know her port from her starboard to a skilled sailor who I would go to sea with any day.
>
> You've shown me that you are brave and fierce yet loving and compassionate, that you have character few could ever hope to match.
>
> So I am asking you to be my wife.
>
> Will you Marry me?"

The tears streamed freely from Caitlyn now, and she nodded yes many times before finally lunging at Mike and hugging him with everything she had before stepping back so he could put the ring on her finger.

Of course, the first thing she had to do was show it to everyone.

Everyone started cheering and clapping, and in an unexpected move Grandpa Stephen stepped up the three steps onto the bridge and pulled the air horn several times.

Then he stepped back down into the Salon and hugged Caitlyn and shook Mikes' hand and said to him.

>Michael, I am glad to see it, I am so glad to see you with this woman, she is good for you and you for her. I hope you have so many happy years together I love you both."

Then it was Dan's turn he shook Mike's hand and hugged Caitlyn.

>"Baby, I am so happy for you, when I was here at Thanksgiving the one thing your mother did was make him prove to me how much he cares.

>That night I gave him my blessing to do this, and I want this for you. He is a good man; he will do right by you."

Monica and Abbey then offered their congratulations; they were both crying tears of joy.

That night after everyone had gone home Mike and Caitlyn sat by the fire in the salon.

>"When should we do it?"

Caitlyn asked Mike.

>"When would you like to?"

>"Soon, I want Grandpa to be there."

Caitlyn responded wary of Grandpa Stephen's deteriorating health.

> "How about we do it now, we go down Monday, get the license, three days later we have the JP do the ceremony?"

Mike replied with a big smile.

> "I would like that very much."

Caitlyn said with a big smile, then she pulled the blanket up over herself and cuddled up to Mikes side and was soon fast asleep.

Christmas morning everyone showed up at the boat together. Warm greetings were exchanged, then breakfast and gifts.

After the gift giving had concluded Grandpa Stephen had one more surprise up his sleeve.

He got Mike and Caitlyn's attention telling them he had something for them.

> "Back in 1953 I met a wonderful, amazing woman while I was up here in Bremerton, her name was Edith, she was the sweetest human being I had ever known."

Then he reached into his pocket and pulled out another ring.

> "I proposed to her with this very ring, she became my loving wife through thick and thin, she worked with me to help me grow my businesses and build my wealth, and we raised an amazing family together.
>
> I found this ring last night as I was going to bed, then it occurred to me I should offer it to you, I know that you already bought a ring Michael, but I should offer it none the less."

Caitlyn sprung up and hugged him.

"Thank you so much, Grandpa!"

She squealed with delight.

Grandpa handed the ring to Michael, and he put it on her finger taking the old one off.

Then Grandpa spoke again after taking a few hits from the oxygen mask.

"I have been worried about what would happen to that ring, would it just sit in a jewelry box somewhere until it is forgotten about?

Would it be lost? Would it be stolen?

I just couldn't bear the thought of it; I am glad it is going to you, I hope it brings you so many years of good luck as it did to my lovely wife and me."

After a moment of silence, Mike spoke up.

"Grandpa there is still one bit of business that needs tending to."

"What is that Michael?"

"Well we have decided to get the license Monday, we're getting Married Thursday. I want you to be my best man."

"Michael, I'd be honored."

With that, the plan was set in motion.

THIRTY-EIGHT

The next morning Mike and Caitlyn drove down to the courthouse, did the paperwork and got their Marriage License.

Then they stopped in to see Judge Harper about officiating the ceremonies; he stated he would. They were going to do nothing fancy, just a small ceremony aboard the Utah Rose.

Then back at the boat, Caitlyn had to do the part she was dreading, at first, she tried calling her mom with no answer.

Then she sent her a Text.

Caitlyn: 2:34pm
Mom, call me.
Caitlyn: 2:41pm
It's important!!!

Caitlyn: 4:45pm
Mom, I'm getting married!

Mom: 4:45pm
WHAT???

Caitlyn: 2:34pm
Just call me please!

Caitlyn waited, she kept picking up her phone and checking the screen to see if she had a new message.

The minutes ticked on, she checked the last timestamp, 4:45. Soon the clock ticked over 5:00 PM, then 5:30, nothing.

Caitlyn's heart grew heavy as she sat on the couch in the salon, Mike walked up behind her and rubbed her shoulders then kissed her on top of the head.

The affection was welcome and helped to melt her icky feeling, but she still didn't feel better.

   "You want to go get some dinner?"

Mike asked hoping the excuse to get out and do something would get her mind off of her mom.

"I'm not hungry. Do you want me to make you something?"

Caitlyn asked as she reached up to her shoulder taking Mikes hand in hers.

"I was thinking about getting some Pizza."

Mike said with a big smile.

"We could order some."

Caitlyn said as she smiled back up at him.

"I think I will do that, what do you want?"

Mike Asked.

"Nothing for me, I am not hungry... Well not for food anyway..."

She responded coyly with a wink and a smile.

Mike took this cue and bent over and kissed her forehead and then spoke with a playful grin.

"Ok, but first PIZZA!"

This made Caitlyn laugh and feel a bit better; then she got an idea.

"You get the pizza; I will get ready."

Caitlyn stood, turned, then gave Mike a hug, and a kiss then headed downstairs.

Mike ordered the Pizza and about ten minutes out from when it was supposed to arrive he fired up all four engines on the Utah Rose to let them warm up.

Caitlyn was kind of surprised that Mike had started the engines, but she carried on getting ready stepping into the shower.

Soon the Pizza arrived, and Mike untied the lines and stepped aboard, and then pushed the big boat off the dock with the bow and stern thruster.

Then he slipped the two inboard shafts into gear, and they began to slowly slip forward out of the no wake zone.

Mike punched in an old route up to an anchorage off Bainbridge Island and locked it into the Autopilot; they would be there inside of ten minutes.

As soon as the no wake zone was cleared Mike brought the other two screws online and the boat picked up speed to 12 knots, not even half her top speed the motors were practically idling.

As Caitlyn finished her shower and began to dry herself, she could feel the boat slow then bob as it slowed to a stop, then came the heavy clanging noise of the anchor chain rolling out up through the hawse pipe around the windlass and out over the bow roller.

The anchor made a big splash as it plunged into the water, then the chain continued to let out as the boat backed up finally setting the hook, Caitlyn could feel the boat strain against the anchor as the engines gunned briefly in reverse.

She dressed in high heels, stockings, a garter belt and a corset, conveniently forgetting to wear a bra. She let her hair down and brushed it out, letting the curls fall over her shoulders.

When she stepped up to the Salon, she found Mike sitting at the Galley bar enjoying a slice of pizza.

He stopped when he saw her; she was absolutely beautiful with her long red curly hair flowing down over her exposed chest held in stark contrast with her pale skin and black Lingerie.

"Lace me up?"

She said with a coy smile. Mike smiled back, then set his slice down and motioned for her to come to him as he wiped his fingers clean with a paper towel.

She turned about and pulled her hair forward exposing the laces of the corset; Mike began working the laces pulling each one to the center where the drawstrings came out, with each pass making the garment tighter around her waist.

When it was fairly tight he stopped, she looked over her shoulder and said:

"All the way please."

Mike smiled at this and continued lacing. Caitlyn could feel the corset squeezing her middle. By the time the back edges had been laced together her normally twenty-two-inch waist had been sucked down to nineteen.

Mike knotted the bows and tucked them and the excess into the laces. Then he patted her on the hip to let her know he had finished.

She playfully tossed her hair back over her shoulders and stepped away turning from side to side for him to admire.

Mike smiled a big toothy grin, and his eyes lit up as he stared right into hers.

"I just want you to know, you're beautiful, and I love you."

This made Caitlyn's insides flutter, she blushed, bit her lip and looked down, with her hands clasped together in front of her and she began to fidget.

After a moment of hesitation she replied:

"I love you too Sir."

Then she peeped back up at him, and he motioned for her to come to him.

She did, and he wrapped his arm around her corseted side pulling her to him in a big side hug then he kissed her on the side of the head.

Then he stood up and lead her into the Salon, he sat on the couch and pulled her into his lap facing him her legs straddling his.

Mike pulled her to this chest so her face went over his right shoulder and he began to caress her rubbing her back.

The gentle touch of his hands caused Caitlyn to soften, the knots eased out of her back, her arms went limp, and soon she was resting all of her weight on Mike with her head resting on his shoulder.

Soon tears formed in her eyes and she sniffled a bit. She sat back and asked him.

> "Sir, I need to feel pain. I am a mess inside."

> "What are you feeling bad about?"

Mike asked genuinely concerned with no hint of annoyance or disgust.

> "Mostly my mom, she tells me I can't be like I am, she tells me I need to be strong, that I don't need a man, that I should be independent.

> And it's just stupid because she is just mad Daddy never wanted her that way for more than one night.

> Every time I talk to her she berates me with it, makes me feel stupid, tells me I am weak."

"You are anything but weak; you're one of the strongest people I know."

Mike replied with sincerity in his voice.

"You really mean that?"

Caitlyn asked with a sniff.

"I do...

Remember when you showed up at my boat after that captain had ripped you off?"

"Yeah." *sniffle*

"Most people would have given up, called the police and then flown back home their tails between their legs, but you overcame it, you found me, you found a way, you didn't let that stop you."

"I guess not."

Caitlyn still sobbed gently.

"Then you learned how to sail, most people who get on the boat just want to go for a ride, they don't care about how it works, but you, you learned everything you could, and by the time we rescued the new boat you were a pro at the wheel."

"I guess you are right."

"Then you took a chance, you got on an Airplane with Grandpa, who you had never met before, flew to California and found me."

"Yeah but I messed that all up."

"No you didn't, sure you made mistakes but you made things right, and in doing so you made everyone respect you."

"Even you?"

"Especially me!"

Mike replied with a huge smile.

Then he leaned in and kissed her then wiped the tears from her cheeks and kissed her once more.

Then he told her to lie across his lap; she did with her butt up in the air.

At first, Mike traced his fingers along her skin causing it to break out in goose bumps, then WHACK! The first blow landed on her right cheek.

The pain stung and Caitlyn winced, then WHACK! WHACK! WHACK! The next three alternated between the sides.

Each time she let out an audible moan.

Mike continued to work for his hand across her backside until it had turned bright red and Caitlyn was once again sobbing.

Then he stopped, again gently caressed his fingers over and back then patted her butt cheek gently to get her to stand up.

She did and then Mike pulled her back into his lap just the same as before and began to caress her again.

This time having had a healthy dose of physical pain it had given her a reason for the emotional pain she felt and Caitlyn now began to sob and cry uncontrollably big heavy wet tears streaming down her face.

Mike just continued to hug her and caress her rubbing her back, and she cried it out.

After about 30 minutes of this Caitlyn could cry no more, she leaned back and pulled a couple of tissues from the box on the end table to dry her eyes.

Then she leaned in and kissed Mike.

"Thank you, sir! I needed that."

She said with a smile obviously feeling better. Then she leaned in and kissed him.

She started with kissing his lips then she grabbed the bottom of his tee shirt and slid it up his torso before he pulled it the rest of the way off.

Then she began kissing him again before dropping down to kiss his shoulders, then his chest then his stomach as she slid onto the floor kneeling in front of him.

Then she untied his boots and pulled each of them off along with his socks.

Then deliberately she slowly pushed her hands from his knees up his thighs to his belt buckle popping it open then undoing the button and the zipper slowly and tediously she opened his pants then tugged gently at the waist in a cute manner suggesting he take them off.

He smiled and pushed his pants and underwear off all at the same time.

Needless to say, with what they would spend the next few hours doing they were going to need to sleep in in the morning!

⚓ THIRTY-NINE ⚓

The next few days flew by, Caitlyn, Monica, and Abbey had a girl's day and bought dresses for the big day.

They arranged for a local seafood restaurant to cater the event with an amazing smoked salmon and pasta dinner.

A handful of close friends had been invited, but there was one thing still eating at Caitlyn, she still had not heard from her mom.

She tried calling and texting several more times, but her mother was having none of it.

Eventually, the calls would go straight to voicemail; it broke Caitlyn's heart that she had to be so petty and could not be happy for her.

Soon the big day was upon them, the crew they had hired showed up to clean the boat.

The caterers set up in the galley, Monica picked Caitlyn up and took her to Grandpa Stephens house to put on her dress. At the same time, she dropped Grandpa off at the boat.

She had picked a simple one piece dress, white in color that hugged her curves, no shoulder straps with a pencil skirt style bottom, it was simple but pretty at the same time. She matched it with some white high heels.

She had her long red curly hair pulled up into a ponytail that dangled down behind her below the bottoms of her shoulder blades; she looked nothing short of amazing.

It wasn't until she saw herself standing in the mirror that the nervousness set in, she was overwhelmed by happiness but at the same time she did not want to look silly or stupid in front of everyone, she wasn't used to being the center of attention in this way.

Then her dad walked in and when he saw her his face lit up with a huge smile.

"Wow, honey! You look BEAUTIFUL!"

He said reaching out to give her a hug.

"Thank you Daddy!"

She replied turning for him to see her before stepping to him to give him a hug.

"Are you ready for this?"

He asked, Caitlyn, paused and thought about it and then smiled.

"Dad, I have never been so sure of anything in my life."

He hugged her again, and when she pulled back, she could see tears welling up in his eyes.

"Dad! Don't do that, because if you cry I am gonna cry, then I will have to redo my makeup!"

He laughed and smiled and rubbed his eyes dry then escorted her to the car.

When they arrived at the boat Monica called Mike and told him to go in one of the forward staterooms and wait until they were onboard, Caitlyn and her father would stay in the owner's stateroom until the ceremony.

As they walked down the Gangway to the Dock, Caitlyn noticed the boat had been well cleaned and was dressed up; white ribbons adorned the rails of the boat with a big bow on the stern.

As well a string of LED lights had been run from the bow up to the mast, then back down to the flag pole, and other lights had been wrapped around the rails with the ribbons.

Inside the tables were covered in white tablecloths and each had flowers in the middle.

Once they were in the stateroom, Dan closed and locked the door behind them. They sat and talked and then all of the sudden they heard the engines start.

Soon the boat was moving, slow at first then faster.

Caitlyn looked at her dad and asked:

> "Did they tell you we were going somewhere?"

> "No one said anything to me?"

He shrugged.

Caitlyn couldn't take the suspense; she texted Mike.

Caitlyn: 3:30pm
Where are we going?

Mike: 3:32pm
It's a surprise. ;)

Caitlyn: 3:33pm
Want to give me a hint?

Mike: 3:33pm
And spoil it? I don't think so!
Mike: 3:34pm
Be about 20-25 minutes.

Caitlyn: 3:35pm
Looking forward to it! =)

The boat picked up speed and Caitlyn could hear music start playing. The ride was mostly smooth with a bit of chop, the sound this time of year could be pretty unpredictable.

Soon the boat bobbed as it began to slow and the wake caught up to it, for a few minutes more they idled then you could hear the anchor drop with a splash and clanging of the chain, Caitlyn figured they were in fairly deep water because quite a bit of chain went out.

Soon she felt the familiar tug of the engine backing setting the hook.

Monica stepped below and told her it would be only a few minutes more.

Caitlyn looked out the portlight and could see they were anchored in the general anchorage off of downtown Seattle. Off in the distance, the space needle pierced up into the dimming sky.

To the east, the sky was turning dark blue, and hung overcast, to the west the sun hung low in the sky partially obscured already by the Olympic Peninsula.

Caitlyn could hear footsteps shuffling above as preparations were being made. She started to fidget with her hands. Dan seeing this stepped over and took his daughter's hands in his.

"You're going to be just fine."

Caitlyn didn't respond, she just smiled. It felt very good to have her dad there supporting her in this.

"Speaking of which I had better change."

He said.

Caitlyn looked confused. Dan stepped into the head and a few minutes later emerged wearing his Navy choker whites with his chief's anchors on the collar and the ribbons on his chest.

Caitlyn had never seen him in this uniform before, and she squealed in delight.

"Daddy you look amazing!"

She said with a huge grin. He tipped his hat to her and smiled.

Soon the announcement was made that everything and everyone were ready. Caitlyn gulped hard and followed her dad up the ladder to the Salon.

There everyone was standing on the back deck with the sliding doors wide open; she was again surprised to find Mike and Grandpa Stephen both wearing their choker whites as well.

They both looked so handsome, clean-shaven, fresh haircuts, although Grandpa still wore his mustache.

Caitlyn smiled so hard it hurt and fought the urge to tear up fanning herself.

> "Awww you guys!"

She said still trying to contain herself.

Abbey was seated being an electric keyboard when given her cue she started playing here comes the bride.

Dan lead Caitlyn by the arm down the center of the Salon out onto the back deck to where everyone stood waiting for them. He stopped just short of where the ceremony was to take place and turned to her, kissed her on the cheek and told her he loved her.

Then he handed her off to Mike who extended his arm.

Then Judge Harper began to speak.

> "Thank you everyone; we are gathered here today for Caitlyn and Mike to join them in celebration of their matrimony.

> At this time, each will recite their vows starting with the groom."

Mike had committed to memory what he wanted to say.

"Caitlyn, since the day you showed up at my boat I have been struck by your beauty, but it was in getting to know you that I discovered how truly beautiful you are on the inside.

In the time I have known you, I have watched you grow as a person, and you have never ceased to amaze me with the depth of your character, your passion, and your kindness.

You have shown me you will go to great lengths to do what is right, and for this, you have earned my respect, my trust and ultimately my love.

This is why I am here to ask you to be my wife."

Caitlyn melted with his words, it all seemed too good to be true.

Then the judge spoke up.

"Now the bride will recite her vows."

"Michael... Mike.

Since I met you I have known there is something different about you, you have always treated me fairly and honestly.

You are not only an amazing man, but you have an amazing family, and you all have made me feel so welcome.

I want to be your wife, and I want to be a part of your family because here with you I have found so much happiness and already have so many fond memories.

I want to spend the rest of my life making so many more with you."

Mike smiled big and wide unable to help himself, tiny tears welled up in the corners of his eyes now.

Caitlyn couldn't contain it, small beads began to run down her cheeks, and she had to ask for a tissue.

Then the Judge asked for the ring which Grandpa produced from his pocket and handed to Mike.

> "Now son, place the ring on her finger."

Mike slid the ring on Caitlyn's finger then held her hand as the Judge continued.

> Michael, do you take Caitlyn to be your Wife? Do you promise to love, honor, cherish and protect her, forsaking all others and holding only unto her?"
>
> "I do!"

Mike replied without hesitation.

Then the Judge turned to Caitlyn.

> Caitlyn, do you take Mike to be your Husband? Do you promise to love, honor, cherish and protect him, forsaking all others and holding only unto him?"
>
> "I do!"

She replied as the tears began to well up again.

The judge turned back to Mike.

> "Michael repeat after me.
>
> I Michael Black, take thee Caitlyn Campbell to be my lawfully wedded wife, to have and to hold, for better or worse, in sickness and in health so help me God."

Mike repeated the words and as he did Caitlyn could feel hear heart race.

Then the judge had her repeat the vow.

Then he smiled and held his hands out to the side.

> "I now pronounce you husband and wife! You may kiss the bride!"

Mike took his hand and swooped his hat off his head taking his other hand placing it on the small of Caitlyn's back and pulled her in for a kiss.

When they finished, the Judge sounded off again.

> "Ladies and Gentlemen, I present to you Misses Caitlyn and Mister Michael Black!"

Everyone started clapping, and Monica snapped photos. Finally getting them to stand at the stern to get a photo of them together, and then a group photo using a tripod of everyone there, and of course, there was the photo with her father. Then one with Grandpa Stephen.

Then naturally one of the three of them all in their whites.

The party sat down for dinner, and well wishes were exchanged. Caitlyn broke down in happy tears more times than she could count.

She had imagined so many times growing up what her wedding day would be like, but she never imagined it could be anything like this.

The sun dropped down out of sight, and the sky to the east turned a deep dark blue then black, to the west the clouds lit up as ribbons of red orange and purple.

To the southeast Mount Rainier peaked out over the cityscape, its snow-covered face bathed in the light of the setting sun turning it a pinkish hue.

Everyone seemed to stop and stare and watch the sunset and enjoy the scenery.

There was just something about being out on the water that made the world seem so different; it made the sky seem so big because you can see so far in either direction.

One thing is for sure nature did its part to make it a day to remember.

⚓ FORTY ⚓

Around 8 pm Grandpa Stephen became very tired, Monica helped him forward to one of the guest cabins.

As she helped him sit on the bed setting his oxygen tank on the floor next to it, he chuckled.

"What?"

She asked.

"I built this boat brand new to share with your grandmother and our family, tonight I find myself in one of the guest cabins I have never slept in before, and yet I couldn't be happier.

I think your brother found a good woman."

He said as he leaned back into the pillows and took a draw off of his oxygen mask.

"I like her a lot too Grandpa; she is very sweet."

"She reminds me of your grandmother at that age, granted your grandmother didn't have the red hair or the temper, she was blonde and very sweet, always taking care of me and everyone else.

I sure wish she could have been here tonight to see."

Monica clasped his hand and held it in both of her own on her lap.

"I know Grandpa; I miss her too, I think she would be proud though.

Caitlyn is way better than Tiffany ever was."

At the mention of her name, Grandpa Stephen went stoic and looked away with an audible scoff.

It was obvious even hearing her name while being aboard this boat was more than he could bear.

"I'm sorry Grandpa, I shouldn't have mentioned her."

Monica said with regret in her voice.

"No! You know you are right, Tiffany couldn't hold a candle to Caitlyn.

Caitlyn has all of the good qualities Tiffany was lacking and has none of the vices that make her an evil human being.

My only regret is I won't live long enough to see any great grandkids...

I bet if they have a daughter she will be as cute as can be."

Monica laughed and replied.

"Can you imagine Mike doting over a little curly red haired girl? He would be a super-protective dad."

"I could see it when she started dating he would probably toss a shotgun shell at the young man and tell him the move a lot faster after 10:00 PM!"

"Well Grandpa! That is certainly something you would do!"

Monica gave him a gentle slap on the arm as she said it. Then Grandpa grew quiet for a moment before he spoke again.

"Monica, I know when you first started dating women I was pretty hard on you, it's just in my generation respectable people didn't do that kind of thing.

In time though I've come around, and I have grown to like that wife of yours. I'm sorry I didn't come to the wedding, I know that must have hurt you very much.

I hope you and she can continue to have many years of happiness together; you two are really good for each other."

Hearing this Monica choked on her tears, it was like an old wound deep inside of her that was now eight years old had all of the sudden ruptured and the emotions came boiling to the surface.

Then as he spoke, it was like that hurt got flushed away.

She didn't say anything; she just kissed his hand then bent over and hugged him.

Then finally she said:

"Thank you Grandpa! I love you!"

And they enjoyed a long moment of solace as the last of a remaining rift between them mended.

Back upstairs the party was still going; Mike kept taking Grandpa's old vinyl records and queuing them up on the record player.

Miles Davis, Glenn Miller, Artie Shaw and Frank Sinatra all played throughout the cabin on the old turntable.

Everyone laughed and carried on until late when finally, the party started to wind down.

Mike could see Caitlyn was getting sleepy, he wrapped his arm around her and kissed the side of her head.

"Are you ready for bed?"

She thought for a moment then smiled.

"I just don't want this day to end; it has been so perfect!"

Then she kissed him.

"Ah yes, but all good things must end."

"I guess you are right."

She said with a grin.

Everyone once more offered their congratulations on such a nice wedding and party. Finally, it was Caitlyn's dad's turn.

"Hey honey, congratulations."

He said giving her a big hug.

"Thank you Daddy!"

She replied before kissing him on the cheek.

Then Mike stuck out his hand out to shake Dan's. They exchanged congratulations and said goodnight; then Mike led Caitlyn down into their stateroom.

Caitlyn slipped off her dress and used the head, she emerged wearing nothing but her stockings and high heels and playfully teased Mike who was just finishing taking his uniform off and stowing it in the garment bag in which he kept it.

He grabbed her and kissed her, and she told him that he had better hurry up as she plopped playfully on the bed.

Mike told her he would be right back and then he stepped into the head, by the time he came back out Caitlyn was fast asleep on the bed.

He stood there for a moment just looking at her rubbing his hand through his fresh high and tight buzz cut smiling to himself, then he pulled her shoes off one by one and moved her under the covers before climbing in himself lying next to her.

Then Mike reached out with his thumb and gave the side of her face a gentle caress, and she stirred a little bit.

"I love you, Sir."

She said in a soft squeaky voice.

"I love you too."

Mike said then kissed her on the forehead and with this she buried her face into his chest.

"Goodnight."

He whispered to her, soon Mike himself had faded off to sleep.

⚓ FORTY-ONE ⚓

The next day was New Year's Eve. Breakfast was held late as everyone slept in.

They were lucky to have anchored a day early so as that they got a good spot to see the fireworks.

For lunch, they took the dinghy to shore and walked around downtown Seattle up through Pike Street Market.

They had lunch at a little Thai restaurant not far from there.

Then they stood up on the walkway and marveled at the big tunneling project the city was undertaking to replace the Alaskan Way Viaduct.

Then they picked up some fresh salmon and shrimp at Pike Street before heading back to the boat.

For dinner, Mike and Dan fired up the big stainless steel grill up on the fly bridge and barbecued salmon fillets and shrimp kabobs.

Once again, they were greeted with an amazing sunset although they did get pegged with a bit of a rain squall, the rain, however, made the emerald city glisten in the fading sunlight.

Soon fireworks were popping and cracking across the bay.

Grandpa turned on the TV, and at 8 pm everyone watched the ball drop in Times Square, that was the bum deal about being on the west coast if you have satellite TV, they don't set the broadcast back for you like they did with cable back in the day.

About 9:15 pm Grandpa decided he had enough for the night. He said goodnight to everyone, and once again Monica escorted him to his cabin.

When she returned, she had a sad look on her face.

"Everything alright?"

Mike asked.

> "It's Grandpa... It's just he is wearing out so fast now, I am getting worried about him."

> "Yeah, not an easy thing to see."

> "No, It's not."

Caitlyn replied the pain she felt obvious in her voice.

Mike hugged her and said.

> "Come on; he will be alright for tonight, let's have a good time."

> "Alright."

She said with a muted smile.

Soon everyone's spirits came back up, and before they knew it, it was 11:55. Everyone made their way up on deck for the big show, and it just so happened the stern was hanging towards the space needle giving everyone a great view of the city skyline.

Then BOOM! SNAP! CRACKLE! POP! POP! POP! The fireworks began to explode from the big display at the space needle.

Then boats in the area began to blow their horns at midnight and much to everyone's surprise onboard the Utah Rose her horn blew as well scaring everyone half to death, as they spun about they found Grandpa Stephen sitting behind the wheel with a big Cheshire Cat grin on his face.

Then Mike looked at Monica and said:

> "I guess he still has some piss and vinegar left in him!"

They both laughed it was the perfect endcap on the night bringing in the new year.

⚓ FORTY-TWO ⚓

After the New Year's holiday, everything seemed to set into the slow frigid routine the first of the year always seems to; the weather was gray and cold.

It snowed several times, and the surface of the water in the boat yard froze into a thin sheet that seemed to amplify the lethargic feeling that set off the new year.

Heavy fog and drizzling rain mixed with the occasional heavy squall would hold for days at a time, then occasionally the clouds would burn off, and the sun would hang low in the sky with a harsh, hard light that made it difficult to look south.

This didn't, however, seem to phase Mike and Caitlyn, they carried on with taking care of the business getting things in place where they needed to be so they could continue sailing in the spring, or whenever Grandpa passed.

That was the foreboding thought on everyone's mind now these days.

It seemed like you could watch him deteriorate daily as the coughing fits worsened and he would have to stop whatever he was doing and take long hard pulls from his oxygen tank often times spitting blood into a rag when he was through.

It became more difficult for Mike to spend time with him, this wasn't how he wanted to remember the man who meant so much to him.

Caitlyn could see he was avoiding it and she understood why.

It didn't stop him from going, but he always procrastinated on the way there and was quick to leave or sit in the other room.

One evening in early February Mike realized that Grandpa had not left his house more than a few times since the wedding. That was very troubling to him.

It wasn't easy watching a man who was once so full of life and vigor, who just a few months earlier had just disappeared hopping on an airplane to fly to Hawaii and find Caitlyn.

Now he could barely walk, barely stand, and the coughing fits, those were the worst. It all summed up to say the great man didn't have long to live.

Soon it was Valentine's day, Mike had planned a nice evening out, and then a better evening in once they returned home.

He had made reservations at a restaurant in Seattle and had planned on taking the Utah Rose and docking her at the downtown marina just off the waterfront.

They set off about 3:00 PM, cleared the harbor and Mike set the throttles down having a little fun but then pulled them back to a more responsible level.

Caitlyn giggled from where she sat perched in the first mate's chair as he did.

For some reason, she just loved watching Mike drive this big boat; it was a complex machine, four throttles, four propellers to control all while steering along with a bow and stern thruster.

Despite her massive size and bulk, the Utah Rose was a quite nimble boat.

Soon they were at the waterfront and tucked into a slip and not a moment too soon as a storm had begun to blow in and the sound was turning to chop with big whitecaps and lots of wind.

Mike had a car pick them up and take them to the restaurant; they were in the lobby waiting to be seated when the call came in.

Mike had not heard his phone ring, so Monica had called Caitlyn, as Caitlyn answered the phone Mike could see her smile change to a very worried look, she held out the phone to him, and he answered, the message was clear and concise.

Grandpa is in bad shape, get here quick!

Was all Monica had to say before she had to go because they were getting into the ambulance.

Mike grabbed Caitlyn and escorted her to the door, he called up another Uber and sat there checking his phone watching the car get closer and closer on the map in the app, his foot began to tap. He couldn't stand still.

Caitlyn felt terrible there was nothing more that she could do other than stand there and hope everything was going to be ok.

Soon the car rolled up; Mike opened the door for her and Caitlyn slid in, and he piled in behind her.

It was the afternoon and traffic was terrible being Valentine's day, they were constantly sitting still, it made Mike crazy watching people on the street walk past faster than the car was moving at times.

The driver battled through the stop and went finally after what seemed like an eternity he had them back down to the Marina.

Mike was off like a shot to get the boat fired up, Caitlyn could barely keep up. Mike jumped aboard and fired the engines, without even being asked Caitlyn started untying lines starting at the bow once she heard the engines come to life.

Then she jumped aboard and made a sweep of the salon making sure there was nothing unsecured before stepping up to the pilot house.

By the time she got there, they were just clearing the no wake zone, and as she sat down, Mike blurted out "hang on" and he mashed the throttles down hard against the stops.

Beneath the decks the four engines roared to life, each making more than one thousand horsepower apiece the propellers sliced through the water driving the massive boat forward causing it to come up high in the water, the boat begin to do the very thing it was designed to do.

GO VERY FAST!

Caitlyn watched the plotter, the speed climbed and climbed, pretty soon they were doing 31 knots! Which is just over 35 miles per hour, which on a boat of this size is flying!

As they cleared the protection of the harbor, they began to smash through the whitecaps. They were short and choppy three to four foot waves coming at a very close interval, and the bow of the boat smashed through them sinking and rising throwing spray every time she cleaved through the next wave.

Behind the boat, the four counter turning propellers were blasting a massive rooster tail out behind the boat along with the huge wake she made.

Mike called Monica and got even more bad news, the Hospital in Bremerton was airlifting him to Madigan Army Medical.

They had already rounded the point at the south end of Bainbridge Island so now they were headed the exact opposite way.

Mike chopped the throttles, slammed the gear boxes into reverse and shoved the throttles part of the way forward again.

This caused the massive boat to throw on the brakes hard!

The bow plunged sending up a huge wall of spray, and the massive wake caught the boat slamming hard against the back of the cabin as it flooded over the transom filling the side and aft decks full of two feet of water that quickly ran out the scuppers.

Then Mike brought the throttles back, threw the starboard screws into forward leaving the port in reverse as he rolled the wheel over hard and rocked the throttles the boat spun about hard.

As it neared the end of the turn, Mike threw the port side back in forward and mashed the throttles back against the stops.

The boat rocketed forward again blasting through the waves just as she had before this time headed south towards Tacoma.

As they shot forward, they could see the Helicopter come over them off of the starboard side. Mike latched onto the sight of it and gave chase as hard as he could before he had to turn towards the docks in Tacoma.

Mike had Caitlyn get on her phone and order another car for the trip to the hospital from the docks at Tacoma.

The motion of the boat made it difficult, she tried to tap the map but then they would plunge through another wave, and the pin would hit the wrong spot.

She tried several times each ending in frustration but soon she nailed it, and the car was on its way.

As she did this Mike called the Marina on the VHF in Tacoma and explained their situation, the Marina explained all of their staff had gone home for the day but that they could grab an outside tie-up and pay when they got back.

Apparently, a few of the liveaboards were listening because when they floated up to the dock, there were about ten people gathered there to help them tie off.

Mike cut the engines and jumped out onto the dock. He thanked the liveaboards for their assistance, but they only told him "GO GO GO!" They could tell what was at stake.

Caitlyn chased Mike up the dock; it was now she regretted not changing out of her high heels even though she could run in them like a pro, Mike was moving like a man possessed!

They climbed the gangway and into the waiting car, the Uber driver had a Chrysler 300C, Mike explained the situation and asked the driver if this thing moved.

The mild burnout pulling out of the parking lot answered that question.

It turned out the driver was a Staff Sargent in the Army, who was driving to make a few extra bucks, he knew Tacoma like the back of his hand and instead of hitting I-5 he went rocketing up the surface streets past all of the commuter traffic slogging it out on the interstate.

Soon they were at Madigan, and Mike handed the driver a card, told him if he ever needed help with anything to please call him, then he thanked him and shook his hand.

Soon they were in the lobby, and a teary-eyed Monica emerged from the elevator to greet them.

As soon as Caitlyn saw her face, she could see it was really bad, and her own eyes ran wet as she ran to her and hugged her.

She looked back when she realized Mike had not followed. He had simply stumbled a few steps then fell to his knees mouth agape with a blank expression on his face grabbing his head with his hands.

In his guts, he knew the day he had been dreading was here, and nothing he could do was going to change that.

It was like the world had just stopped and his ears began to ring.

Finally, his hands dropped to his sides, and he slowly stood up still blank and expressionless.

There is something that happens to you when your body fills full of adrenaline, at first you become hyper aware, you become very strong, and everything intensifies.

Then when the moment passes you crash, and you crash hard.

This combined with the news of what was happening hit Mike like a ton of bricks as he tried to stand he found himself tired and sluggish, difficult to move his heart was still pounding in his chest so hard he could hear it in his ears.

But the fight that was ever so present in him had evaporated like a splash of water into a volcano.

⚓ FORTY-THREE ⚓

As they rode the elevator up Monica explained to them that Grandpa had had a heart attack and that the doctors were currently working on him.

He was in rough condition unconscious but alive.

Fortunately, she had been there when it happened and immediately called for help and began CPR and used the automatic defibrillator she had insisted on purchasing months before.

Soon the doctor found them in the waiting room, Monica and Caitlyn sat talking softly, Mike sat in a chair staring blankly forward.

As the doctor approached, he stood, and the women joined him, the doctor spoke to Monica first as they had already been introduced.

> "It looks as though you saved his life; you got very lucky having that defibrillator on hand.
>
> Your grandfather has had a pretty serious heart attack, we performed emergency coronary angioplasty and installed a stint near his heart, I would also recommend a replacement of his heart valve because it too is failing however at this time in his present condition the surgery is not an option.
>
> It is highly likely this is what is making him so weak."

Monica and Caitlyn dove into gear asking questions both dutifully taking notes. They asked about treatments, options and what could be done, the truth was not much with cancer chewing away at his lungs.

Soon they were told he was awake and they could see him.

Monica burst into the room and hugged him; Mike was still slow and lethargic.

Caitlyn just felt awkward, there was a feeling looming overhead, that was this time he wasn't coming home, and this made her feel very bad.

Monica started going into "nurse" mode as Grandpa called it going through the options putting a plan together for treatment but she was cut short as Grandpa held up his hand and spoke.

"I signed a DNR; I am refusing any further treatment."

He said. With this Monica began to cry and shrieked:

"No! Grandpa! NO! you can't do that to us!"

"It's my time; I am tired of being poked and prodded and hooked to these machines. I just don't want to do it anymore."

Monica began pleading with him, and Caitlyn looked to Mike and asked what a "DNR" was when he muttered the words "Do Not Resuscitate" the shock of what had just happened hit her full force, and she buried her head in his chest and began to cry.

It wasn't until now that she began to realize how special the old man had become to her.

Grandpa looked to Mike and spoke.

"So Michael, how's that for Irony, I almost died of a broken heart on Valentine's day!"

Mike couldn't help but laugh which upset Monica greatly, but there was something about military men civilians just couldn't understand is that when faced with death they would laugh in the very face of the grim reaper himself before stepping off into eternity.

This was hardly surprising with Grandpa Stephen; he had spent his life cheating death, first at Pearl Harbor, then at the Sinking of the USS Helena, again in Korea and Vietnam.

He had fought in three major wars, circumnavigated twice, for all of the danger he had faced in life, it was such irony that what was finally killing him as the Asbestos that had been used in the shipyards all those years.

The next two weeks went by slowly, Grandpa was moved out of intensive care and up to a general room.

He kept saying how he wanted to go home but Monica fought like a tigress defending her cub to keep him in the hospital.

She made Mike swear not to bring him home, and for once he relented and agreed.

Then one day they came to the hospital to start their visit for the day and the room was empty, grandpa was gone.

Monica went running to the nurse's station to find out what had happened but it was already plain as day to Mike.

Grandpa had called up one of his old Navy buddies and had had them pick him up. Apparently, the old man wasn't as helpless yet as Monica perceived him to be.

Mike wound up laughing at his tenacity, and this only served to make Monica that much angrier.

She proclaimed over and over that it wasn't funny, but Caitlyn could see the humor in it.

They drove back to his house, and there they found him sitting in his chair drinking a cup of coffee, he hadn't even tried to disguise the fact he had spiked it with a little rum and had left the bottle sitting right next to the Coffee pot.

Monica began pleading for him to return to the hospital but now it was Grandpa's turn to put his foot down.

> "Monica, honey I love you, but you have to stop with this! I built this house, I raised a family in this house, your grandmother died in this house and so will I!
>
> That is the end of it!"

She began to protest, but he just held up his finger and spoke again.

> "If you cannot respect that you can find somewhere else to stay until after I have passed."

Grandpa had had enough of being worried over, he wanted peace, and he was going to have it whether or not she was willing to give it to him.

Monica finally accepted defeat. She began to cry, and she hugged him. He comforted her and told her everything was going to be ok.

Then he suggested they all get lunch at the diner. It was clear Stephen Black was going to live his life to the very last, not wither away in a hospital bed somewhere!

⚓ FORTY-FOUR ⚓

The wind whipped through the harbor slamming the Utah Rose against the dock causing the fenders to groan as they rolled down her steel hull.

The waves beat against her starboard side with a steady intensity and even inside of the protected anchorage small whitecaps were breaking, and bits of salty spray were being carried through the air.

Every once in a while, the Pacific North West was subjected to a blow like this, and this storm was particularly fierce.

The afternoon was flooded by a sticky gray light that permeated through the fog and the clouds obscuring everything in the distance.

Caitlyn sat next to Mike on the couch in the salon under a blanket, the fireplace crackled in the corner and the wind howled over the boat, and the constant shifting caused her woodwork to creak and groan making sounds you would expect to hear in an old pirate movie.

Then it came loud and hard with a massive flash lightning struck a tree on the opposite side of the narrow waterway.

The thunder clap scared Caitlyn, and she let out an "Eeep!" as she jumped slightly.

Then another a bit further away burst with a flash and a bang.

"I'm just glad we are not out there in this."

Mike said in a reassuring voice as he reached over and put his hand on her knee. The affection was soothing, and Caitlyn cuddled up to his arm and rested her head on his shoulder.

The storm continued, and soon Mike had to get up and stoke the fire.

When he sat back down before he could pick his book back up, Caitlyn pounced on him sitting down on his lap wrapping her arms around his neck.

"So, it's the middle of the day, and something tells me with this storm no one is going to bother us."

She said with a playful grin before giving him a little playful kiss.

Mike grabbed her and rolled her over on the couch and got on top of her and kissed her back.

"They won't notice the boat rocking either!"

He said with an evil grin.

They proceeded to start pulling off each other's clothes as they made out kissing and touching each other.

There was just something about a stormy day that made them not good for doing much else!

This had become their routine, on days when the weather was decent enough to go out they would check on the business, visit with grandpa and spend the evenings alone together.

On days when it was bad, they spent them alone together aboard the boat.

Sex was becoming a big part of the relationship, and it was making them closer than ever before, sometimes like this, it was sweet and playful, sometimes it was romantic, sometimes it was wild crazy and kinky!

One thing was for certain was that Mike and Caitlyn were developing a deep, profound affection for each other.

This winter, in particular, had been cold and brutal, but in the closeness, they began to share it didn't matter what the weather outside was doing, they had each other, and that made anything going on outside of their walls much less significant.

The next day the storm had calmed down, and Mike got up early and sprinkled salt on the docks to melt off all the ice that had formed from the rain.

After breakfast, he and Caitlyn hopped in the old GMC and headed up to Grandpa's. Monica was heading up to Canada for a few days to prepare for another gallery show and Abbey was going with her which left Mike and Caitlyn to watch over Grandpa.

Grandpa's house was built in such a way that there were a large series of picture windows in his Livingroom that looked out over the harbor. You could see the Navy Yard; you could see his boat yard, you could see the Utah Rose on her moorings.

As well off in the distance, you could see the mountains of the Olympic Peninsula jutting off into the sky. It was one of the better pieces of property in town, and he had been lucky enough to purchase it so long ago before land prices had gone through the roof.

In 1951 he paid a paltry twenty-five hundred dollars for the piece of dirt that today was easily worth several hundred thousand.

When he built the house, he set up the picture windows in a way that allowed him to see his life's work, not realizing now that as his life was drawing to an end that it would give him a place to sit in his chair and admire all he had accomplished.

A place to sit and look out and think about the good ole days.

Mike came in and found him sitting in his chair, oxygen mask in his left hand he would occasionally pull off of, a cup of coffee in his right.

He plopped down next to him in the other recliner.

"Good morning."

Mike said with a smile trying not to notice how weak and feeble Grandpa was looking.

"Good morning Michael."

"You want to go get some breakfast?"

"No, not today, I already had a bit to eat, and really I'm not that hungry."

Mike frowned at this. He knew the truth was Grandpa just didn't have the breath in him to get up and get going. He had been spending much more time in his chair lately.

Soon Monica was packed up, and she and Abbey were on their way north to Canada.

Mike threw a DVD in the player for Grandpa and then he and Caitlyn went down and grabbed some lunch.

The previous day's low that had brought the massive storm had been replaced by a high that brought clear sunny skies.

The air was still cold and crisp, the sky a pale blue and the sun was still low towards the southern horizon, causing the light to be hard and abrasive.

On the way back from lunch they stopped and got some groceries, then headed back to the house.

They pulled into the drive and parked, then marched up the steps into the house. Mike opened the door carrying a bag of groceries, he called out for Grandpa but got no answer, he set the groceries down on the counter and stepped into the living room.

Grandpa was still sitting in his chair; Mike stepped around to see his head was hunched over and his oxygen mask was laying on the floor.

His skin had already started to turn gray; it was then he knew.

Mike sat down in the chair next to him and just sat. He didn't cry; he didn't get angry, he just sat there reeling in what had just happened.

This moment had been coming for so long that in a strange way he felt a sense of relief knowing Grandpa was no longer suffering.

Then Caitlyn walked in, Mike looked up at her she looked at grandpa then back at him, and her eyes began to flood, her hands went to her mouth, and she started "No! No! No!"

Mike stood up and hugged her, and she began to sob into his chest. It was at this point his eyes teared up too.

After a moment, he led her out of the room and had her sit down at the bar in the kitchen; he then called the coroner's office to report Grandpa's death.

Now Mike had to do something he really didn't want to, he picked up his phone again and Dialed Monica. She answered after a few rings.

"Hello?"

Mike cringed before he spoke:

"Hey, where are you guys at?"

"We're on the Port Townsend ferry almost to Whidbey, why what's up, is Grandpa ok?"

Mike swallowed hard and replied.

"You'll want to turn around and come back. I don't know to say this, so I am just going to say it Grandpa has passed."

The other end of the phone went silent for a minute. Then Monica replied.

"I will be back as soon as I can. Please make sure to call the coroner and ensure grandpa gets taken care of."

"I have already done so, is there anything else?"

"No, I'm prepared for this, please just let me handle it."

Mike hung up the phone and looked back to Caitlyn; she sat in the chair at the bar staring over at Grandpa in the chair.

"It will be alright; he is not suffering anymore. He is at peace. He went the way he wanted to in his own home, quietly uneventfully. No one is hovering over him."

Caitlyn just nodded and looked away from him.

Soon the van was in the driveway, and Grandpa was carted off to the Morgue.

Monica arrived about an hour later, she and Abbey hugged Mike and Caitlyn, then they set to work planning the funeral and making the calls that needed to be made.

Mike took a piece of paper from a notebook in the kitchen and began to write:

Master Chief Gunners Mate Stephen Paul Black United States Navy, May 11th 1921 - February 26th 2017.

To me, he was just known as "Grandpa"...

FORTY-FIVE

The next few days were spent arranging the funeral, Monica turned into a force to be reckoned with caring for every detail. She even coopted Caitlyn into service handling tasks to her to help ensure everything was ready for the Friday evening service.

Mike had many things to tend to himself; he had to meet with the attorney who was going to meet them in Hawaii after the spreading of the ashes to read the will.

He already knew he would be taking over running the companies, but he didn't know all the details of Grandpa's wishes yet.

Even so, there was still plenty to be done; several people had to be notified, several meetings had to be held.

The hardest call Mike had to make was to Allen who was not surprised but not happy with the news either, he and Grandpa had been great friends for decades.

Allen closed the call simply saying he would see Mike when they were ready to shove off for Hawaii and informed him he would not be attending the funeral because he would rather remember Grandpa for how he lived, not how he died.

Mike said he understood, which he did more than anyone could know, himself he really had no desire to attend the funeral.

Then he looked over seeing Grandpa's Liquor cabinet, and he got an idea. There was a bottle of Scotch that Grandpa had just opened a few days before. It had only one or two shots taken out of it.

It occurred to him that no one else had drank from the bottle, so he took it and hid it away behind the seat in his truck.

Then he ordered 15 shot glasses from a local shop that did engraving, after explaining the situation the shopkeeper was more than willing to rush delivery and he had them the next day.

The funeral was Friday and was split into two parts; there would be a viewing that went on through the morning and then a small ceremony that would follow in the afternoon.

Friday arrived, and the family assembled, everyone dressed in black.

Grandpa Stephen was laid out in his coffin that was painted a beautiful navy blue and polished to a near mirror finish with stainless steel handles. The inside was lined in white silk where he lay dressed in his Navy Dress Blues, his hands folded across his chest, his cover lay atop them.

On a stand next to the casket hung his shadow box with the folded American flag and all his ribbons including his Master Chief pins and his Surface Warfare pin and various medals spanning the three wars he served in.

To the other side was a cork board Monica Abbey and Caitlyn had spent hours putting together with photos of family and friends over the years.

The family had a small private viewing first, and then they took their seats. Then the doors to the church were opened.

What they were not prepared for was the flood of people waiting outside, person after person flowed into the church to stand at the casket and pay their respects then passed the family giving them well wishes.

Some stopped to tell stories; others simply told how sorry they were, others had nothing to say at all. Some stopped to pray on their way in our out; others simply meandered through.

After a while the sheer volume of people became exhausting.

The reason why was obvious, though, Grandpa Stephen had touched so many lives, he owned several businesses and property all up and down the west coast, but he always made a point of it to get to know people.

He could walk into a business and remember people and remember details about their lives and this endured them to him.

Some people had come to work for him back in the 1950's when he had just started in owning businesses, and they had worked their entire careers at his companies, then their children had found jobs with him, and even some of their children's children.

One man had brought so much prosperity to all of these people and with the news of his death a tidal wave of them came to pay their respects.

Many already knew Mike, for this, it was difficult for him because person after person offered their condolences knowing how hard it must have been for him and they would wish him luck in assuming his new role.

Finally, at Noon it was announced the family was going for lunch and would be back for the service.

The service, however, had to be moved back twice because there were still people trickling in who wanted to pay their respects.

Around 5:00 pm the service was finally held. Many speeches were given, and finally, it was Mikes turn to speak.

> Master Chief Gunners Mate Stephen Paul Black United States Navy, May 11th 1921-February 26th 2017.
>
> To me, he was just known as "Grandpa" My whole life he was my hero, my friend, my mentor.

He inspired me to Join the Navy when as a boy he would tell me stories, many of which I can assume he wouldn't want to be repeated here today!"

Mike smiled and paused as the audience laughed.

"He taught me to sail and fed my sense of adventure; he taught me about business and what it means to be a man.

I could not be the man today I am today were it not for him.

In fact, I wouldn't have my lovely wife Caitlyn were it not for him.

You see she and I met last year when she came and crewed on my sailboat on my trip up the inside passage, we became close, but at the end of the summer, we had to go our own ways.

Well, Grandpa seeing how I really liked her, he found out where she was in Hawaii, got on an airplane and went and found her and brought her to me in California.

Mind you this was after he had been diagnosed with terminal Mesothelioma!

There was nothing going to stop him when he decided he wanted to do something and I think that is what we admired the most about him.

That was the thing about Grandpa he was a very caring man, he took care of his people, and because of that he formed very strong bonds in the community, I know we will all miss him incredibly and that his legacy will survive many years past his death.

With that, I want to thank you all for being here today.

And for helping celebrate the life of a great man, it means so much to all of us in the Black family."

The audience roared in applause; many people broke out in tears. Caitlyn looked to Mike beaming in pride; she could see it in him that he was quickly becoming a great man such as Grandpa Stephen was, and she could see in his lifetime he would be revered by many as well.

After the funeral, there was a dinner for friends and family, then the following day Grandpa was Cremated and his ashes placed in a silver urn.

Mike and Caitlyn spent the next couple of days packing and soon they were on their way back to California.

It was time to put the Stephen Black back in the water!

FORTY-SIX

The straps of the crane went taught, and the jack stands fell loose under the massive boat, the workers pulled them and the blocking away, then the massive travel lift crawled towards the pier.

Mike and Caitlyn watched as the crew very carefully and nimbly moved the big vessel back out and lowered it into the water.

Once floating again, the straps were pulled away, and they climbed aboard. Mike started pulling the covers to the bilges inspecting below to be sure there were no leaks

When he was satisfied, there were none he began opening all of the seacocks and checked again to make sure the boat was not taking on water.

As soon as they were sure she was floating and not leaking the engine was fired, and they pulled her back over to her usual tie-up on the dock.

Whenever a boat sat on the hard for a period of time there was always a process of waking it back up; tanks had to be filled, dust cleaned up, the hull had to be washed, cabinets restocked.

Luckily for Mike and Caitlyn, no rodents or insects had gotten into the boat.

They set to scrubbing and polishing laundering the sheets and towels, stowing their clothing.

Mike took a pair of teak blocks and fashioned a set of clamps for Grandpa Stephen's urn that he screwed to the shelf above the dinette in the galley with some brass screws.

After a couple of weeks, the Australians showed up, they pulled into the harbor blowing their horn and as they did Mike and Caitlyn emerged on deck.

Mike yelled out to him.

"Hey, you goofy fuckin Australian! How was Colombia?"

"Beautiful country! Very lovely place!"

Jim yelled back with a big smile.

Mike and Caitlyn jumped down on the dock and helped them tie off.

Hugs and handshakes were exchanged, then it was decided they needed to go out for dinner that evening to tell the tale of their trip.

As it turns out they had spent the winter having quite the adventure.

The next few days were spent getting Jim's boat hauled out and returned to Allen after they had cleaned it all up, then the process of provisioning the Stephen Black for the Hawaii crossing had to happen all over again.

Having been through this all before Caitlyn took charge, she recruited Mary and Tania to help her, and within a couple of days, they had the boat stocked full to the gunnels.

Meanwhile, Mike and Jim set to working on the boat, checking fluids and hoses and electrical systems, checking the rigging, checking the sails, making sure everything was ship-shape for the voyage.

Monica and Abbey flew down from Seattle to see them off, Allen was there, then Caitlyn got an even bigger surprise when her dad showed up.

Everyone enjoyed a barbecue aboard the boat that night, many stories were told, and a healthy bit of alcohol was consumed.

The next morning, they were up early getting ready, Mike checked the weather and the forecast had not changed, they were still good to go.

Allen, Dan, Monica, and Abbey showed up about 7:00 and everyone got to say their goodbyes.

Dan expressed his regrets to Mike and Caitlyn that he could not join them for the trip, but his boss at work did not want to give him the time off. So instead he would fly to Hawaii for the funeral then fly back.

Soon they slipped off the lines and pushed off of the dock, everyone who was flying out waved from the dock as they pulled away.

They cleared the breakwater, but they were facing a headwind, so they stayed under engine.

Within forty-five minutes they were nearing the Golden Gate Bridge, as they rounded the point the wind shifted, and they were able to raise sails.

The sails filled and the big boat heeled over and started slicing through the water.

As they cleared out into open ocean, they started riding over the swells up and back down again pushing forward out into the Pacific.

The wind was cold, and the sky was gray, everyone was bundled up in their foul weather gear when they were topside.

Mike set the course into the plotter, and the Auto Pilot took over, and he and Jim set to work keeping the sails trimmed for maximum speed.

This is what this boat was built for; she was long enough that the swell didn't affect her the same way it did smaller boats.

In My Way, they would have been rolling and bobbing to a much greater degree, but the Stephen Black was a much longer boat, and the length made her ride very well through the waves.

Caitlyn sat in the cockpit looking back at land, soon it too disappeared over the horizon, and all anyone could see in any direction was the Pacific.

The further they got from land the clouds started to break up, there were wide stretches of blue mixed with dark black ominous clouds that hung in the distance behind them, to the west light fluffy clouds lingered in the distance.

As the sun dipped to the horizon, they were treated to a spectacular sunset that glowed red and orange before fading to black.

Caitlyn made a stew for dinner which was easy to eat from a bowl on a pitching bucking boat.

After dinner, the watch schedule was set, Mary would have the 20-24 watch, Mike would take the 00-2, Jim would take the 2-4, and Tania would take the 4-8.

This was a good way of splitting the watch because your two mid watches were only 2 hours each.

The 20-midnight watch was four hours, but whoever stood it could sleep from midnight to 8 am, the midnight to 2 am could sleep from 2-10 am if they so desired, really the only tough one was the 2-4 which meant having to split your night's sleep.

By rotating the watch however you could keep it where someone only had to stand this watch once every four days.

That night Jim relieved Mike at 2, then Mike sleepily crawled down the companionway stripped off his fowlies and made his way back to his cabin.

When he stepped into the cabin he was surprised by what he saw, Caitlyn had turned the lights down low and gotten all dressed up for him.

She had dug out the handcuffs and sat with them on patiently waiting for him on the bed.

Mike smiled a big grin and looked her over; there was something about the sight of her that just seemed to wipe all the tired off of his face.

"Good evening Sir!"

She called out to him in a very playful voice.

"I thought you could use some entertainment after your watch."

She said with a smile.

Mike jumped onto the bed and pushed her cuffed hands up over her head pinning them down; then he kissed her deeply.

"I think you missed me on watch."

He said with a grin.

"Maybe just a little."

She said with a wink and a giggle.

Above decks Jim was seated in the cockpit warming his hands on the little radiator, he could hear the giggles below deck turn to moans.

He smiled and laughed to himself, he thought about knocking on the deck over their cabin but decided not to as that sort of thing had a way of starting shenanigans at sea, and he figured Mike was the type he didn't want to be receiving payback from!

The next day the weather evened out some, the swells dropped in size some, and the ride became very pleasant.

As the ride smoothed out, the boat picked up speed and soon they were making nine knots through the water.

The weather was still cold, and they were still relegated to their fowlies when above decks, but below decks, it was much more casual.

There wasn't anything to see topside, so Mike and Jim tended to stay topside while the girls stayed below in the salon.

After about a week of this the temperature started to rise. First, everyone stopped with the foul weather gear, then they were all down to wearing their swimsuits.

It was funny because there was a stark contrast between Mary, Tania, and Caitlyn, Mary and Tania had just spent the winter in Colombia, and because of this they were tan, and Caitlyn who had just wintered with Mike in Washington was as pale as a ghost.

This meant Mike had to lather her up frequently with sunscreen, and eventually she did get a bit crispy on the shoulders which meant having to stay below or cover up.

She did tan a bit, though, and soon her freckles came out everywhere like crazy.

Then one day Tania surprised her, she came up on deck and sat down in the cockpit across from her and pulled her shirt off and was completely naked other than her bikini bottoms.

Tania apparently caught her staring because she blushed and said:

> "Oh! Is it not ok if I go topless?"

Caitlyn blushed at being caught, then tried to speak but stumbled over her words.

"Oh no… It's just… well… you're… You are."

Caitlyn couldn't say what she was thinking; she was thinking how pretty Tania was.

Finally, she had to do something to break the silence, so she grabbed her shirt pulled it over her head undid the string on her bikini top and tossed them aside then sat back in her seat.

This brought on a big laugh from both of them, and Caitlyn looked back to see Jim Laughing sitting at the wheel.

He then shouted out:

"Ah Tania, you have to remember, Caitlyn is from the old country, she's never been toe to toe with a free-spirited Sheila before!

They're more reserved back in the old world!"

Caitlyn's Irish accent became more prevalent when she shot back at him:

"Said by a man from one of Her Majesties former penal colonies!"

Everyone started laughing at that and as the laughter died off Caitlyn leaned back and began to read from her book again, although she kept having to steal glances at Tania across the way.

She had never really taken note of her before, she was about five foot four inches tall, platinum blonde with a very well defined chin that gave away her Dutch ancestry, she was quite pretty, and her body left little to be desired as well.

A couple of times as she snuck a peek she caught Tania looking back at her, and with this, she could feel the tension between them start to build.

That night when he came off his watch, Mike found Caitlyn waiting for him in their stateroom.

She bluntly asked him:

>"Sir, what do you think of Tania?"

The question caught him off guard, but he replied.

>"She is very nice."

Caitlyn hesitated then spoke.

>"I think she likes me..."

She bit her lip waiting for Mike's response.

>"Does she now? Why would you think this?"

>"Kept catching her staring at me earlier today when we were both sitting topless on deck."

>"I see."

Mike said rubbing his chin, then he continued.

>"Do you fancy her?"

>"Do you?"

Caitlyn replied hoping Mike would say it first.

>"She is pretty, albeit I wouldn't trade her for you."

He said with a wink and a smile. Then he tackled Caitlyn on the bed, pushed her hands up over the top of her head and pinned them down which he knew she loved.

Then he put his face just inches from hers and asked:

"Do you want to fuck her?"

Caitlyn didn't hesitate she immediately responded:

"Yes Sir I do!"

Then she lifted her head and gave Mike a playful kiss.

"Then you have my permission. By the way, her watch end's in two hours. Maybe you should go invite her to join us and see how it goes."

Caitlyn smiled and responded with the customary "Yes Sir" then Mike let her up, and she decided to slip into something sexier.

She put on a black bra and panties then wrapped herself up in a white bathrobe and stepped out to find her.

On deck, Tania was sitting in her usual seat when Caitlyn emerged from the companionway. Tania made eye contact and spoke with a bit of surprise in her voice.

"I thought you two would be well into your evening routine by now?"

Caitlyn blushed a bit. Apparently, everyone on board was aware of their after-hours escapades. Caitlyn didn't say anything, she just walked over and sat down next to her and looked at her letting the robe fall open a little bit.

"I figured you might come and join us if you want to."

She finally said with a coy look and a smile, bit her lip then leaned forward, Caitlyn sensing the cue leaned in and kissed her.

Quickly hands started groping before Caitlyn pulled back.

"Now now, we can't be distracting you on watch."

Caitlyn said as she stood up and backed towards the companionway a smile beaming across her face her robe wide open giving a good long look at her body before closing the robe.

"You are such a tease!"

spurted out at her, then continued:

"But I will be there, don't start without me!"

She promised with a big smile.

⚓ FORTY-SEVEN ⚓

The next morning the three were awakened by Jim pounding at the door in a panic.

"Hey mate! Wake up! It's Tania! She's gone overboard!"

He shouted through the door.

Mike shouted back:

"It's fine! She's in here; we will be out in a minute!"

"Oh! Alright then, false alarm!"

Was the only response that came through the door after a brief pause.

About ten minutes later they were dressed and emerged from the Stateroom. Tania was more than just slightly embarrassed and when Jim noticed the red marks around her wrists from the handcuffs, she practically died.

In his usual fashion, he laughed it off.

Everyone just let the issue die and didn't speak any more of it.

Caitlyn too was paying for the previous day's adventures, her chest had absorbed a bit more sun than she should have allowed and she was now very tender, it wasn't super bad, but it would peel in places.

Mostly it was just enough to be mildly uncomfortable.

In an unusual move, Tania helped her cook breakfast and some of the sense of closeness from the night before reared its head again.

Occasionally the boat would rock, and they would bump into each other unintentionally which only served to build the tension between them.

The next few days found Tania joining them several more times, Caitlyn and she began to have some girl time in a way that she had never experienced before, they dressed each other up, they did each other's hair and helped each other paint their toenails.

It was a lot of fun because they got to forget about being adults for a while and just enjoy the experience.

Mike enjoyed himself as well, it was obvious, but what man especially a sailor wouldn't!

But underneath the exterior, something was getting to him, and it was like the closer he got to Hawaii the colder he became.

Soon the smell of land permeated the air, the plants, the dirt, the exhaust; it was Jim that notice it first; crying out "LAND HO!" pointing to a small green lump under a cloud on the horizon.

The land grew out of the water all day, and by the afternoon they found themselves cutting between Oahu and Molokai.

The beauty of these islands was unmistakable, jagged mountains covered in green tropical vegetation over their saw-toothed backs clawing at the sky that was near the color of the beautiful light blue water that surrounded them.

Around the periphery of the islands were the cities and villages and the roads mankind had cut into the islands to make them habitable.

Everyone was awestruck by the beauty except for Mike.

Caitlyn noticed him standing at the wheel staring forward not looking at the islands. She did not bother him but made a mental note to check on him later.

Soon they were at the dock they had reserved, tied off snug and sound their journey over.

The Australians were incredibly excited about being in Hawaii and wanted to check out the town immediately, but Mike remained hesitant to step foot on the dock, he told them to go ahead and said they should call later to make plans. They said they would, and the three of them scampered off into town.

As they left Caitlyn caught Tania looking back at her and when she did Tania blew her a little kiss and grinned probably figuring she was missing out on some fun they were going to have while they were away.

However, this wasn't the case.

Mike stepped below and crashed into the seatee, he just sat there stoic and seemingly void of emotion.

Caitlyn came and kneeled in front of him grabbing his hands in hers, she looked up at him and without saying anything conveyed she was there for him.

A few minutes passed, and he looked at the urn and fixing his eyes on it, he began to speak.

> "I've not been back…"

His words trailed off choked out by emotion before he mustered the strength to continue.

> "I've not been back since Stevie died. After the divorce, I sold everything. I just wanted to leave so badly, but I felt trapped here by the home I had bought for us, my home became a prison rife with memories so sweet that with his death turned so sour I could not bear them.
>
> Day in and day out they tormented me, but I had to go on, the house had to stay clean so the realtor could show it, I wound up having to paint the walls, but after I did, I didn't put any of the pictures back up.

I couldn't bear to see her face after what she had done.

Finally, after six long months the house sold, I sold my pickup, I had already sold most of the furniture, the rest I gave away, I flew to Washington on the first thing smoking and bought My Way sight unseen off of an add I had seen on the internet.

She was a wreck, and I had to completely gut her before I could move aboard, but I didn't care.

One day Grandpa found out I was sleeping in the pickup I had bought under a camper shell staying next to my boat in the boat yard, he showed up and offered to move the boat to his yard and let me stay on the Utah Rose.

When I turned him down it rubbed him wrong; it's one of the few fights we have had.

He felt like I was acting too good for him, he just didn't realize I couldn't be where the Utah Rose was because that was the last place I had seen my son alive.

I couldn't stand to remember, and I couldn't make myself forget.

That is whey when you met me I was docked over in Seattle. I never took My Way to Bremerton, I sailed her as far south as Argentina, as far north as the Bearing Sea, I almost even took her to Japan, but never Hawaii, never Bremerton."

As he paused, Caitlyn could see the tears forming in his eyes. Mike was fighting them as hard as he could, but small droplets seeped out and wetted his eyes before small drips came part way down his cheeks before they evaporated.

Caitlyn kissed his hands and tried to comfort him without saying anything.

Then Mike motioned with his hand for her to climb into his lap which she did and he wrapped his arms around her in a big giant hug.

They stayed like this for what felt like an eternity and slowly Caitlyn could feel him soften and relax.

Finally, when he let go, she kissed him, then told him she loved him and kissed him again.

He responded with a warm touch caressing her cheek which caused her to bury her cheek in the palm of his hand and to cradle his hand with hers.

As he pulled his hand back he said "I love you too" and he smiled for the first time in a couple of days.

Later Mike and Caitlyn decided to go into town for dinner, they had eaten meal after meal aboard the boat, and by now Caitlyn had more than had enough of cooking all of the meals.

She got dressed up in a beautiful black dress that contrasted nicely with her hair, the sunburn was all gone and the bit of a tan she had now made her freckles stand out more than ever before.

She also got to indulge her 6" high heels which were nearly impossible to wear on a bucking pitching boat on the sea.

Mike put on a royal blue button up shirt and some gray slacks. He shaved his sea beard and looked very respectable other than the fact that his cheeks had much less color than the rest of his face!

As they stepped from the pier they got another surprise, a woman's voice called out.

"Oh, Caitlyn! Mike! Is that you?"

They both wheeled about to see Caitlyn's mom walking down the pier towards them in a white dress, sun hat and a ridiculously large black and white purse clomping along in white high heels with black bows.

Caitlyn was stunned because the last time they had talked was the fight in Bremerton, now she was here unexpected and acting as though nothing were wrong.

Mike went tense, and Caitlyn could tell he was not ready to deal with her tonight it was the worst timing possible.

She had to act quickly because now her Mother was almost there.

"Mom! What are you doing here?"

Caitlyn questioned her as she approached.

Melany just broke out into a big hug and said:

"Oh, I missed you so much I wanted to see my darling daughter and her new husband."

Mike wasn't having it; his face was stone cold, and Caitlyn thought quickly.

"Well mother I am afraid you caught us just leaving for dinner, we have reservations already."

"Well can't they just add one more to the list?"

"They told us they were full up!"

Caitlyn lied, and Mike agreed realizing what she was doing.

"Oh well then cancel then, we can eat aboard the boat!"

Melany interjected, and Caitlyn folded. She looked at Mike, and he reluctantly nodded in approval.

They hadn't made it ten steps into Hawaii from his boat; really they hadn't even made it to Hawaii yet because they hadn't stepped from the dock onto dry land, but it would have to wait for tomorrow.

They reluctantly stepped back aboard and canceled their reservations and Caitlyn set to work scrounging something up from the ship's stores which were running pretty low after the crossing.

Mike and Melany sat at the dinette with an awkward silence between them; Mike finally decided he was going to go up and "Check the lines before the sun went down."

It was really just an excuse to go topside by himself.

As he closed the companionway hatch behind him, Melany was on Caitlyn immediately.

> "You did very well."

She said to Caitlyn who responded with a puzzled look:

> "What do you mean mother?"

> "He is very wealthy!"

She shot back in her thick Irish accent. Caitlyn just looked at her and didn't say anything.

> "If you divorce him you will be very rich!"

Melany then exclaimed not even attempting to mask the excitement in her voice.

> "Mom! I didn't marry him for money!"

Caitlyn shot back the fire beginning to burn in her eyes. Her mother had always been the opportunistic sort despite being a militant feminist.

"Well, when it doesn't work out at least you will be well taken care of!"

Melany retorted hoping Caitlyn would see it her way.

Caitlyn caught herself before she flew off into a rage, she choked it down then simply replied.

"No, not it wouldn't..."

She paused and as she did her mom tilted her head quizzically before Caitlyn continued.

"Look, I signed a prenup; I get what I have earned for myself, nothing more nothing less."

"Are you bloody stupid!"

Melany screamed at her and Caitlyn fired a volley back in her very thick Irish accent:

"Mother, I married him because I love him because he is the strongest man I've ever known and I love him with all of my heart and if you cannot accept that you can get the hell out of here!"

Then Mike's voice boomed through the boat.

"WHAT THE FUCK IS GOING ON HERE?"

He roared in the voice a military man uses when addressing his subordinates.

Unable to keep up the act Melany challenged him.

"I was just discussing my daughter about this silly agreement you manipulated her into signing when you married her.

I thought I had raised her to have some good sense and to look out for herself but then here comes the likes of you and that goes all out the window, mister big fancy man in his big fancy boat winning her over making her fall all over you to be your submissive little housewife!"

Then she pointed to the collar around Caitlyn's neck and continued.

"And what the fuck is this, is this some kind of collar, is she nothing more than a dog to you? Is that all she is?"

With this Caitlyn snapped and began to scream at her.

"MOTHER! YOU HAVE NO RIGHT TO JUDGE"

And then Mike cut her short as he shouted the words:

"Caitlyn Kneel"

And without hesitation she dropped to her knees and placed her hand's palm up on the tops of her thighs and looked up staring at him obviously not happy he had cut her off, and even more displeased that he had made her do this in front of her mother forcing her to be completely disarmed.

But the feeling didn't last because then he swung down into the salon all of the way making a heavy thud as his feet slammed down on the teak deck.

Mike stood up straight and broad letting his mass tower over Melany, and he began to speak very deliberately and very slowly pointing his finger at her.

"Now, Melany, you listen to me, this woman right here, your daughter is the most unique and special woman I have ever met!

She is kind, she is loving she is extremely intelligent, it also just so happens she is a people pleaser, she likes to make people happy, she is a submissive.

But don't you for a second confuse that with being weak, because weakness is not something she is rife with at all, she is very strong!

She has strength in her I have never seen in a woman before so don't you dare sit here and tell me or her our relationship degrades her because it gives her the very thing she needs more than anything and that is the ability just to be herself!

This may sound silly to you but in living this way she has found real freedom and happiness and so have I!"

By now Melany had backed several feet across the cabin, and Mike had followed not backing down.

"Now you get this through that head of yours, because of who she is I love her more than I ever thought it was possible to love someone and I will be damned if I am going to let anyone harm her or put her down INCLUDING YOU!

And if you can't deal with that I will drag your ass off of this boat and dump you in the Pacific!

DO YOU UNDERSTAND ME? Because you had better understand I will move heaven and earth if I have to see that she is safe, happy and well cared for!"

With these words, Melany reeled back and didn't know what to say, and Caitlyn was shocked when the words "Yes sir!" passed her mother's lips!

It was at this moment Caitlyn realized that her and her mother were not that different after all, they both had that famous Irish temper, they both had a habit of testing every man they met.

Now it was so obvious; her mother was simply reacting to having been hurt so many times this is what made her bitter angry and conniving.

She had been let down so many times that somewhere along the way she began to look at men as tools to get what she wanted, not people to have relationships and life experiences with.

And with this, it dawned on her had it not been for meeting Mike she could have turned out very much the same way!

Her thoughts were broken when she realized Mike was reaching out his hand to her. She took it, and he helped her to her feet.

He kissed her and told her he loved her then he stepped back into the stateroom.

Caitlyn looked at her mom, and Melany looked back at her, they both broke out crying and hugged each other, and it was as though an invisible wall had broken down between them and it just came pouring out of them until dinner began to burn on the stove.

⚓ FORTY-EIGHT ⚓

After re-making dinner, Caitlyn found Mike in the stateroom answering emails on his tablet when she entered he set it down and looked up at her.

Caitlyn practically burst upon him and hugged him and began to cry.

> "I am so sorry, at first I was mad at you for making me kneel, but then just... your words...
>
> You showed me how much you love me, and you showed me she is just like me only full of pain, and I can see that is how I'd have become if I had not found you!"

Mike hugged her back and comforted her, then he wiped her tears away and kissed her.

> "I meant every word of that."

He said somewhat stoic but affectionate.

> "I never had any question you did!"

Caitlyn replied with a huge smile and then she hugged him again.

They emerged from the stateroom and were able to have a pleasant meal; the conversation turned to small talk about the voyage and the pending funeral.

Everyone would be flying in in a few days and then they would be scattering Grandpa's ashes would be deposited aboard the Utah where she capsized.

Soon all of the guests had arrived and the morning was upon them. Smitty was there, so was Allen, Monica and Abbey had flown in, Caitlyn's dad as well.

He and Melany were able to be surprisingly cordial, Caitlyn suspected if her mother misbehaved she would be worried that Mike would make good on his promise to throw her in the Pacific!

Everyone including the Australians piled into the stretched limousine that had been rented by Allen for the occasion along with the urn, and they sped off towards Pearl.

Once on Ford Island, they met with the Park Ranger and retired Navy Chaplain who as it turns out was a newly minted ensign at Grandpa Stephen's last command.

As well the base's captain and a handful of staff officers tagged along, this was a fairly monumental event for all of them.

They gathered at the water's edge at a dock near where the Utah had been birthed; there they boarded a navy boat that would take them to the wreck of the mighty ship.

As they floated closer, the funeral party could see the rusting hulk of the ship partially visible above the waves her turrets and superstructure cut away; but starboard side of her upper works and the rail of her deck jutting slightly out of the water as the last remnant of the ship that seemed to defy the deep.

They pulled alongside her, and the coxswain held his station and the Chaplain began to speak.

"Ladies and Gentlemen, we are gathered here today to celebrate the life of a great man, Master Chief Stephen Black, United States Navy, Loving father and grandfather and businessman.

We are here to celebrate a life that touched so many lives in our lifetime including my own and today it is our duty to perform one last act in his life depositing his ashes here today at the location his ship the USS Utah was attacked and sunk during the attacks of December seventh nineteen forty-one.

Many of his shipmates perished that day when the Utah sank and capsized an initial attempt to salvage her was made but when it was discovered she was still too badly damaged she was abandoned and the men who died on her are still entombed here today.

It is Master Chief Black's wish for his ashes to be deposited here with his shipmates. Petty Officer Thompson, a Navy diver, will perform the honors."

With this, the Navy diver stepped forward clad in his wetsuit. He slid into the water and dawned his fins; then the urn was passed through the attendees so they could touch it one last time before being handed down to the driver so he could place it in the wreck.

The diver held the urn between his hands and kicked his feet remaining above water until he reached the hulk of the ship.

Signaling that he was ready, the Chaplain shouted the command "Hand Salute!" with this Mike, Allen, Dan and all of the officers in attendance popped a salute in the direction of the ship.

Then he dove below and deposited the urn through one of the portlights and as his head emerged from the water he gave a hand salute signifying that the deed had been done, and with this, the Chaplin signaled to the bugler to play taps, and with this from shore came the twenty-one-gun salute.

Then came the command "Ready TWO!" and all at once the salutes dropped.

Then the Chaplain thanked everyone for coming, and Mike interrupted him.

"One more thing!"

He said producing a case he had brought with him. He set the case on one of the seats and produced the bottle of Scotch he had collected from Grandpa's house.

"For those of you who do not know me, I am Senior Chief Mike Black, Stephen's only grandson. The day he died I pulled this bottle of Scotch from his liquor cabinet, he had only taken one shot from it the day before.

Today I would like to ask you all to join me in a toast to a great man and a life well lived!"

Then he produced the glasses which bore an inscription with the Master Chief's anchor on one side and Grandpa's portrait on the other encircled by his name and birth and death dates, and a quote etched into the bottom that read:

"Twenty years from now, you will be more disappointed by the things you didn't do than those you did. So throw off the bowlines. Sail away from safe harbor. Catch the wind in your sails. Explore. Dream. Discover." — Mark Twain

Mike poured each shot and distributed the glasses poured two for himself then made the toast holding his high.

"To my Grandpa, Master Chief Stephen Black, a hard-fighting sailor and a hell of a man who truly showed us all you have to grow old, but you don't have to grow up! Here's to you may you rest in peace and contentment with a life well lived!"

Everyone shouted out the customary "Here! Here!" and downed their glasses, some opting to clink theirs with those next to them.

Mike downed one of the glasses and then held the other over the side of the boat.

"Grandpa here's to you!"

He said as he let the glass slip from his grip and fall to the ship lying entombed below. Then he saluted one more time and about faced to the crowd.

There was not a dry eye on the boat.

FORTY-NINE

The next day came the reading of the will. They gathered aboard the boat with the lawyer who was very businesslike. He gathered everyone around wasting very little time on pleasantries; he began to read aloud:

"I Stephen Black of Bremerton Washington declare this to be my last will and testament. This will shall make any previous wills null and void.

Article I – Funeral expenses and payment of debts.

By the time of the reading of this will, my funeral should have been completed as I have left explicit instructions for doing so, if this will is being read before my remains have been deposited on the USS Utah.

Please carry out this task before reading any further; it is my express wish to have my remains entombed there before my assets are divided.

At the time of writing, I am leaving no debts other than monthly bills to which my accountant is part and capable of making payments for the time being.

Article II – Money and Personal Property.

At the time of writing my cash value is worth approximately twenty million dollars, and stocks worth another eighty million.

I wish for the funds to be distributed as follows:

To My Darling Monica, you have been so kind and so caring through my sickness, your love for me was clearly so strong, and to you, I leave twelve million dollars cash, and half of my stocks, a value of forty million dollars.

To your lovely wife, Abbey, I leave you one million dollars and the hopes that you two may enjoy many happy years together!"

A general sense of shock began to take place around the room, everyone knew Grandpa had done well for himself, but no one had realized how well and mouths around the room hung agape.

The Lawyer continued.

"Michael, you have already done very well for yourself financially, and seeing as that you are already a self-made millionaire I have decided instead of leaving cash funds to you I am going to give you the other half of the stock portfolio approximately forty million dollars.

To your lovely wife Caitlyn, I leave you another million dollars in cash. Please use your best judgment in handling this money, Michael is very smart, he can help show you what to do with it to make it grow."

Caitlyn was floored, she had not expected anything, she had never so much as seen this much money in her life let alone thought she would ever have that much, it was as though she was dreaming!

If she was, she never wanted to wake up!

Then the next surprise came as the lawyer continued to read:

"To Dan, Caitlyn's father. I only knew you for a short time, but in that time I grew to see you loved your daughter very much, I can also see you struggled very hard over the years to provide for her and to make a life for yourself as a single father trying to support two households.

I commend you for that, and I am leaving you one million dollars and a piece of property to be discussed in the next section."

Dan was shocked, he had been struggling with his new job and had been having a row with his new boss, the news that he was now a millionaire was more than he ever expected.

When Grandpa Stephen had told him he had left him a little something, he thought maybe a painting or a trinket, possibly a gun, never in his wildest dreams did he think he would receive so much!

The lawyer continued to read:

> "To Jim Coates of Australia. I admire your adventurous spirit, you reminded me of yourself when I was your age, and it is my desire to help you achieve all you can in this life, so to you I leave one million dollars and as per my Discussion with Allen, the Yacht you sailed to Colombia over the winter. She is yours do with her as you wish, please just continue to take good care of Mary, she is a fine lady. And so is her sister Tania."

it was Grandpa's wish that the remaining four million be used to build a memorial to the Utah and her crew and enclosed was a Check that Mike and Monica were to personally present to the base commanding officer before leaving Hawaii.

Then it came time for the property, Article three.

> "Allen, you have been a dear friend of mine for many years, as we had discussed in California all you wanted was the old set of stainless Colt forty-five revolvers I bought all those years ago at that estate sale we attended, as per our agreement they are yours."

Allen smiled and nodded; it was indeed all he had asked. The lawyer continued.

> "With my boat, the Utah Rose, Michael building this boat with you while you were stationed in Bremerton was one of the fondest memories of my life, I ask that you always keep her as she is named for my dear

mother, and there is so much of our family history on her.

We built her to go anywhere at any time in any weather and a finer craft I could not build.

This brings me to the businesses. Michael, I am leaving one hundred percent of my businesses and land holdings to you with the exception of my home in Bremerton which is to go to your sister. She loves that house, and I would hope that she can live many happy years in it as her home."

Monica smiled and sighed a sigh of relief, she had always loved the house, and now it was hers. She had practically grown up there with Mike and Mike had shown little interest, he preferred to be on the sea anyways, so there were no hard feelings.

Finally, the piece of property Grandpa had left to Caitlyn's dad:

"Dan, as I mentioned I am leaving you a piece of real estate, there is a home I own in Coronado, it is a lovely place although I have not been there in a couple of years due to my health.

It is on the water with a private dock large enough that you can park your own boat there and have enough room for Mike and Caitlyn when they come to visit.

You had told me how much you love the area down there in Coronado and how you had always wanted to buy a home there, so please, take this home and make it yours."

At the conclusion of the reading, everyone was shocked, as it turned out at the time of his death Grandpa Stephen the humble old man from Bremerton Washington was worth close to two hundred million dollars yet still drove the old GMC pickup he had bought new in 1972.

The humble, unassuming man had touched so many lives, and now a great responsibility had been passed on to Mike to tend to this empire, the weight of it was something that settled on both he and Caitlyn.

They now had a myriad of businesses and properties up and down the West Coast stretching from Alaska to San Diego, and as far west as Hawaii, that they were responsible for.

It was a lot to take in, but after a few days the shock wore off, and everyone returned to themselves.

Finally, the routine of preparing the boat for a trip back across the Pacific to Bremerton had begun, they re-provisioned her and tested her systems.

The day then came for them to push out across the Pacific. Dan surprised them all when he showed up with a suitcase.

"Captain, would you have room for one more?"

He said to Mike with a big grin. Mike smiled and responded:

"Welcome aboard!"

Then he nudged Caitlyn and continued:

"My first mate here will show you to your accommodations, good sir."

Caitlyn nudged him back in the ribs a bit harder than was playful but she smiled just the same.

She lead her dad down to the cabins forward and set him up, and as she was making the bed, he stopped her.

"Sweetie, there is something I have to tell you."

Caitlyn stopped, for a moment a bit of panic struck her because his voice was very serious, the thought that he might be getting ready to level bad news started to make her grow anxious, what was it, was everything ok?

After a long Pause, Dan spoke.

> "I know I haven't always been there for you and I feel horrible about that, being gone so much had to be very hard for you as well as all of the traveling growing up back and forth between California, Hawaii, and Ireland.
>
> I watched you have difficulty making friends; I'd be out to sea and get a message that you had got in another fight, or that you had run away from home again.
>
> I always felt so guilty for that, and I am sorry I have not been a better father to you."

Caitlyn's eyes ran wet, and she lunged at him hugging him as tight as she could.

> "I love you daddy!"

She exclaimed in a soft sweet tone.

Then he continued:

> "But I have to tell you something..."

With the long pause, Caitlyn stepped back with a look of puzzlement on her face, what was it, was he dying, was he going away? Is that why he had come???"

> "Things at work haven't been going well for me at work, and this morning I was thinking everything over, I already have an income from my Navy retirement, as well I have some small investments I made, along with the windfall from Mike's Grandfather, I don't have to work anymore.

So I called, I quit my Job, and I resolved to come spend some time with you if you will have me that is..."

With this Caitlyn launched into him and hugged him again practically knocking him over as she hugged him.

She was tiny, but her exuberance told him she was very happy he was going to be there more to spend time with her, it truly did mean so much to Caitlyn.

Soon the massive boat pushed away from the dock; they maneuvered her out of the harbor and into the vast wastes of the Pacific headed to the North of the Pacific high, so once they had cleared it they could turn east to Washington and have the wind with them the whole way.

As the day began to fade into night, they were treated to an amazing sunset full of vibrant colors that danced off the clouds and the water.

Caitlyn came to where Mike sat enjoying the sunset and sat next to him wrapping her arms around his resting her head against his shoulder.

"I love you Sir."

She said with a smile.

"I love you too!"

He responded before kissing her on the head.

"What will we do next?"

She asked him not knowing what the future would bring.

"I was thinking about building a new boat, a catamaran."

Mike said with a big smile.

"A catamaran?"

Caitlyn asked not being very familiar with them.

"Yes, they have two hulls, they are much faster, and the living space in them is amazing!"

Mike said with a confident tone and reassuring smile.

"You had me at more living space!"

Caitlyn retorted with a smile.

Then they just sat in silence, two people who had found the perfect balance in each other watching the sunset over the Pacific, the struggles of life seemingly behind them or so they thought...

⚓ FIFTY ⚓

At a marine salvage yard in Anchorage the dejected hull of My Way sat mostly stripped of anything valuable, The massive gash torn in her side still boarded over with now crumbling plywood that had turned gray and back and rotted away in the harsh Alaskan winter.

A man stood examining the boat rubbing his chin, madness in his eyes. He pulled a flip phone from his pocket and dialed a number.

> "Charlie? It's Amos; I need you to run down a boat for me, it's registered out of Seattle Washington, the name on the stern is "My Way.""

The man paused and listened to the man on the other end of the line.

> "Michael Black, out of Bremerton Washington?"

> "Yes, if that is the man who owned her, that is the man who killed my brother!"

To be continued...

⚓ RESOURCES ⚓

If you enjoyed this book, please visit my website for more information and news on future projects.

http://www.albertreichard.com

Additionally, if this book made sense to you and you want to explore more about Kink please visit:

http://www.albertreichard.com/resources

⚓ DISCLAIMER ⚓

TAMING OF THE
SIREN

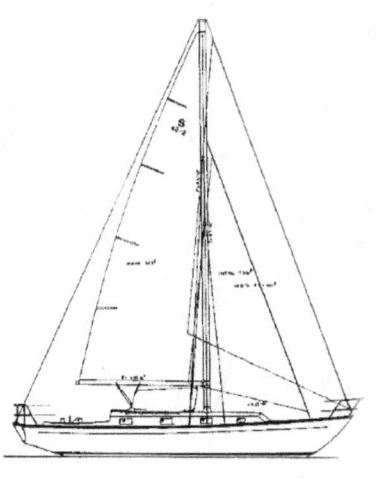